DEATH
BY
DUMPLING

"Vivien Chien serves up a delicious mystery with a side order of soy sauce and sass. A tasty start to a new mystery series!" —Kylie Logan, bestselling author of *Gone with the Twins*

"*Death by Dumpling* is a fun and sassy debut with unique flavor, local flair, and heart."
—Amanda Flower, Agatha Award-winning author of *Lethal Licorice*

"A charming debut, with plenty of red herrings. The heroine's future looks bright." —*Kirkus Reviews*

Also by
Vivien Chien

DEATH BY DUMPLING

Available from
St. Martin's Paperbacks

DIM SUM

OF

ALL FEARS

VIVIEN CHIEN

St. Martin's Paperbacks

DIM SUM OF ALL FEARS

Copyright © 2018 by Vivien Chien.
Excerpt from *Murder Lo Mein* copyright © 2018 by Vivien Chien.

For information address St. Martin's Press, 175 Fifth Avenue, New York, NY 10010.

ISBN: 978-1-250-12917-8

Our books may be purchased in bulk for promotional, educational, or business use. Please contact your local bookseller or the Macmillan Corporate and Premium Sales Department at 1-800-221-7945, ext. 5442, or by e-mail at MacmillanSpecialMarkets@macmillan.com.

Printed in the United States of America

St. Martin's Paperbacks edition / September 2018

St. Martin's Paperbacks are published by St. Martin's Press, 175 Fifth Avenue, New York, NY 10010.

10 9 8 7 6 5 4 3 2 1

For Rebecca,
Best friend and soul sister

Thank you for sharing the milestones

ACKNOWLEDGMENTS

I am eternally thankful to the following people:

Heartfelt gratitude goes to my wonderful agent, Gail Fortune, for being my cheerleader and guide throughout the publishing process. I'm extremely fortunate to have you by my side. To Hannah Braaten, my editor and second set of eyes, thank you for "getting" me. To Allison Ziegler, Sarah Schoof, and Nettie Finn for the amazing jobs they perform. To Mary Ann Lasher, for making my book covers looks delicious. And, to all of St. Martin's for being one heck of a publisher. I am so proud to write for you.

To the Sisters in Crime, both locally and nationally, I applaud you for the support and direction you provide to so many. Big hugs go to my NEOSinC buddies Amanda Flower and Cari Dubiel for their continuing guidance, their expertise and friendship. To Casey Daniels (who is also Kylie Logan) for being the best fairy godmother a gal could ever ask for.

Many thanks to Tina Roberts for helping on the topic

viiiACKNOWLEDGMENTS

of retail property. To Kim Hammond for answering my random legal questions. And, to Michael Wojciechowski for his behind-the-scenes casino knowledge. (All errors or adjustments to reality belong to yours truly.)

To Paul Corrao who is one heck of a dad. You never cease to amaze me with the confidence and faith you have in what I do. To my mother, Chin Mei Chien, who gifted me with this sass and sense of humor. My sister, Shu-Hui Wills, for always looking out for me and telling me I'm "smarter than that." I will never find the appropriate words to properly thank Rebecca Zandovskis who has remained with me through thick and thin and provided me with such an amazing friendship. You continue to inspire me. Much appreciation goes to Holly Synk for all of her support and also coming along while I walk the path of my characters. Huge thanks to my gal pals: Mallory, Lindsey, Tiffany and Alyssa, I don't know what I'd do without you.

To my very favorite boss lady, Kelly Antal, who has shown me so much support through this process since day one. Thank you for allowing me to jump around in your office and for putting up with me on a daily basis. To Christopher Foster for his enthusiasm in my work away from work. And, also for entertaining all of my silliness. (I haven't jumped around in your office yet, but it's coming, I'm sure.) Richard Foster, I am grateful for your kind words, encouragement and allowing me to be myself, teal hair and all.

To my readers . . . I would hug all of you if I could. You make this even more fun for me.

And lastly, but never least, to the unnamed friends and family who have shown belief in this "little engine that could" . . . I thank you.

CHAPTER 1

"Ai-ya!" my mother bellowed from across the crowded restaurant. She stood up from the table, her hands squeezing her hips. My sister and father turned in their chairs to see what she was looking at with such disdain.

It was me. Lana Lee.

The gawking eyes of just about everyone in the room—including staff—followed me as I slunk across the restaurant to the table where my family was seated. Of course they had to be sitting all the way in the back.

The best way to describe our family of four is similar to the game "one of these things is not like the other," with my dad—the solo white guy—being the odd man out. Even though my sister and I are only half Taiwanese, you wouldn't know it by looking at us. If I had a dollar for every time someone said, "That's your dad?"—well, I probably would never have to work another day in my life.

On Sundays, the four of us gathered for our traditional dim sum outing at Li-Wah's on Cleveland's east side. And because of this, we opened our own restaurant, Ho-Lee Noodle House, at noon. This meant my sister and I didn't have an excuse to skip out on family time.

"Shhh!" I hissed at my mother as I slipped into the empty seat next to my sister. "People are staring at us!"

"Your hair is blue!" my mother screeched, ignoring my plea. "Why is your hair blue?"

My mother, though petite, did her best to tower over the table. At times, it was hard to take her seriously because she was so darn cute with her chubby cheeks, but it was all in the eyes. And today, the eyes let me know that she was not amused.

I lifted a hand to my head, running my fingers through the freshly dyed hair. "Not all of it."

Okay, so maybe it wasn't the best time to dye my hair with streaks of blue. I hadn't really thought that part through when I'd set up the appointment.

Not only was I springing a daring new hairstyle on my parents, who were both on the old-fashioned side, but I was also getting ready to tell them that I had been interviewing for a new office job in the hope of quitting my stint as server at our family's restaurant.

Most of the positions I had been looking into were for data entry, but there was one company that stood out among the others I had applied to, and the position was a little higher on the totem pole. It was for an office manager, and the pay was great. The benefits package was great, the office itself was great . . . everything was great. And, added bonus, it came with three weeks of paid vacation.

I'd interviewed with them the week before, and it

had gone exceptionally well. They had called this past Friday to set up a second interview for this upcoming Thursday, and I had a good feeling that by the end of it, the job would be mine if I wanted it. Which, of course, I did. After all, a gal can't peddle sweet-and-sour pork her entire life. So alas, it was time to let my parents know they needed to start looking for new help.

"Betty." My dad, the calm and collected one of the family, put a gentle hand on her forearm, nudging her back into her seat. "Let's all sit down."

Anna May—older sister and picture-perfect daughter—gave me a once-over. "And you did this on purpose?"

After stuffing my purse under the table, I shimmied out of my winter coat and hung it on the back of my chair. "Yes, I did it on purpose. Not all of us want to be so plain all the time." I gave her a pointed once-over back.

"Interesting." My sister ran a French-manicured hand through her pin-straight black hair. It fell just below her shoulders, and gleamed. "I suppose you're right, though, not all of *us* can pull off a classic look."

My own nails, painted teal, were chipping. I hid my hands under the table before she could notice. "If that's what you want to call it . . ."

My mother continued to analyze my hair, her eyebrows scrunched low over her eyelids. "Why did you do this?" Her lips pursed as she landed on the question mark.

With a shrug, I replied, "I don't know. I felt like it." *Lie.* I did know. However, I didn't want to admit to them, or to anyone, that it was because of what had happened to me only a few short weeks ago. Of course, no one would say anything once I explained that it was because my life had been threatened at gunpoint, but part of me didn't want to say that out loud. Saying it out loud made it more real.

Since then, I've decided to stop putting things off until the elusive "tomorrow." Procrastination is nobody's friend.

My savvy stylist, Jasmine Ming, was more than thrilled to swap out my gold peekaboo highlights for some bright-blue ones. I didn't want to go overboard, but I'm pretty sure I saw a glint in her eye when she added the first touch of blue.

I reviewed the plates on the table and avoided eye contact with my mother. Placed in front of me were plates of baby bok choy in garlic sauce, noodle rolls, turnip cakes, and pot stickers. I busied myself with unwrapping my chopsticks and grabbed a rice noodle roll stuffed with shrimp.

My dad looked at me with a soft smile. "Is this because of what's-his-name?"

"No, Dad," I huffed, my chopsticks involuntarily tapping my plate. "I couldn't care less about him."

Okay, that wasn't totally true, either. What's-his-name was my ex-boyfriend, whom we did not mention by name. Ever. Not unless you wanted me to sprout snakes out of my head à la Medusa.

Anna May snickered. "No, Dad, she's dating Detective Trudeau now, didn't you know?" She clasped her hands together next to her face and batted her eyelashes. "He's sooo dreamy."

"Would you all stop it?" I jabbed the noodle roll with my chopsticks. "You're making a big deal over nothing. I've been thinking about doing this for a while, and I decided to stop putting it off. That's all."

I twisted in my chair to properly face my sister. She looked a little too amused at my expense. "And for your information, Adam and I have only been out on three dates. I hardly call that dating. Not that it's any of your business."

Anna May turned her nose up. "Well, I won't be looking for my wedding invite anytime soon, but still, close enough."

"I kind of like it . . ." My dad cocked his head at me, nodding his acceptance of my hair. "Now, about this Adam character . . . he's a cop, so he's no slacker. Does he drive American?"

"Bill," my mother said, clucking her tongue. "This is no good. My daughter looks like a cartoon."

"Oh, honey, she looks fine," he said, squeezing her hand. "Let's just enjoy our lunch before we have to head to the restaurant." He tapped his watch. "Besides, we still have the news we need to tell the girls, remember?"

My sister and I glanced at each other.

"What news?" Anna May asked.

My mother set down her chopsticks and shifted in her seat. "Your a-ma called this morning. She is very upset and has been crying for many days now." She shook her head. "Your uncle does not know what to do with her."

My "a-ma" is my grandmother in Taiwan. Because of her declining health, she was now living with my mom's younger brother and his wife, along with their three children, two of whom were toddlers. I guessed the living quarters were starting to feel a little cramped.

"So . . ." my father started, urging my mother along.

"We are going to Taiwan for a couple of weeks to help take care of A-ma." My mother said this in one long blurt while avoiding eye contact with my sister and me.

"A couple of weeks?" I yelped. No, no, no. They couldn't leave now. Not when I'd just found the perfect office job.

"Right before Chinese New Year?" Anna May glanced between the two of them. "Can't you wait until after it's over?"

My parents looked at each other.

"Who will run the restaurant?" I asked, fearing the answer. Any way you spun it, it wouldn't be good.

Anna May perked up beside me, straightening in her seat. "Well, that's obvious, it's—"

"Lana will run the restaurant," my dad announced before Anna May could continue. He put his arm around my mother and gave her another squeeze.

"What?" my sister and I shouted in unison.

My dad held up a hand. "This makes the most sense. Lana is already working there full-time. And besides," my dad said, eyeing Anna May, "you've got school. You don't have a lot of time to run a business."

I threw up my hands. "Oh, of course, Anna May and her law school stuff again. What about my stuff? Does anyone ever think of what I have going on in my life?"

"Lana." My mother gave me her masterful look of disapproval. "This is something to help Mommy. Why would you not want to help Mommy? I changed your diaper when you were a baby."

I sighed. The diaper argument. Every time.

"I can't believe you're leaving her in charge." Anna May slouched in her seat. "Lana isn't responsible enough to manage the restaurant unsupervised. I'm going to end up putting in extra time to help."

"Are you kidding me?" I turned to glare at her. "I'm sitting right here."

She returned my glare with one of her own. "I know."

"Okay, girls," my dad interjected. "That's enough bickering. This is our decision and it's final. Anna May, you have too much going on in your life to give the restaurant your full attention. Lana has more time than you do right now and this makes the most sense. End of story."

Anna May folded her arms over her chest. "Yeah, I suppose you're right. She doesn't have anything going on besides hanging out at that stupid bar where Megan works."

I stiffened in my seat. "First of all, Megan's bar is not stupid. And I do have stuff going on. Just because I don't tell you every single thing I do doesn't mean I'm not doing anything."

"Right . . . so do you want to tell us what that supposed stuff is, exactly?"

My dad shushed my sister and then turned to me. "Lana? Is there a reason you don't want to be in charge of the restaurant while we're gone? If there's something going on, Goober, you need to tell us."

If I didn't speak up now, it would be too late and I could kiss my chance of leaving the restaurant goodbye. By the time they were back from their trip, the position I was hoping to take would more than likely be gone. I weighed my options as my family stared at me, waiting for a justifiable answer.

My mother finally got to me. Her stoicism usually drove me crazy, because I never knew what she was thinking. But today, her emotions were written all over her face. She was obviously tired and stressed. It had been a long time since my parents had made the trip to Taiwan, so I knew it had to be urgent. With my sister canceled out as an option, I knew they would be solely dependent on me for this. Knowing my mother, she would not let someone outside of the family run the restaurant. She'd rather close up shop.

I looked away, feeling defeat. "No, there's not."

"Good, then it's settled," my dad said, rubbing my mother's back. "See, Betty? I told you everything would work itself out."

"When are you guys leaving?"

My mother looked down at her plate. "We leave in three days."

"Three days!"

Anna May chuckled beside me.

Great.

I'd like to say that this was my biggest problem, but unfortunately, this was going to turn out to be one of my better days.

CHAPTER
2

After dim sum, I headed home, a little on the blue side. The hope that I'd been holding on to for getting back to my former life was starting to slip away. In the past few months, things had progressed from bad to worse, starting with breaking up with what's-his-name and drifting in a downward motion toward walking out of a more-than-decent job, a mounting pile of credit card debt, and an obsession with doughnuts that gained me a pant size. (In the wake of emotional disaster, there is nothing I find more comforting than pastries and retail therapy.)

The battle back upward had been a difficult one and I gave in to taking a job at my parents' Chinese restaurant so I could get caught up with my bills again. Turns out bill collectors are not very sympathetic to your breakup-induced depressions.

Don't get me wrong; Some people like being in the service industry. But me . . . I'd had my fill. Ho-Lee

Noodle House had been a part of my family since before I was born. There wasn't a time I remembered it not being there. But I needed a change of pace.

I don't think it had originally been my mother's dream to open a restaurant, but regardless, she and my father poured everything they had into making their business succeed. The plan was to keep Ho-Lee Noodle House alive for as long as possible, which for them meant keeping it in the family.

With two daughters, you wouldn't necessarily think that the burden would be left on my shoulders. You'd think that it would go to the eldest. But you'd be wrong.

Anna May, the scholar of the two of us, had her whole life planned out in a detailed outline that she'd started when she was around sixteen and read her first John Grisham novel. From there, talk about criminal law was just as common in the Lee family household as talk about noodle recipes.

Of course at that time, being two years her junior, I was still concerned with rock band posters and how I was going to get out of third-period gym class. I had no ambitions that could rival my sister's legal dream.

Maybe it was the pressure of comparing myself with her that led me down my eventual path of idealism. I became the dreamer of the family, the lover of arts and literature, taking joy in things that were made with creativity. I wanted to do something meaningful . . . to be driven by passion. I wanted to have something more than simply "a job."

I just wasn't sure what that entailed exactly. I had my interests, but nothing had stuck in terms of "lifelong."

And as most twenty-somethings come to realize, having a dream doesn't actually pay the bills. After college, I floundered around aimlessly looking for jobs that would at least sustain my life as an adult, all the while knowing that if I didn't find a grand career scheme like my sister, my fate would be chosen for me.

All of this tumbled through my head as I walked into the two-bedroom apartment I shared with my best friend, Megan. It was a modest garden-style apartment in North Olmsted, which was only a hop, skip, and jump away from Asia Village. It made my commute easy and was one thing I could put on the "pro" side of my list.

Kikko, my black pug, waddled to the door to greet me. Her curly tail wiggled as she spun around my ankles. I knelt down to give her a pat on the head. She approved and scampered off in search of something acceptable to bring me.

Meanwhile, I found Megan sitting at the kitchen table with a cup of coffee in hand and paint swatches scattered in front of her. She was still in her pajamas, makeup-less, and her blond hair was swept away from her face by a thick black headband. Without looking up, she said, "Oh good, you're home. I was just about to text you. I was thinking we could go to Home Depot today. I've decided on this mermaid theme for the bathroom, and this teal is the perfect color to paint the walls." She held up a swatch to show me her recent selection. "I also need to grab a new flashlight and some window cleaner."

"A flashlight? We have one under the sink."

"I want one for my car. I'm putting together a whole kit of tools to keep in the trunk."

I studied the paint swatch. "This works for me," I

said, with little emotion. I was too bogged down with my current pity party to give a more enthused answer.

"It kind of matches your hair." She looked up and frowned. "What happened? Did your mom give you a hard time about your new dye job? Because you said you were anticipating that, and we decided you weren't going to let it get to you, remember? We both know she doesn't do well with change."

I nodded, sitting across from her, still in my coat. "Yeah, but that got overshadowed real fast."

"With what?"

"My parents announced that they're going to Taiwan for a couple of weeks to help take care of my grandmother."

Megan sipped her coffee, unimpressed with my news. "What's the big deal with that?"

"They're leaving me in charge of the restaurant. They leave on Wednesday." I slouched in the chair.

"Wednesday!" Megan shouted.

Kikko came barreling into the dining area, stuffed duck flapping in her mouth. She dropped it at my feet and looked at me in anticipation.

I knelt down and picked up the duck, throwing it into the hallway. Kikko happily scuttled after it. "Yes, Wednesday, the day before my interview. The interview I'm not going to make because I now have to work."

"But didn't you tell your parents that you were trying to get this job?"

I looked at the floor.

"You did, right?" Megan insisted.

"I didn't think it was a good time . . ."

"Lana! How else are you going to get out of that place if you don't speak up?"

"It wasn't a good time to bring it up. It's really important to my mom that she go to Taiwan right now, and I didn't want to cause more problems for them," I said, trying to justify my actions. "Who else is going to do it?"

"What about Anna May? Can't she run the restaurant?"

"They think it would get in the way of her school stuff. And it probably would."

Kikko came back with her duck, dropped it on the floor, and nudged it with her nose.

"I can always try again when they get back."

"Of all the times for your parents to choose to go to Taiwan, of course it's now." Flustered, Megan stood abruptly, startling Kikko, who in turn grabbed her duck with indignation and pranced into the other room. "Well, we'll figure out a plan together. You have to get that job. It's not going to wait around for you." She sighed. "In the meantime, I'm going to get dressed and then we're going to Home Depot . . . this bathroom project will cheer you up."

"What will cheer me up is if we stop at the doughnut shop on the way."

Bright and early Monday morning—my least favorite time of all—I pulled into the parking lot of Asia Village, passing the dragon-coiled arch on my way in, the sun barely touching the tops of the pagoda-lined plaza. The parking lot had been freshly plowed, and my tires crunched over the remaining snow and rocks of salt.

I walked with care through the lot, keeping an eye out for patches of ice as I made my way to the main entrance. My riding boots were more fashionable than practical.

I stamped my boots on the entrance mat as I entered the building, the sound echoing through the near-empty plaza. A few shop owners sprinkled the establishment, lifting gates or unlocking doors in preparation for opening.

With its cobblestoned walkways, skylights, and koi pond—Japanese footbridge and all—Asia Village is what you'd call picturesque. The Asian-themed enclosed shopping plaza contains all the treasures of the Orient. Literally. That's what it says in the brochure.

We've got all the latest Chinese films and TV shows, a variety of pastries from moon cakes to egg tarts, and a full-sized grocery store that sells everything from bamboo shoots to red bean Popsicles. Hey, don't knock it till you try it.

I circled left around the red-painted fence enclosing the koi pond, passing Asian Accents hair salon, Wild Sage herbal shop, China Cinema and Song, and our newest addition, City Charm Souvenirs. The space in between Ho-Lee Noodle House and China Cinema had been filled at long last.

I could see my newest friend and one of the proprietors, Isabelle Yeoh, through the window, tinkering around at the cash register. She noticed me and waved. She was a cutesy sort of girl with a round face, apple cheeks, and eyes that crinkled when she smiled.

Isabelle and her husband, Brandon, had only joined our community a few short weeks after the whole ordeal with Mr. Feng. I was relieved they hadn't had to experience those traumatic events.

City Charm Souvenirs was the first of its kind in

Asia Village. Not only did it represent Cleveland with the standard city pride paraphernalia, but it promoted the shops in the plaza as well. You could find snow globes, shot glasses, and mugs touting the Asia Village name.

Once Isabelle and Brandon were more situated, they planned to do specialty items for the surrounding businesses. Most of the shops in the plaza had already put in requests.

I was so preoccupied with daydreaming about logo designs, I hadn't noticed that Peter, our head chef, was waiting for me. He stood from the bench he'd been sitting on, a mass of black clothing and shaggy hair.

"You're here early today," I said, pulling the restaurant keys from my pocket.

"Whoa . . . dude," Peter said, ignoring my comment. "Your hair is blue."

I unlocked the door and we shuffled inside. With an hour left before open, I made sure to lock the door behind me. I had already learned my lesson. "Yeah, I had it dyed this weekend. What do you think?"

He nodded in approval. "Right on. I totally like it."

Peter and I had formed a sort of special bond over the past few several weeks. Though we'd known each other for years, it wasn't until Mr. Feng's death that we'd solidified this new relationship.

Through no fault of his own, Peter had been the patsy of the situation, and while many had turned their backs on him, I wasn't willing to follow the herd. Of course, that's what led to me being held at gunpoint, but in the end, it was worth it.

That's not to say I wasn't still reeling from the experience. We both were.

We wove through the black lacquered tables toward the kitchen. He turned to me with a smirk on his face. "What did your mom say? I bet she totally freaked."

I groaned, remembering her outburst at the restaurant. "You would not believe . . . she made a complete scene while we were out for dim sum yesterday."

Peter covered his mouth to stifle a laugh. "Oh man! I wish I could have been there to see that. Mama Lee does not disappoint."

Through the swinging doors, we entered the kitchen, and Peter flicked on the light. We passed through the kitchen to the small back room that housed my mother's office and a makeshift living room. It had become a communal hangout area for the employees when we needed to get away from the customers. Its original purpose had been to keep me occupied and entertained after school when I was still a kid. I'd spent many an afternoon doing homework in this room.

He removed his black baseball hat from the hook hanging by the door, smoothing his hair before slipping it on. He turned to me. "Your mom is way cool, but she is seriously stern. If my mom was like that . . . I don't know what I'd do."

I snickered. "Well, let's just be glad there's only one of her around here."

We went back into the kitchen, and I lined a tray with soy sauce bottles while Peter turned on the grills and burners.

Both of us had our own morning rituals, and it was kind of nice to work in sync with someone. They did their thing, you did your thing, and everyone was happy. Maybe it wasn't going to be so bad staying at the restaurant after all.

*   *   *

Around lunchtime, my mother and Esther Chin showed up bundled in their thick coats and matching cabbie hats. My mom, known for her love of hats, was sporting one of her favorites—a white knit, with a sparkly pink butterfly pin on the side of the brim. It came with a big pom-pom on top and everything.

Esther's eyes widened as she took in my hair for the first time. "Ai-ya! You are like a Hong Kong movie star now!" She came up to me and slapped my arm, her bangle bracelets jingling from inside her coat sleeve.

Esther is my mom's best friend, and also the owner of Chin's Gifts. I've known her all of my life, and she's like an aunt to me . . . a kooky aunt . . . but still, an aunt. She helped raise me and my sister at times, honing us to be what she considered proper ladies.

My mother gave her a sideways glance.

"You like it?" I asked, beaming at the irritation on my mother's face.

Esther nodded, gushing with pride. "This is very high fashion now in Hong Kong and Tokyo." She nudged my mother. "You do not have any taste, Betty."

My mother snorted. "She is too old to dye her hair like this. She cannot find a husband this way. No man will want a wife with blue hair."

My eyes narrowed. "Mom . . ."

"Okay, okay, I know what you will say." My mother bobbled her head as she mimicked me. "'It's too early for this talk, Mommy.'" She waved a hand at me as she walked past. "We will eat lunch and go back to the casino. Mommy will not bother you today."

"You're going to the casino again?" I asked, a little

shocked. I don't know why I was all that surprised. Jack Casino, housed in the old Higbee Building—the very one featured in the classic movie *A Christmas Story*—was a newer edition to the downtown area. From the minute the doors reopened in their newfound glory a few years ago, my mother and Esther couldn't wait to claim their titles as slot machine champions. "Don't you have things to do before you leave for your trip? Like packing?"

"It will be okay. I am going to take an empty suitcase and buy things while I'm there. It is much cheaper this way."

"I thought we were going to go over things you wanted me to do while you're gone."

"We can do that tomorrow," she said, dismissing me.

Esther squeezed my arm and followed my mother to the back. They were Peter's problem now.

I was just about to sit down on my hostess stool when the bells above the door tinkled and Isabelle walked in, smiling from ear to ear. "Happy Monday, Lana!"

An eye roll escaped. I swear, it was like a disorder I couldn't help. "I don't know about all that."

"Oh come on, it can't be that bad!" She scanned the restaurant. "At least you can ease into the week; it's not very busy in here today."

"True," I replied thoughtfully. "What brings you by? Need some lunch?"

She shook her head. "No, Brandon brought me lunch from Tea House Noodles. He had to run an errand downtown and thought he'd surprise me. Isn't that sweet?" Without waiting for me to respond, she continued. "But I will definitely need dinner later on tonight. I told Brandon I'd stay at the store and close up while he finishes his other errands."

"You're working late again? That's the fourth day in a row." I tried to hide my surprise, but my emotions tend to live on my face. Poker face has been a work in progress longer than I care to admit.

She shrugged. "That's the life of a business owner, am I right?"

"I suppose."

"Well, anyway," she replied, shaking it off. "I stopped by to see if we're still on for our weekly book date tomorrow?"

"You bet we are! I have my list of must-have books all ready to go."

"Meet me at Modern Scroll and then we'll head to the Bamboo Lounge for some dinner and drinks?"

I nodded. "Yup, I'll meet you there at five thirty."

She clasped her hands together. "Great! I'll make sure that Brandon knows he absolutely has to stay at the store tomorrow."

She waved goodbye and fluttered out just as Esther came back up to the hostess station. "That girl is always so cheerful," she commented as she watched Isabelle disappear from view. "You should learn to be more like her."

I laughed. "Even if I wanted to, I don't think I could ever be that positive."

At five p.m. on the dot, Vanessa Wen, the alternative bane of my existence—second only to Anna May— waltzed in the door looking very much like a ski bunny.

She bounced over to the hostess station, the pom-poms dangling from her hood swaying back and forth with every step. "Hey girl!" she spouted with enthusiasm. "It's getting cold out there; I hope you wore your heavy coat today."

Sometimes I wanted to put my hands on her shoulders and say, *Calm down, stand still*. Curbing that urge, I went with a tight smile. "Yeah, I did."

Satisfied with my answer, she traipsed into the back room tracking snow through the dining room. I groaned and reminded myself that I was learning to practice patience. After all, she was only a teenager.

She came back with the same spring in her step, ponytail swinging like a pendulum. She froze in place, gawking at me. "O . . . M . . . G . . . I just realized that your hair is blue!"

"Yeah, I had it done on Saturday." All of my energy focused on keeping my face still as I said it.

She leaned in and whispered, "Are you having a midlife crisis now? I mean, I know you're almost thirty . . . and that's super old and way scary to deal with. I mean you're not even married, you know?"

And . . . patience gone. I let out a deep breath. "No . . . I'm—"

"Is it because of the whole almost-being-shot-to-death thing?" She formed a gun with her fingers. "Because I totally get it. I mean, I would do all kinds of stuff if that happened to me. Like . . . I'd get tattoos or something."

The heat rose in my cheeks. "No, I dyed my hair because I felt like it, okay?"

"Oh," she replied, her shoulders sinking.

"And I'm too young for a midlife crisis anyway. I'm only twenty-seven."

She looked away, mimicking a toddler put in time-out. "Sorry."

Without saying anything else, I stomped through the kitchen into the back room to grab my coat and purse. "Peter, I'm leaving . . ." I said as I came back through. With frustration, I jammed my hand through the sleeve of my coat.

"Whoa, what's got you riled?" He was cleaning the grill and waiting on our night cook, Lou, to arrive.

"Not even worth telling you."

"All right. Well, I'll see you in the a.m. then."

I gave a flippant wave and barreled through the double doors. "Try not to burn the place down," I said to Vanessa as I passed her.

In my extreme desire to exit in a way that would make a statement, I almost ran smack into Brandon and Isabelle on their way into the restaurant.

"Hi Lana!" Isabelle chirped, unfazed by my close proximity.

"*Oh!*" I stumbled backward. "I didn't see you there!"

"Where's the fire?" Brandon chuckled to himself, stepping out from behind his wife. At six foot two, he towered over Isabelle and me as we stood in a triangle of sorts.

"Sorry about that, my head is elsewhere." My eyes—like every time I talked to him—drifted up to his forehead, which I found to be exceptionally oversized and shiny. The overhead lights in the lobby bounced off it and created a shadow underneath his narrow eyes.

"We were just at the salon. Brandon wanted to get his hair lightened before he went home. We thought we'd grab some dinner before he left for the night," Isabelle explained. "Are you leaving for the day?"

"Yeah, I'm heading home," I told them, noting the lightened tips of brown in his otherwise black hair.

"That's too bad." He sank his hands into his pockets and rocked back and forth. "I feel like we're always missing each other. Isabelle has such nice things to say about you all the time and I've hardly gotten a chance to know you."

"Likewise," I replied. I wanted to add that maybe we'd know each other better if he didn't dump Isabelle at their store day after day, but I held my tongue. Point for me.

"Thanks for helping out, by the way. Sometimes these errands keep me running all over town. I'm glad there's someone to keep Isabelle company."

I forced a smile. "Not a problem. Anything to help a friend." The poor girl did need a bathroom break once in a while. In the past few weeks, he'd been disappearing more often. I had to wonder what all these errands were that he was so busy running.

"One of these days we'll all have to go out for dinner. I hear you're dating a cop? Maybe we can make it a double date." He winked at Isabelle.

"That's a great idea!" she said, beaming up at him.

I blushed at the mention of Adam. "We're not really—"

Isabelle cut me off. "Oh, you stop it. You guys are the cutest new couple in the world."

"Not as cute as we are, of course," Brandon bragged, slinking an arm around Isabelle's shoulders.

Stifling a groan, I faked another smile and said, "I'll check with him and see when he's free. He's been slammed with work lately so it might be hard to schedule."

"Set it up, and it's a date." Brandon nodded with resolution.

"We'll let you go home now." Isabelle stepped aside to let me pass. "I'll see you tomorrow. Have a good night and be careful out there! I hear everything's turning to ice."

I waved my goodbyes and scurried out into the already cold, dark evening, muttering to myself. Yeah, Adam on a double date? He was just going to love this.

CHAPTER
3

Anna May had come in to the restaurant the next morning so that my mother and I could go over the details of running things while she was gone. I knew how to do most of what my mother did, but there were a few tasks that she reserved for herself, like completing food orders and dealing with payments to vendors and suppliers.

My mother's work space was a complete mess, but she had it down to a science. She knew where everything was, and the way she flowed through the stacks of papers and folders impressed me.

She showed me all of the order forms, the contact lists, and the database system she used to keep track of sales.

"It is very important that we keep track of how much people like certain dishes," my mother said to me. "This way we know what specials to make if business becomes too slow."

"I don't think we'll have that problem right now, Mom," I replied. "With the holiday coming up, you know we should have good business no matter what's on the menu."

She clucked her tongue. "Can you just listen to Mommy? I am trying to teach you something very important."

"Okay, sorry . . . go ahead."

We spent the next hour going over the specials she had planned for while she was gone and the scheduled shifts that all of us would work. According to her master plan, everything would work perfectly if we followed her exact instructions.

After we finished, my mother sat back in her chair, observing me. She nodded to herself. "This is going to be very good for you."

"Yeah, it's going to be great."

She narrowed her eyes. "I wish you would not act this way about everything that Mommy thinks is good for you. You are still too young to know what is good. One day you will thank Mommy for all her help."

"I'm not too young to know what's good for me. I'm not a little girl anymore."

She waved a hand at me. "This is nothing. You have so much life to live yet."

"Yes, Mom, I know," I said through gritted teeth. "But in order to live my life, I have to start living my life."

My mother cocked her head at me. "Sometimes when you talk, I don't know what you are saying to me. You are living your life, yah?"

I huffed. "Never mind. I wish you would trust me with making my own decisions. I know what I want to do and it's not running this restaurant. I want to do something else, okay?"

The minute it came out, I was filled with regret. I hadn't meant to have this conversation with my mother before her big trip, but it had been so heavy on my mind the past few weeks, it slipped out.

My mother stiffened in her chair. "I want you to have a good life. That is what Mommy is trying to help you do. If you do not appreciate this . . ." She twisted away from me, focusing her eyes on the computer screen.

"Mom . . ." I gave a heavy sigh. "It's okay, I know. I'm just frustrated lately, that's all. I don't mind working at the restaurant."

She perked up, turning back to face me. "If you had a boyfriend, that would make you happy, yes?"

I buried my face in my hands. This argument, which had been going on for months on end—ever since I broke up with jerk-face—was our never-ending battle. Time and time again, I had told her that I was just fine on my own. Even with Adam somewhat in the picture, she hadn't let up on her argument about me finding the perfect match to solve all my worries and woes. I didn't know how else to tell her that finding the perfect man wasn't always the answer to life's problems.

She'd met my father early in life, and things had worked out swimmingly for them. My dad was truly one of a kind. He had the patience of a saint, and even when my mother was at her most difficult, he kept his cool and worked alongside her moods. On top of that, he was thoughtful, always putting my mother's needs before his own. Call me a daddy's girl, but I admired my dad, and I wasn't ashamed to admit it.

Anna May tapped on the door. "Excuse me, Lana . . . I hate to break you away from your oh-so-important training session, but you have a visitor."

I looked up at her. "Who is it?"

"Detective Trudeau . . . or should I say . . . *Adam*. He's waiting at a table near the front. I told him you were busy but he won't go away."

"Anna May!" I looked at my mother for support. "Do you see what I put up with?"

My mother shrugged.

I marched past my sister and made my way out into the dining room, spotting Adam at a table toward the front, right where my sister said he'd be.

My stomach did flip-flops.

Adam was a classic sort of handsome. His strong jaw-line was covered in a five o'clock shadow more often than not, and the prominence of his cheekbones gave him an excellent profile. And his eyes . . . I could go on for at least an hour on how green they were and how I'd never seen eyes more beautiful than his. The reddish tint to his brown hair helped bring out the color, and when he was dressed in all black, like he was today, they became even more intense.

A crooked smile appeared on his face as we made eye contact, and a small part of me melted at the dimple that formed in his cheek.

"You dyed your hair blue. I like it."

"I didn't expect to see you today." I sat down in the chair across from him. "What brings you by?"

"I had this sudden urge for noodles, so I thought I'd stop in," he replied with a wink.

Stomach flop. "Oh, I can get you something . . ." I started to get up, my nerves getting the best of me. "Do you want to take it to go?"

He put a hand over mine and squeezed. "Lana . . . sit down. Your sister is taking care of it."

I blushed, sitting back in the chair. "Right. Anna May."

"She told me that you're training with your mother while she goes to Taiwan? She's really leaving tomorrow?"

"Yup. She's all ready with her empty suitcase."

"Huh?"

"Never mind," I said, dismissing the topic. "There was actually something I wanted to talk to you about."

He folded his hands in front of him on the table. "Okay, shoot."

"So, you know my friend Isabelle, right?"

"The one that works in the new souvenir shop?"

"Yeah, her." I squirmed in my chair.

"Okay . . ."

"Well, her husband—Brandon's his name—he asked if we would want to go on a double date with them."

He stared at me with a blank expression. For a minute, I wasn't sure that he'd heard me.

"I told him that you were really busy and it would probably be a pain even to schedule something like that with everything you have going on. But they insisted that I tell you. So now I have and I'll tell them no for us so you don't even have to think about it." I took a breath. There.

He laughed. "Why would you tell them no?"

My eyes widened. "You mean, you would consider it?"

"Yeah, if it's something you really wanted to do."

I couldn't believe what I was hearing. I thought for sure that he'd think it was the lamest idea in the universe.

He seemed to read my thoughts. "You underestimate

me, Lana Lee. I'd be more than happy to go on a double date with you and your friends."

Mentally, I did a dance of joy. I couldn't wait to tell Isabelle.

Adam stopping by and his acceptance of the double-date idea carried me on a cloud through the rest of the day. Not even my sister and her negative comments about me running the restaurant could dampen my mood.

After work, Isabelle and I met up for our bookstore adventure. We stood shoulder-to-shoulder staring at the spines of the books in the mystery section. Neither one of us spoke as our eyes skimmed the titles, searching for our favorite authors.

"I wish I could be like one of these women in the books we read . . . solving mysteries and serving justice." Isabelle turned to me. "Do you ever wish that you were a detective?"

I glanced at her from the corner of my eye. "Not really. It seems like it would be kind of dangerous."

"Yeah, you're probably right," she said with a sigh.

I waited for her to say more, but she didn't.

Instead, we focused back on the books in front of us, picking out a few more titles before heading to the cash register.

The Modern Scroll, one of my favorite places in the plaza, was run by Cindy Kwan, a small woman a few years older than me. If there was any one person who loved books more than Isabelle and me, it was Cindy.

"Well, hello ladies!" Cindy stood behind the register peering at us through her black, thick-framed glasses.

A name tag was pinned to her sweater and read I'M A BOOKWORM! under her name. "I see you're replenishing your winter reading piles."

I set my books down on the counter. "My parents are leaving for Taiwan tomorrow, and they're leaving me in charge of the restaurant."

Isabelle turned to me. "You didn't tell me that. When did you find out?"

"Sunday."

"Sunday!" the two women exclaimed.

"Right? They hardly gave me any notice."

"You had an interview lined up, didn't you?" Isabelle asked, and then quickly covered her mouth. "Oops . . . sorry to spill your news."

"It's okay, I don't mind if she knows . . ." I said, eyeing Cindy. "Just don't spread it around."

"Oh, don't worry, this one I will keep to myself." Cindy chuckled, sliding my books closer to her side of the counter. "I don't want the wrath of Mama Lee coming down on me."

"So what are you going to do?" Isabelle asked.

I shrugged. "The interview is for Thursday, so I have until at least tomorrow to figure it out. I'm keeping my fingers crossed that I can get someone else to cover for me. But even if they do, who knows if they'll wait until I'm able to start."

"How long will your parents be gone?" Isabelle asked.

"They said at least a couple of weeks. And then, of course, we'll have to find someone to replace me, and who knows how long that will take."

"Well, you can try at least and see what happens,"

Cindy suggested. She started to ring up my books. "Honestly, I'm surprised that you would want to leave. It seems to be going well over there, and you even joined Ian's new board of directors."

"Yeah, I suppose." I answered noncommittally. "I was kind of hoping to get back to office work, you know? Get away from the public and stare at something other than noodles and dumplings all day. Maybe work myself up the corporate ladder or something."

Cindy scoffed. "The corporate ladder? That doesn't even sound like you, Lana! You need to be doing something you love. Like how I love books." She thrust her arms out, waving at the volumes that surrounded us. "My favorite thing to do is come in and set up that table you see when you first walk in. I get to show everyone my very favorite picks . . . guide them on their next fictional journey or help them learn a new hobby. You need something like that in your life."

I groaned. "I'm not entirely sure what I love anymore . . . I've felt so lost since . . ."

All three of us knew what I was thinking, but none of us wanted to comment on it.

"Lana, you love noodles!" Isabelle chimed in.

"I'm not that great a cook."

Cindy leaned over the counter. "Maybe you should learn then. I have some great cookbooks with Asian recipes if you don't want to ask your mother or Peter. You could even surprise them with your new culinary skills."

"I don't know . . . maybe."

Cindy tapped her chin. "Maybe you're right . . . scratch the cooking thing. You like to be in charge of things, right? Well, here's your opportunity to test that out. Why don't you see how this shoe fits before trying on a different one?"

Even though I didn't want to admit it, she was right. I hadn't really given the restaurant a fair chance since I'd started working there full-time. In the back of my mind, it had been a temporary solution until something better came along.

Isabelle linked her arm in mine. "Well, however you want to look at it, I for one am glad that you're not going anywhere. You help keep me company most days. If it weren't for you, I might go insane."

After we finished at the bookstore, we headed over to the Bamboo Lounge for drinks and a light dinner. I told her about Adam accepting the idea of a double date, and when she didn't respond the way I had anticipated, I knew something was wrong.

"Okay, spill it," I said. "What's going on with you? You've been acting strange since we met up."

"Everything is fine." She forced a smile, looking at something over my shoulder.

"Liar."

Her eyes focused back on me, and for a second, I thought she was teary-eyed.

"Whatever you tell me will be in total confidence. I promise." I held up my hand in oath.

"It's Brandon."

"Okay . . . what about Brandon?"

"He's been acting strange lately . . . disappearing . . . and I'm afraid that he . . ." She turned away from me again.

I could see her eyes blinking rapidly and I suspected that I was right. She *was* getting teary-eyed.

She took a deep breath. "I'm afraid that he's getting bored with me."

My eyes widened. "Seriously? Are you kidding me? I see the way he looks at you, Isabelle. He's definitely not bored with you."

"You really think so?"

"I would bet money on it, in fact." Those are the words that came out. The ones that didn't were questioning where it was that he was disappearing to every time he left Isabelle at the store. "Maybe you should come right out and ask him."

"You don't think that makes me sound like a crazy person?"

"Not at all. It's a valid question."

She seemed to mull it over and then nodded in agreement. "You're right, there's no reason I can't ask him. I am his wife, after all."

When we were done and ready to leave the plaza, we walked together to the main entrance, finalizing our double-date plans. But before we could make it through the door, Brandon flagged us down.

"Hey, are you ladies done with your book escapades?" Brandon asked, jogging up to us.

He was dressed in his coat and gloves and caught up to us where we stood in front of Asian Accents, car keys in hand.

"I'm heading home right now to get dinner ready for you," Isabelle said, giving Brandon a peck on the cheek.

"Change of plans, sweetheart." He swung an arm around her neck and pulled her against him. "I have to run a quick errand, and I need you to close up shop." He looked down at her with an innocent smile. "You don't mind, do you?"

I stifled a groan.

Isabelle remained silent for a minute, and I imagined that after our little talk, she was having an inner battle with herself. "Can't the errand wait until after you close up? I'm exhausted tonight and I'd really like to get home. I've had to work late every night for the past week."

"I know, babe, but it's just this once. I promise that I will open and close tomorrow."

"Where is it that you need to go?" Isabelle asked. "Maybe I can go for you."

"No can do, but I appreciate the offer."

She looked down at her feet, a slight pout forming on her face.

It wasn't lost on me that he'd avoided answering her other question.

A gust of wind blew against my back, and I turned to see a tall man with what I couldn't help but describe as William Shatner hair standing behind us. And when I say William Shatner, I mean the Captain Kirk era. This guy's hair was a lot darker, but the style was exact.

As if on cue, he ran his fingers through his hair, shaking his head in that slow-motion sort of way that men do in movies. In reality, he was just removing the snowflakes from his head, but it looked pretty rehearsed if you asked me.

I turned back around, focusing my attention on Isabelle and Brandon.

"It's really important." Brandon noticed the tall man standing behind me and then glanced at his watch. "I have to get there before eight thirty and if I leave right now, I'll just be able to make it in time. You understand, don't you?"

Isabelle let out a deep sigh. "Okay, but tomorrow, I get to sleep in."

He chuckled as he kissed her forehead. "Deal." He waved a goodbye to me and jogged toward the tall man, giving him a pat on the shoulder.

I watched them as they left the plaza. *That's weird. How come he didn't introduce us to his friend?*

"Well," Isabelle said, turning to me. "I guess I'll see you tomorrow." Her shoulders dropped as she headed toward the souvenir shop.

"Do you want me to stay with you?" I offered, following after her. "I could keep you company."

"No, that's all right, you go. I know you have to take your parents to the airport early in the morning."

"You're right . . . ugh." I shook my head. "Okay, I'll see you tomorrow. When you get here, stop in and I'll make you something special . . . on the house."

"That sounds great!" She tackled me in a hug, causing me to almost lose my balance. "I'm so glad that I met you, Lana . . . what would I do without you?"

CHAPTER
4

Cleveland Hopkins International Airport is no LAX, but as far as airports go, it holds its own. As I drove my parents around the bend to the second-level departure lanes, a sense of wistfulness passed over me—the same feeling I got every time I came to the airport—and I wished that I was the one bound for a different destination. Palm trees, sandy beaches, and drinks in coconuts danced through my head as I waited for the stoplight to turn green.

"Now," my mother lectured, interrupting my daydream. "Do not forget to lock the money in the safe all the time. When Anna May comes to work, you take the money to the bank. Make sure to write everything down every day, and save the receipts for Mommy to see when I come home. Do not go to the bank at nighttime because then Mommy will worry about you every day."

"Yeah, yeah." I waved a hand at her. "I know what to do."

I could feel my mother staring at me out of the corner of my eye. "Why are you so crabby this morning? Are you not sleeping good again?"

"I slept fine; I just haven't had enough coffee." Early morning is not my most graceful time. "I'll be fine once I get to Starbucks."

My mother huffed. "You drink too much coffee. This is no good for you and will make you very nervous."

"She probably gets that from me, Betty," my dad said from the backseat. I could hear the smile in his voice. "There's nothing better than a morning cup of joe."

In front of their airline's drop-off entrance, I double-parked next to a family of four all saying their goodbyes. No matter what city you're in, the story is the same. Get in and get out. Unload and go. The goal is to beat the airport monitors before they can make it to your car to signal you off.

The three of us hustled out of the car, and I helped unload their bags from the trunk. We quickly hugged and I scooted back into the car, taking off with a cheery honk before the family of four had finished their send-off.

The time display on the radio told me there was still time to get coffee and beat Peter to the plaza . . . if I didn't get stuck in traffic. It must have been my lucky morning because the roads were clear of snow and traffic was light. I made record time, pulling into the plaza parking lot thirty minutes later. It was still dark out, and only a few cars speckled the employee parking section. I noticed that Isabelle's car was there and covered with a thick layer of snow. Strange. It hadn't snowed since last night.

I parked next to her car, and just as I was getting out, Peter came whipping through the parking lot in his beat-up Chevy Malibu. He slid carelessly into the spot next to mine—a little too closely—and turned off the engine.

"Whoa . . . there's still ice everywhere," he said, getting out of the car and testing the pavement with his combat boot.

"Yeah." I scowled at him and hugged the warm cup against my chest. "Be careful, you almost hit my car . . . and I almost dropped my coffee."

"Nah, don't sweat it, I'm an expert in the snow."

We crunched through the parking lot and made our way inside. The short time we'd spent outside had turned our cheeks and noses red.

"So," Peter said, with an amused grin on his face. "Are you ready to be the boss lady or what?"

I groaned. "I don't really have a choice . . ."

"You're gonna do great. I'm totally excited for you to be the boss of me."

"Uh-huh."

In front of City Charm Souvenirs stood a petite Asian woman with big curls and a long trench coat. She looked as if she was waiting for the store to open.

"Wonder who she sneaked in behind," I mumbled to Peter.

"Probably didn't want her to stand outside in the cold or something. It is way frigid out there."

As we passed, she turned to face us, her wide, inquisitive eyes looking between me and Peter. To say that the woman was beautiful would be a severe understatement. She was striking. The only time I've ever seen cheekbones that well defined, they had been on a model.

Next to me, I think I even heard Peter gasp.

"Excuse me," she said, stopping us in our path. Her

pouty, fuchsia-tinted lips formed a brilliant smile showing perfect white teeth. "Could you tell me when this
store opens? I see the light is on, but there doesn't seem
to be anybody around."

I looked past her at the well-lit store, expecting Isabelle to be there, standing at her usual spot behind the
register. But the woman was right: No one was around.
"Um, the plaza doesn't open until nine. You still have
some time left, but there's a bench you could wait on."
I pointed past her to the bench that sat against the koi
pond's fence.

"I was hoping to catch the owner before the store
opened." Her eyes fixed back on the store and she craned
her neck to get a better look toward the back. "I was sure
that he'd be here."

"Usually his wife opens the store," I told her. "Brandon isn't much of a morning person."

She laughed to herself and then turned back around
to face me. "Of course he isn't." She removed a pair of
knit gloves from her jacket pocket. "I'll stop by another
time then. Thank you."

She tipped her head, giving Peter a more prominent
smile, and then walked back toward the entrance.

"Hm, what the heck was that about?" I asked, watching her leave the plaza.

Peter whistled. "She is hot. Like . . . super hot."

"Better not let Kimmy hear you say that."

He blushed. "Huh?"

"Never mind," I said, stifling a laugh. Kimmy Tran,
who worked at China Cinema and Song, was a childhood friend of mine. And, she was also maybe Peter's
new girlfriend. They were keeping things quiet at the
moment.

My eyes fell back on the store. Hadn't Brandon promised to open this morning? Where was he? And where
was Isabelle?

Peter nudged me. "What's up with you?"

"Nothing, I guess . . ."

"You have 'something' face."

I turned to him. "It's just that Isabelle's car was already here, and she made a deal with Brandon that she
could sleep in today if she closed up for him last night."

"Maybe his car broke down and he took her car this
morning."

"But there was snow on the car . . . it hasn't snowed
since last night," I reminded him.

"Or her car broke down and he took her home, you
know? And they're not here yet."

"But the lights are on . . ." I pointed at the window.

"She probably just forgot," Peter said, shrugging it
off. "I don't think it's a big deal."

"Yeah, maybe that's it." Convincing myself that Peter had to be right, I pushed down the uneasiness that I
felt and we continued on to Ho-Lee Noodle House.

The restaurant was cold, and I cranked up the heat
knowing the Mahjong Matrons, our first customers
every morning, would complain about the cooler temperatures. I went about my morning duties while Peter
banged around in the kitchen.

At nine o'clock, I unlocked the front doors in anticipation of the four elderly women's arrival. They did not
disappoint.

The four women marched in, single-file, bundled in
their oversized jackets and hats. They never bothered
with waiting to be seated. Instead, they headed straight
for their designated booth near the front window that

looked out into the plaza. Pearl and Opal, who were sisters—and the oldest of the bunch—took their places nearest the window while Helen and Wendy filed in after them.

I greeted the women as a formality. I already knew what they were going to order because it was the same thing every day: rice porridge, pickled cucumbers, century eggs, and Chinese omelets with chives. Nothing more, nothing less.

For a few months, I'd anticipated some type of change, but they hadn't surprised me yet. I didn't even bother with menus anymore. Not that what they ordered was on the menu.

"And how are you ladies doing this morning?"

"Cold," Pearl, the eldest of the bunch, replied. She removed her hat, smoothing down her graying hair. "We are very much excited to have our tea this morning."

That was my cue. I headed back into the kitchen, grabbed the ladies' tea, and placed their order with Peter.

When I came back out, Opal, Pearl's younger sister, looked up at me. She was the quieter of the two, and a slip of a woman. Sometimes I had to strain just to hear her. "Did your mommy and daddy leave for Taiwan today?"

"Yeah, I took them to the airport this morning." I placed the teapot in the center of the table.

Helen, the mother hen of the group, reached for the pot and poured a cup for each of the women. "I will pray that they have safe travels," she said with a curt nod.

An elderly couple walked in and I excused myself from their table. Usually I tried to seat people a reasonable distance from them. They were prone to gossiping, and sometimes they would try to get other tables in-volved. Even though it was harmless, a lot of people didn't like to be disturbed during their meal.

I went back into the kitchen to grab more tea. Peter was busy on the grill, bobbing his head to the heavy metal humming from his kitchen radio. "The food is just about done."

I gave him a thumbs-up and took my tea service out into the dining room.

Within five minutes, I was back with the new table's order and ready to pick up the food for the Matrons. As I started to place the food on the tray, a loud bang came from the back room behind the kitchen. I jumped, nearly dropping a plate of pickled cucumbers.

Peter looked at me with confusion, turning down the volume dial on the radio. "Is someone at the service door?"

The banging continued.

"Must be," I said, wiping my hands on my apron. "Do we have a delivery coming this morning?"

He shook his head. "No . . . no deliveries before ten. It's a Mama Lee rule."

I scurried to the back room behind Peter to see what all the commotion was about. When he opened the door, it flew back in his face. Kimmy Tran barreled into the restaurant from the service hallway; her already messy hair, piled in a bun, was teetering to the side of her head. Her face was flushed and her chubby cheeks looked like two beets.

"There is blood everywhere!" she screamed. "Every-where! Call the police!" She waved her hands in a frantic circle around her head.

"Kimmy . . . calm down, what are you talking about?"

She started to hyperventilate. "I was taking out the trash . . ." She looked behind her at the door.

"Okay," I said, trying to keep my voice steady. "And then what?"

"I was walking past City Charm and the door was open a crack," Kimmy said, turning back to me. "And I thought maybe Isabelle forgot to close the door or something. But when I went to stick my head inside, they were both lying on the floor . . . blood everywhere!" She started to panic again, and looked at Peter. "Call the police!"

Peter stared at me, his eyes wide.

"Call the police," I instructed him. "I'll be right back."

"I don't think you—"

But I was gone before he could finish his sentence. I was out in the hallway, not thinking about anything except that my friend was in trouble and I had to get to her.

The door was still nudged open from when Kimmy poked her head inside. Afraid to touch the handle, I stood at the threshold and took a deep breath. Slowly, I stuck my head in the opening. I took one look and let out an involuntary scream. There they were, husband and wife lying next to each other on the floor. All my eyes saw were flashes of red and blank stares before they squeezed themselves shut.

In that moment, I wished I'd never left the restaurant.

CHAPTER
5

I'm not sure how I made it back to the restaurant. I want to say that Peter came and walked me back into the sanctity of Ho-Lee Noodle House, but I'm not sure.

While I had been next door seeing what couldn't be unseen, Peter had called the police and remembered to rush the food out to the Mahjong Matrons. In my state of panic, I had left the restaurant completely unattended. My only hope was that they wouldn't suspect something was going on when I didn't show up with their food.

Kimmy and I sat in the back room, side by side, on the small couch my parents had failed to replace since my childhood. The couch was worn from years of use; when you sat down, the cushions sank to an uncomfortable level. I stared at my knees trying to stop myself from thinking about the bloody scene I'd witnessed next door.

Two uniformed police officers from the Fairview Park Police Department had shown up and informed us that Detective Trudeau—Adam—was on his way. The first officer to arrive was a young guy with sandy-blond hair, freshly buzzed. Given his youth and demeanor, I had the distinct impression that he'd just graduated from the academy. With the precision that came from being new, he asked us a series of questions from a list in his notebook, checking things off as we commented on this or that. After he was finished, he instructed us to wait for Trudeau. I didn't think that'd be a problem. Kimmy, for once in her life, was speechless.

Peter poked his head in the doorway. "I called Mrs. Feng and Ian," he informed us. "They're on their way."

"Oh good." I took a breath. Mrs. Donna Feng was the widow of Mr. Feng, who had been the Asia Village property owner. Since her husband's untimely demise, Donna had taken a backseat and given herself the position of "silent partner" while Ian Sung took the reins. Previous to Mr. Feng's murder, Ian had been his partner and handled various other smaller properties owned by the Feng family.

"I also put up the CLOSED sign and cleared out the old couple, but the Matrons won't budge. They want to know what's going on back here."

I sighed, pinching the bridge of my nose. "I'm not surprised."

"What do you want me to tell them?"

"Maybe tell them there was an accident and the police have ordered us to clear everyone out. Make it sound like we don't know anything, either. That might get them to leave easier."

"You got it."

"Oh, and Peter," I said as he started to disappear. "Thank you for taking care of everything."

He poked his head back in the room. "No problem, boss. Holler if you need me." And his disembodied head disappeared back into the kitchen.

Kimmy scrunched her face. "Boss? Where are your parents?"

"They're on their way to Taiwan," I told her. "Your parents didn't tell you?" Nearly everything that happened in the plaza was common knowledge. Trying to keep a secret in this place was like trying to keep a millennial off social media.

She shook her head. "No, they didn't mention it. When did they leave?"

"This morning."

"And you're in charge?"

"Yup."

"Did Anna May crap her pants?"

"Yup."

She blew out a deep breath. "Man, they are going to freak when they find out about this."

I put my head down. I hadn't even thought of that. My parents were definitely going to flip out. How was I going to tell them two people were found dead right next to their restaurant as soon as they left town?

"Go figure, Asia Village is a crime scene again!" She sank deeper into the couch, her face filled with disgust.

The young police officer showed up in the doorway with Detective Trudeau standing behind him. "They're both in here, sir." He gestured to us and then stepped out of the way.

Adam stepped through the threshold, giving us both a pensive look. "Ladies, are you all right?"

Kimmy looked up at him. "I could use a smoke."

He nodded with understanding. "Miss Tran, why

don't you step outside and I'll speak to Miss Lee until you get back."

Kimmy turned to me, raising her eyebrows. "Your boyfriend calls you Miss Lee? Now, that's some discipline." She smirked and hoisted herself up from the couch. "I'll be right back."

I blushed. When she left the room, I snuck a glimpse at Adam. "I'm sorry, I didn't . . ."

"Don't worry about it," he said with an amused smirk. "I know how these things work with women." Just as fast as the smirk appeared, it faded and he was back in detective mode with the grim expression I'd come to recognize as his no-nonsense face. "What can you tell me?"

I shook my head. "Not much really. Kimmy came pounding on our back door and Peter and I let her in. She wasn't making a whole lot of sense, and all she told us was that there was lots of blood. I rushed over there thinking maybe . . ." I looked down at my hands. "I probably shouldn't have, but I wasn't thinking about *that*. I thought maybe there was something I could do."

He exhaled. "The scene in there is hard to take in, that's for sure. I'm sorry you had to see that."

I peeked at him from the corner of my eye. "What happened? Do you think they were robbed?"

"The coroner is on his way, but from what we can tell so far, it looks on the domestic side. Looks like they argued, maybe he pushed her and she fell wrong, hitting her head pretty hard on that cement floor. His gunshot wound is self-inflicted."

My eyes widened. "That's impossible."

He cocked his head at me. "Why would you say that?"

"Because they were in love . . ." I whispered. "They just got married . . . they were happy."

He sat down next to me, making the couch feel even smaller than it already did. Our knees touched and even though it was the slightest contact, it was comforting. "Lana." His voice softened, and he sounded more like Adam and less like Detective Trudeau.

A tear trickled down my cheek, dangling on my chin. "And . . . she was my friend." I sucked in my lower lip, trying to hold back the waterfall that was threatening to come pouring out. "We were all going to get dinner, and everything was going to be great . . ." I trailed off, knowing a full-blown babble was about to occur.

Adam must have sensed the breakdown was coming on because he rushed to shut the back door to give me some privacy. When he returned to the couch, he wrapped an arm around me and nudged me closer to him. I sank into his chest and let it all out.

Anna May showed up a little after Adam had gone back to the crime scene and I'd put myself back together. She had offered to skip her next class to help close up the restaurant while I went to the police station with Kimmy to fill out an official statement.

On a regular day, Anna May gave me a hard time on just about everything, but today my older sister was rife with compassion, knowing that I had formed a bond with Isabelle. "You going to be okay, little sister? I can rush through things here and meet you there."

"No, I appreciate it but I'll be fine. Plus, Kimmy will be with me, so I won't be totally alone." I forced a weak smile. "Thanks, though."

We hugged, which isn't a usual occurrence for us, but it was nice to have her support. I needed all that I could get right now.

After I made a quick call to Megan filling her in on what happened, I said my goodbyes to Peter and Anna May. Kimmy was driving with me to the police station, and we planned to meet in front of China Cinema and Song.

However, when I walked out of the restaurant, I found an entourage of people circled around her that I didn't expect. Front and center were the Mahjong Matrons, who huddled around her asking for her firsthand account of what had been going on. On the outer layer of people stood a few of the other shopkeepers, a couple of random stragglers, and Ian Sung. He happened to turn around and make eye contact with me as I came up on the crowd.

"Oh good, Lana, you're here." He stepped away from the crowd to greet me. In his usual ensemble of Armani business wear, he looked more like a *GQ* model than a property owner. He placed a gentle hand on my elbow. "I was worried about how you were holding up."

I took half a step back, and he removed his hand. When I'd first met Ian, he'd made it extremely clear he was interested in more than a business relationship with me. Though I found him attractive, there was something about Ian that sent warning signals to various regions of my brain and parts of my gut, too. He'd seemed to have slightly gotten the message and had backed off in recent weeks. I did my best not to encourage him. "I see Kimmy is getting her fifteen minutes of fame." I nodded toward the crowd surrounding her.

"This is terrible," Ian said, shaking his head in dismay.

"Asia Village can't afford another . . . disaster. Not while I'm trying to get this place up and running to its maximum potential."

"Is that what you're worried about? Bad publicity?" The outrage in my voice rose with every word. "Two people are dead."

He put his hands behind his back and straightened his shoulders, his chin lifting as he spoke. "As a businessman, I have to look out for the well-being of the plaza, Lana. This affects everyone."

I didn't have the stomach to talk business strategies versus human emotion with him . . . not after what had happened. "Where is Donna?"

"She's on her way. I guess she was at some conference near Hudson." He glared at the crowd. "My only hope is that some of these people disperse before she gets here. I don't think it's going to help her state of mind. You know how she feels about gossip after . . ."

"Allow me to help with that," I said, and shoved my way through the crowd. "Excuse me, everyone, but we've got to go. I'm sure Kimmy can chat with all of you later." I grabbed Kimmy's wrist and dragged her toward the entrance.

"Hey," Kimmy snapped. "What's the big rush?"

"Let's get out of here before Donna shows up," I said, raising my eyebrows at her.

"Oh right. Good point."

I let go of Kimmy's wrist and we left through the main entrance, hurrying to my car. It had started to snow, and a light dusting had begun to blanket the cars.

I cranked up the heat and waited a few minutes for the engine to warm up. "Hopefully this won't take too long." I thought back on my previous visits to the police station. I wasn't looking forward to returning.

"Does it really matter at this point?" She leaned back in the seat, closing her eyes. "I'm not exactly in a rush to get home."

I looked at her out of the corner of my eye as I backed out of the parking space. "Why not?"

Her eyes popped open, and she turned to face me. "Are you? I mean, out of everyone you were the closest with Isabelle. Do you really want to go home and be alone with your thoughts for the rest of the day? You saw what I saw, and it ain't pretty."

I pulled the car out onto the street and headed down Lorain Road. "I didn't think it bothered you that much."

"Oh, you mean back there?" she asked, jerking a thumb over her shoulder. "Sometimes you have to put on a little show for people."

CHAPTER

6

After the police station, I took Kimmy back to the plaza to pick up her car. While we'd been giving our statements, the police had partitioned off part of the plaza to seclude the souvenir shop, and Donna had officially closed the plaza for the day.

Anna May had sent a text to let me know that she'd closed the restaurant and to call her if I needed anything.

The roads were starting to get slippery, and I took my time getting home, not anxious to sit—like Kimmy had mentioned—with too much idle time to think. I was exhausted, but too restless to fall asleep. I contemplated the pile of books I'd just bought on my last trip to the bookstore with Isabelle.

My heart lurched at the memory of us standing in the mystery aisle at Modern Scroll. It had been just another average day at Asia Village. Hard to believe that it had been less than twenty-four hours since we'd been there. It felt like a lifetime ago.

As I thought back to the conversations we'd had only

yesterday, my mind stuck on her comment about wishing she were a private detective. Was that a pointed inquiry? Had I dropped the ball? Should I have asked more questions or gone along with her line of thinking? Maybe her concerns about Brandon's extracurricular activities were more serious than I realized.

I pulled into the parking spot that I'd claimed as my own, then shuffled down the sidewalk to our apartment cluster. The grounds people had sprinkled enough salt on the walkways to ensure there were no lawsuits this year.

Kikko rushed the door as I stepped inside.

I gave her a little pat on the head and made my way into the living room, where Megan was perched on the couch with a ball of yarn and knitting needles, entertaining her new craft of the month. She was in the process of making her first full-sized blanket. I was confident that she'd give this up as soon as the weather warmed. The process beyond frustrated her and she'd already started the blanket over three times.

She looked up from the couch, her hands frozen in place for the next stitch. "There you are!" Megan dropped her needles, and the ball of yarn tumbled to the floor. She stood up and wrapped her arms around me, suffocating me in her tumble of blond hair. "How are you holding up? I've been sitting here like a nervous wreck waiting for you to get home. I wish you'd let me meet you at the police station."

"It's okay, really. Kimmy was with me and the two of you in a room together . . ."

She released me from the hug and studied my face. "I can behave myself, you know. I wouldn't start a fight with her in the police station."

"Plus, why sit there when you don't have to?" I asked, tugging off my boots.

"So tell me what happened . . ." She ushered me to the couch. "There hasn't been anything on the news or online."

"They might not have gotten ahold of the families yet, I don't know." I sat on the edge of the couch, searching for the right words. Flashes of the crime scene skipped through my head. I squeezed my eyes shut, willing the images away.

"It's okay if you don't want to talk about it. I'm really sorry you were the one to find them that way. I know you liked her very much."

Tears were starting to well in my eyes. "It's just so unexpected . . . so strange. They seemed so happy. I don't know what could have gone wrong."

"Well, you see it on the news all the time. Husband goes crazy—maybe gets jealous—kills the wife. Do you think that's what happened?"

Kikko jumped up and plopped herself on my lap, looking at me expectantly. I gave her head a pat.

"I'm not sure; I can't see it going that way. Not that I cared much for the guy, but he didn't seem like the violent type. Or the suicidal type, for that matter."

"So what would be another scenario?"

"Trying to come up with another explanation is hard because I don't have many details right now. I left before the coroner came out. Adam said it's possible that it was an accident. Maybe he couldn't save her and he didn't know what to do. The way she fell . . ." I shook away the image of her distorted body. "I don't know, it still doesn't seem right. If she was hurt, I don't see him giving up without getting her some kind of medical attention."

She sat back on the couch, her face covered in disbelief. "Wow, either way I still can't believe it. It's one thing to hear about it on the news, but for it to happen in your own town . . . to someone you know? He did seem nice the one time I met him. Who could have seen this coming?"

"Maybe she did," I said, thinking back to the conversation Isabelle and I had at the Bamboo Lounge. "Maybe I'm being blind to the whole thing."

"What do you mean by that?"

"Well, he took advantage of Isabelle sometimes when it came to running the store. He would leave and stick her with closing after she'd been there since open and was always rushing off to run supposed errands."

She crinkled her brows. "What kind of errands?"

I shrugged. "She started to think he was seeing someone else . . . but didn't know anything for certain. He never told her where he was going or how long he would be gone. I tried to convince her that wasn't the case . . ."

"She was probably right. You know how women have a sixth sense about this sort of thing. Sounds to me like something suspicious *was* going on. He could have been cheating on her . . . or gotten wrapped up in something," Megan said, tapping her chin. She had that look on her face. I knew it all too well.

"Oh no, don't even think about it." I wrapped my arms around my legs, hugging my knees to my chest. "Not this time."

"What?" she asked, holding up her hands in defense. "We can speculate, can't we?"

"Speculating, sure . . . but I know that face. Whatever is going on, Adam can figure it out," I assured her.

"Are you trying to convince me of that? Or yourself?"

"You. We need to stay out of it. I have to run my parents' restaurant, and I don't have time to run around figuring out what the heck is going on. *If* anything is going on at all. For all we know, it was an accident just like Adam said." Even as I said it out loud, I didn't believe it. I couldn't shake the feeling that something wasn't right about all this. And could I really stay out of it when I felt that way?

The doorbell rang and Kikko jumped up from my lap, scuttling to the door. She sniffed under the crack, snorted, and proceeded to bark.

"Who's that?" I asked.

Megan darted for her purse on the kitchen table, pulling out her wallet. "Oh, that's the pizza. I ordered it just before you got home. I thought you might need some comfort food."

"Oh." Now that I thought about it, I hadn't eaten all day. "Did you get it with a side of doughnuts?"

She snorted. "You wish."

CHAPTER
7

The shrill ringing of my cell phone jolted me awake. I squinted at the glow of light in my otherwise dark room. Without checking the time, I knew that it was too early for anyone good to be calling. I slapped my hand over the phone, struggling to grab it from my nightstand. A string of numbers stared back at me along with the knowledge that it was only four a.m.

International call.

"Laaa-na . . ."

"Mom?" I mumbled into the phone.

"Yes, it's Mommy. I am calling to tell you that me and Daddy made it okay to Taiwan."

"Oh . . ." I rubbed my eye and sat up, leaning against the wall. "Good, that's good."

My mom chuckled. "I forgot it is still very early there. Sorry."

"Don't worry about it; I'm glad you guys made it there safe. Was the flight smooth?"

"Yes. How is the restaurant?" she asked. "Everything okay?"

I thought about the events that had taken place the previous morning. That image of Isabelle twisted and lifeless on the floor flashed through my mind, followed by Brandon lying next to her in a crumpled heap . . . all that blood . . . "Yeah, everything is fine, Mom."

"Good," she said, sounding relieved. "You know that Mommy worries about you."

"I know, Mom . . . I'm fine, and we'll be okay until you get back. You just . . . try to have fun there."

After we hung up, I tried my hardest to fall back asleep, but my fib was weighing on me and the imagery was lingering. I didn't have the heart to tell my mother what was really going on at home because I knew she had enough to deal with. And knowing her, she would get right back on a plane and come home, which was senseless because there was nothing any of us could do. On the other hand, if she talked to my sister—or anyone else from the plaza for that matter—she'd find out that I'd lied to her. And my mother wasn't the type of person to care if my intentions were good or not. I could imagine my mother and sister talking right now, and Anna May callously blurting out the news about what had happened, sending my mother into a frenzied state.

I reached for my phone again and called my sister, hoping that she was up, too. The call went to voice mail, and I hung up without leaving a message. I'd try again tomorrow.

Tossing and turning, I tried to convince myself that I'd deal with it when it happened. *If* it happened.

Instead of running through possible outcomes resulting from my lie, I tried to think of anything but. My mind ran over the new responsibilities I'd have at the restaurant and the schedule I would have to follow. That's when it hit me. Today was the day of my interview! With everything going on, I had completely forgotten to ask anyone to cover for me. I made a mental note to do it as soon as I got up for the day.

I fell asleep rehearsing what I would say to my not-future employer if I ever got my interview.

Running on a few hours of crummy sleep, I dragged through the excruciating process of getting ready for work and stuffed myself into my freezing car. The windows were iced inside and out. I blasted the heat and sat staring at the steering wheel remembering the warmth of my bed. On the radio, the weatherman announced that today was the beginning of a series of below-zero days. Joy.

While I waited for my car to unthaw, I tried calling my sister again. This time she answered.

"Talk fast, I have class in half an hour, and I'm already running late," Anna May said. She sounded out of breath.

"Oh, so you have school today?"

"Yes, Lana . . . I have class every Thursday. You know that." She paused. "Why? Are you not up to going to work today because of what happened?"

"Well . . . speaking of what happened, did you talk to Mom?"

"No, she called last night, but I was passed out," my sister told me. "I don't have time to call right now, so I figured I'd wait until tonight. Did you tell her?"

"I don't want to worry them . . . I was thinking maybe we shouldn't say anything until they get back."

There was silence on the other end, and I could envision my sister sliding her eyes back and forth as she contemplated. "If she asks me about the plaza, I'm going to tell her."

I groaned. "Anna May . . . please."

"She probably won't ask me about the plaza since they decided to leave you in charge. But you should really tell them what's going on. You're going to make it worse by not saying anything."

"If she says anything about the plaza, just change the subject. You're good at that."

"Lana, I don't have time for this. I have an exam today. Look, as far as covering for you goes . . . I've been studying my butt off all week. It's really important that I be there today. So if you don't think you *really* need me, then . . ."

I knew how important school was to my sister. And even though I wanted that job, it felt a little selfish with everything going on. "I'll be fine."

"I'll check on you later . . . but I gotta go." And she hung up.

I stared at the phone in my hand, thinking about what to do about my parents—primarily my mom. If I called now, I'd have a lot of explaining to do, and I didn't have the mental capacity to deal with it this early in the morning. Best to take some time and think through what I was going to say.

I tried Nancy next. Nancy—Peter's mom and my honorary aunt aside from Esther—is our other full-time server. She usually works the split shift, picking up slack and covering lunches for me and the others.

When the call went to voice mail, I started to leave a message, then decided against it. Maybe this was a sign.

The drive in was less hectic than it had been over the previous weeks, and I rejoiced that the bigger holidays were behind us. There's a certain calm that falls over people after the first of the year, and it comes with a sense of relief for me. Aside from the Chinese New Year preparations taking place at the plaza, the excitement of holiday shopping had evaporated and the majority stopped rushing from one location to the next, avoiding winter as much as they could.

I trudged down Lorain Road cautious of black ice. At these freezing temperatures, you never knew what to expect.

Asia Village was still dark, the only light coming from a few headlights reflecting off the building.

As I turned the corner, I noticed that a stream of vans were parked along the side street leading to the service entrance of the plaza. A small huddle of people stood gathered together on the sidewalk near a bright beam of light illuminating a woman in a thick coat and furry hat. I pulled my car through the crimson archway, the dragons' golden scales covered with a thin layer of snow.

I parked my car facing the news vans to get a better glimpse of what was happening without being seen. The woman in the furry hat held a microphone and talked to someone in a black jacket and fedora, but I couldn't make out who it was.

A tap on my window startled me.

It was Peter.

I rolled down my window. "What are you doing out here? It's freezing."

"Watchin' the show." He pointed toward the news

vans. "Ian's over there giving them some kind of state-ment."

I squinted, studying the figure in black. "Of course he is," I sighed. Figures. I should have known it was him. Who else would it be?

"He's been there for twenty minutes already."

"Have you gone over at all?" I asked.

He shook his head. "Nah, I'm not much for the spot-light . . . especially after what happened last time."

"This is ridiculous, I'm going inside." I rolled up my window and turned off the engine.

Peter stepped back so I could open the door. "Mrs. Feng is going to be so mad."

"Well, that's Ian's problem now."

We walked to the entrance together, passing by a few Asia Village employees on our way in. Apparently everyone wanted to see what was going on.

As we headed toward the restaurant, we caught sight of a short woman with straight caramel-brown hair in a black coat and dress pants standing outside City Charm. Her hands were cupped around her eyes, trying to look inside the store.

My defense alarm immediately went off. "Excuse me, do you need something?"

Startled, the woman jumped and turned to face us. "Oh hi, I didn't hear you coming . . ."

"Can I help you?" I walked up, inches away from her, straightening my back.

She stuffed her hands into her coat pockets. "I was wondering what you could tell me about the owners of this store."

"And you are?" I folded my arms across my chest.

She looked past me at the entrance. "Um, I'm with

the *Plain Dealer*. I was hoping I could get a different story from what my partner is reporting outside. Do you think you can help me?"

My arms fell to my sides and I tried my best to keep my anger under control. "Reporters are not allowed in the plaza unless invited by someone, and I don't believe we invited you . . . so you can leave now." I pointed toward the entrance.

The woman appeared offended that I would deny her a story. "I'm trying to get something more personal for the community, and if you don't want to help with that, I have to wonder if you even cared about them at all."

I felt my nostrils flaring. Peter put a hand on my arm, reminding me he was there. "Look, if you want to get your story so bad, you can speak to the property managers. You're not welcome here. Now, unless you want me to have you removed legally, I suggest you be on your way."

We stood staring each other down like two cowboys in an old Western at sunrise.

She puffed up her chest. "That won't be necessary." Her eyes flicked toward Peter before she stormed off.

I watched her stomp out and noticed that a few people who had been loitering at the doors were watching us. When they caught me looking, they quickly turned away.

"You cool?" Peter asked, nudging my arm.

"Yeah, fine." I dug into my purse for the store keys and let us in. "Let's just try to get through this day without any more drama, if that's possible."

"You got it, boss," Peter said, giving me a salute.

Fifteen minutes later, Ian was knocking on the door, signaling me to let him in. "It *is* freezing out there today," he said as he rushed in, rubbing his hands together. "I thought they'd never let me leave." He removed his hat and ran a hand over his hair.

"What were you saying to them?" I asked, my hands naturally gravitating toward my hips. I could feel myself looking like my mother.

"I told them this whole thing was a tragedy and while we're devastated over what happened, it has no bearing on the shopping quality of Asia Village." He turned away from me and headed toward a table. "Would you mind getting me some tea? I need something to get rid of this chill."

"Ian!" I yelled to his back. "Two people are dead and you're talking about how it's still safe to shop here? That's so insensitive!"

He whipped around, his expression filled with shock. "Insensitive? Practical, you mean. We're going to lose business if we're not careful, Lana. This is the second incident to happen at Asia Village in a matter of months. I have to think of the well-being of the plaza." His tone was condescending and it only helped fuel my fire.

"That is such a business thing to say."

"It's the truth." He removed his coat, draping it over the back of a chair and placing his hat on top. He pulled out the chair next to it and sat down. "Now, some tea if you don't mind . . ."

I started to say something but thought better of it and stomped off to the kitchen, pushing the swinging doors a little harder than I meant to. The right door smacked against the stainless-steel counter that was behind it.

Peter jumped at the sound. "Whoa!"

"Sorry." I grabbed a teakettle off the shelf.

"What happened out there?" he asked, nodding toward the dining room.

I filled the kettle with hot water from the water dispenser. "Oh, nothing. Ian just needs some tea. You know, to warm him up after telling the news crew that it's safe to shop at the plaza . . . because it's not our fault that two people are dead."

"Wow, that guy is . . ." Peter shook his head. "I don't even know the word for it, man."

"I know a good word for him." I prepped a tray with the teakettle and cup, taking a deep breath before returning to the dining area.

"Do you want something to eat, too?" I asked with a hint of contempt as I set down the tea in front of him. It took everything in my power not to slam it on the table.

His cell phone rang before he could answer. He held up a finger signaling me to wait, and answered the phone. His voice raised an octave. "Good morning, Donna, I'm so glad—"

I could hear her voice on the other end of the phone, and she didn't sound happy in the least.

"Well, yes, absolutely, I understand—"

She cut him off again, and I could hear her talking a mile a minute.

"No, I didn't mean—" He closed his eyes and exhaled. "Yes, I'll be here. See you then."

He hung up and looked at me. "I'll be back later. I have to meet with Donna soon." He poured himself a cup of tea and leaned back in his chair, seemingly preoccupied.

"Fine, I have some things to do before we open." I left him to his thoughts and his tea, rushing back to the office to make my dreaded phone call. I wasn't really in the mood to deal with this, but maybe the best thing for me was to get away from this plaza. Too many things happened around here, and I longed for the quiet isolation of a cubicle.

A receptionist answered the phone and instructed me to hold while she patched me through.

"Hello, Mr. Forester?" My voice came out soft and unsure. I cleared my throat, scrounging up some courage. "This is Lana Lee. We had an interview set for later today."

"Oh yes, Miss Lee, how nice to hear from you," he replied, good-naturedly. "How can I help you?"

"Well, I'm afraid I won't be able to make today's interview. It turns out that my parents had to make an emergency trip overseas and they've left me in charge of our family business."

"I'm sorry to hear that. I hope that everything is all right with your family."

"It is, thank you." I twirled the phone cord between my fingers. "I'd really like an opportunity at this job, and I think I'd make a great fit at your company. I was wondering if there would be any way we could reschedule. Maybe I could come in when they get back?"

"When do you anticipate them to return?"

"It wouldn't be for at least two weeks."

"I will say that you were my favorite candidate for this position. And I've had the same thought about your place at this company." I heard him take a deep breath over the phone. "But I'm sorry, Miss Lee, we need this position filled as quickly as possible and we have quite a few people interested who can start immediately. I'm sure you understand."

"Of course, that makes sense." My shoulders sagged as the reality hit that I had officially lost my chance at this job. "Thank you for your time. I appreciate you taking my call."

"Take care, Miss Lee. I hope everything works out with your family."

I thanked him again and hung up. There were still a few minutes before I had to unlock the doors, and I used that time to remove the disappointment from my face. We hadn't even opened yet, and I couldn't wait to go home.

The Mahjong Matrons filed in and took their usual seats by the window. They wore worried expressions on their faces, and spoke hurriedly among themselves.

When I greeted them with their tea, Pearl was the first to speak. "This is bad luck," she said, staring up at me with concern. "That store is bad luck."

I set the teakettle in the center of the table. "It's just a coincidence," I said, trying to keep my voice calm. I didn't want to egg them on, knowing how fast they could spiral out of control given the right ammunition.

Wendy shook her head. "No, this store"—she pointed at the wall that stood between the restaurant and City Charm—"this store is bad luck. You do not want this bad luck to follow you."

The four women looked at one another.

"What?" I asked, eyeballing the four of them.

Opal reached into her purse. "We brought you this." She pulled out a beaded jade bracelet and handed it to me. "You keep this with you all the time. It will help keep away evil spirits."

"Um . . . thank you." I took the bracelet and slipped it over my hand.

"Trust us. This will help you stay safe." Pearl reassured me.

"I'll make sure to wear it every day."

All four women nodded in satisfaction. They had accomplished their mission for the morning. Now it was on to their next feat: breakfast.

Ian reappeared as the Matrons were getting ready to gather their things and leave. However, now the sudden rush they were in dissipated as they watched him claim a table.

"You're back early," I said, noting the two hours remaining until lunch. "What happened to your meeting with Donna?"

"She rescheduled for later this afternoon. Something else came up that she had to handle right away." He tapped the table with his index finger. "By the way, tomorrow morning before the plaza opens, Donna wants to call a plaza employee meeting. You need to be here an hour earlier."

"Fine. Do you want something to eat now?" I asked, feeling impatient. I was still aggravated with him for his actions earlier that morning. Plus I knew the Matrons were hovering to see if they could pump him for information. The gossip mill does not rest, especially in times of crisis.

"Maybe just some egg drop soup for now. I'm not sure if Donna wants to eat when she gets here."

I nodded. "Fine, I'll let Peter know."

When I came back out, Ian was talking with the Matrons from across the room. My only saving grace was that no one else had come in to witness their conversation.

"I think you should not open this store again," Pearl said with force. "It is bad luck. Every business that moves there will be cursed."

"That's nonsense," Ian replied. "There is no such thing as curses."

"The young people don't understand," Wendy said to Pearl with a sigh.

I eased through the dining room hoping they wouldn't suck me into their conversation. For the sake of argument, or lack thereof, I had gone along with their superstitious beliefs and taken the bracelet without comment. I didn't want them to use this in their argument against Ian.

I didn't have to worry, though, because Ian was starting a speech on why superstition was silly, and I managed to make it all the way up to the hostess station unnoticed. I plopped down on my stool and tried to eavesdrop without being obvious.

". . . problem with the older generation, and we can't live by those standards today," Ian told the ladies in a matter-of-fact tone. "These are new times, and no one believes in those things anymore."

"You be careful, young man," Pearl lectured. "We have lived a long time and know many things you do not understand. You are still a baby."

Ian snorted. "I'm hardly a baby."

The bells above the door jingled, and a woman wearing a black fur coat and leather gloves stepped in. Her eyes were covered by large, round sunglasses. A plump man in a tan coat followed closely behind her. He held a leather briefcase in his right hand and looked around the restaurant with apprehension.

The woman stepped up to the podium, removing her glasses, revealing eyes that were hardened and judgmental. I slipped off my stool, throwing on my smile designated for customers. She returned the gesture with a tight-lipped smile that told me she didn't mean it. She gave me a once-over, spending extra time assessing my hair. She shook her head, mumbled to herself, and took a deep breath of exasperation.

"Would you like a table for two?" I asked, ignoring the scrutiny.

"No, thank you," she replied, her voice deeper than I had expected. She was a thin woman with narrow features. In a manner of speaking she was attractive, but in a handsome sort of way. "I'm trying to find the property manager. I stopped at the office, but the doors were locked." She glanced over her shoulder in the direction of the property office. "Do you know when they'll be in?"

"Oh, he's actually right over there, waiting on a food order." I twisted in his direction, pointing at his table.

"Very good," she said, looking past me at Ian. "Thank you." She headed straight for his table, and the plump man behind her followed, giving me an anxious glance as he passed.

I watched Ian and the woman interact. The smile he greeted her with slowly started to disappear. She gestured toward the man standing behind her who gave Ian a terse nod, both of his hands now gripped tight to the handle of his briefcase.

The woman turned an about-face on the heel of her

designer boots and marched out of the restaurant with the plump man struggling to keep up.

Ian stood from his seat, smoothing out the wrinkles in his dress shirt. He buttoned his suit jacket and squared his shoulders, looking both determined and agitated.

"Lana, I'm going to need you to deliver that soup, if you don't mind." He didn't look at me as he said it; he just stared at the door, his eyes narrowing.

"Why?" I asked. "What was the deal with that woman?"

"That is Constance Yeoh . . ."

"Constance Yeoh?"

"Yes," he hissed, finally making eye contact. "Brandon's ex-wife."

"Ex-wife?" My eyes flew to the door, but she was gone. "He was married before?"

"I guess so. And to top off that surprise, she claims his store belongs to her now."

CHAPTER

8

"I can't believe he was married before and it never came up," I said to Peter. After Ian left, the Matrons lost interest and headed out themselves. Before they left, they made me promise I would update them should I learn anything interesting. The restaurant was now empty and I'd hunkered in the kitchen waiting for Ian's soup.

Peter poured the soup into a plastic container. "Maybe it was a sore subject or something," he offered.

"I don't know, I guess. It just seems weird to me that Isabelle never brought it up when she basically told me everything else about their life."

"Except where Brandon was disappearing to all the time . . ." Peter looked at me sideways as he put the plastic container into a paper bag.

"You noticed that, too?"

"Oh, for sure. He would disappear constantly. Sometime I had to help her with shipments because the boxes were too heavy for her. I asked where he was and she would always say the same thing—"

"Let me guess: He was out running errands." I finished for him.

He nodded. "How many errands can you have?" He stapled up the bag and started to remove his apron.

"Where are you going?" I asked.

"I'm going to run this over to Ian."

"Can I take it?" I asked. "I kind of want to see what's going on."

He shrugged his shoulders. "It's your call, dude . . . I mean, boss."

I smirked, taking the bag from his hand. "I'll make it quick."

I rushed out into the dining room only to find Adam standing at the podium with his hands in his jacket pockets staring at the ceiling. Against my will, a symphony of butterflies danced around in my stomach as I made my way up to the podium. "What brings you by, Detective?"

"Good morning, Miss Lee," he said, his voice low and soft. "There's a crew coming to handle a few things next door." He jerked a thumb over his shoulder. "And I thought since I'm already here, I'd come by to see how you're holding up."

"Oh? There's still more to be done over there?"

"Just wrapping up a few things . . ." he said, his gaze traveling to the bag in my hand. "Are you going somewhere?"

I looked at the bag as if it were a foreign object. "Oh . . . I'm bringing Ian some soup."

Adam stiffened at the mention of Ian's name. "Soup? Is he sick?"

I laughed. "No, he ordered it. I'm not bringing it from *me* personally."

His body relaxed and he let out a deep breath through his nose. "Oh . . . well, I'll walk over with you then." He gestured to the door, and I stepped in front of him, leading the way.

"So you were saying something about the scene of the crime?" I reminded him.

He stopped walking and turned to face me. "I was going to wait until we could sit down to talk about this . . . but I know how upset you are over what happened." He reached for my empty hand and gave it a squeeze. "The gunshot wound is not consistent with a suicide. The angle is wrong, and there should be gunshot residue on his hand but there isn't."

My hand felt slick in his. I jerked it away, rubbing my palm on my pants. "Meaning?"

"Meaning that even though the shot was taken at a close enough range for a suicide, someone staged it to look that way. The murder weapon was incredibly clean." His eyes studied my face as I processed what he was saying. "We just notified the families that this is now being treated as a double homicide."

"I knew it!" I said, a little too loudly. "I knew he couldn't have done it!"

"Lana . . ." His jaw clenched. He glimpsed around to see if anyone was staring. "As of now, my team and I are opening an investigation, and we want to go over the crime scene again before releasing it. With this new information, we may find something we missed before. At least that's the hope."

"So this means Brandon is in the clear." Mild relief washed over me as I said it. Even if he didn't commit the crime, he was still guilty of something. Staging a murder felt too calculated to be a random act of violence. Whoever this person was wanted Brandon to look guilty.

"And I need you to stay out of this. No digging around like you did with the Mr. Feng case."

It was almost as if the man could read my thoughts. "But—"

"No buts, Lana."

We continued our walk, the wheels in my brain moving at full speed. I turned to him as we reached the door to the property office. "It's just that . . ."

"Just what?" I could see the patience slipping from his eyes.

I stared at the door to the office. "Ian's inside talking to Brandon's ex-wife and her lawyer."

He raised an eyebrow. "And?"

"Wait, you knew?"

"Of course I knew, didn't you?" He cocked his head at me. "You were friends with them, right? Isabelle never mentioned it?"

My face reddened. "No, I didn't know."

"His parents told us about her when we notified them of what happened. I guess she's the executor of his estate."

"I can't believe you didn't tell me." I shook my head.

"That she's the executor of the estate?"

"No! That he had an ex-wife."

"Lana, I thought you knew. How was I supposed to know that you didn't know? You guys were friends . . . I just assumed."

My shoulders slumped.

"So what's the big deal?"

I gawked at him. "The big deal is that she's in there talking with Ian about taking over the property the day after her ex-husband dies. She just happens to be the executor of his estate. They're divorced . . . how does that even happen? And you don't find that the least bit suspicious after what you just told me?"

He contemplated this, then glanced up at the door. "Maybe I better take that soup in. It wouldn't hurt to join their chat."

After I left Adam with the soup, I returned to the restaurant in the hope of keeping busy. Of all the days to be slow, of course it had to be today. With no customers to tend to, I paced in front of the entrance to the restaurant, waiting for the door of the property office to open. In an effort to occupy myself, I called Megan to fill her in on everything that Adam had told me.

"Maybe they just forgot to mention it," Megan suggested when I told her about the mystery wife.

"How do you forget something like that?" I asked. "We talked about everything else. She told me all the details of how they met and how long they'd been together. Their first apartment, the way he proposed. Everything."

"Do you think maybe she didn't know?"

I thought it over. "I guess it's possible."

"You did say you thought he was keeping secrets from her all the time about where he was going. So why not about his past, too?"

"I suppose you're right."

"That's usually the case."

I pretended to gag. "Careful, your head might not fit through the doorway the next time you try to walk through."

"Har har."

I snickered into the phone.

"Well, what now. I mean, we have to look into this, right? Brandon was clearly being set up by someone. Do you think it could be this ex-wife?"

I thought about how Adam had just instructed me to stay out of it. "Maybe. I don't know . . . shouldn't we let the police handle this one?"

"Things got a little dicey toward the end when we were digging into the Mr. Feng case, but would they have solved it without our snooping around?"

She had a point, but I didn't have time to think about it at that moment because the door to the property office started to open. Adam slipped out, mouthing something over his shoulder.

"Ooh! Adam just left . . . I'll call you back and let you know what happened."

"Okay, we can talk about this more later, but just one thing before you go."

"Yeah?"

"Does he look dreamy today?"

I hung up to the sound of Megan snickering.

Adam's demeanor had changed since he'd entered the office, and the expression on his face led me to believe his hair might light on fire at any minute.

"Well . . ." I prodded. "What's going on in there?"

"That woman is a piece of work, that's what's going on in there." He tugged at his tie as he approached me, loosening the knot. "She had the nerve to tell me how to run my investigation. *My* investigation."

"What did she say?"

Before he could tell me anything, the door to the property office flew open and Constance Yeoh stormed out with her lawyer in tow. He scrambled to keep up with her long strides. Ian stood in the threshold with his hands behind his back, seemingly dissatisfied.

Constance marched up to us—Godzilla-style—and planted a gloved hand on her hip. "Mark my words, Detective, that property is mine, and if anything in there is damaged from your little investigation, I'll be coming to the police station for compensation."

"Constance," her lawyer whispered. It was the first thing I'd heard him say since they'd shown up. "Maybe it isn't wise to speak to the detective in that tone."

She held a finger up to his face. "Don't *you* tell me how to talk to someone. I pay you to work for me, remember?"

The lawyer put his head down and took a step back.

"Ms. Yeoh," Adam gritted through his teeth. "I can guarantee the property will be just fine when we're done with it, but I cannot let you in until my team is finished. Those are the rules."

"What's left to look at?" Constance said, inching toward City Charm, giving the exterior a disgusted glare. "The bodies are gone . . . what more do you want?"

"We're collecting evidence," Adam said in a flat voice, refusing to elaborate. "Until we're certain that we're finished, nothing can be contaminated by an outsider. My team is very careful."

"What evidence could possibly be left? My ex-husband killed that poor, moronic girl and then shot himself. Case closed."

"Constance . . ." her lawyer pleaded.

Adam's neck began to turn red. "Actually, Ms. Yeoh,

the case is *not* closed. New evidence has been discovered revealing that your ex-husband is not responsible for either death."

Her eyes bulged. "What do you mean, 'new evidence'?"

"Brandon Yeoh is not responsible for these murders. Someone set him up to take the fall for this, and we are reexamining the crime scene to see if anything was left behind that might lead us to the actual killer." He crossed his arms over his chest; a tiny sliver of self-satisfaction fell over his face as he watched her struggle for words.

She dismissed him with a flick of her wrist. "Fine, whatever. Collect your evidence. But trust me, I'll be going over everything with a fine-tooth comb and if there is anything disrupted from your . . . equipment, then I'll be speaking directly with the chief about you, Detective." She snapped her fingers and sauntered out with her lawyer tagging along behind her.

Poor guy.

Ian came up behind us, shaking his head. When they were officially through the entrance doors, he gave a low whistle and said, "That woman is scarier than Donna."

I turned to glare at him. "What?"

"I didn't say anything."

Adam nodded. "I have to agree. Mrs. Feng can be quite intimidating from what I've seen, but this woman is on a whole other level. Completely out of control."

"Is it true what you said?" Ian asked. "Brandon is really in the clear?"

"Yeah, he absolutely did not kill himself, and him killing his wife is not likely considering the circumstances. Someone took time to make him look guilty."

"But I still don't understand . . . how could she possibly own the property?" I asked. "Wouldn't it go to next of kin or something like that?"

"She has a will stating that at the time of Brandon's death, he relinquishes everything to her. And a living trust that gives her the right to take it over as soon as possible," Ian explained.

"Her?" I asked. "But what about his own wife?" Not that it mattered, but I couldn't imagine how someone's ex could be in charge of their personal matters after death.

"Isabelle's not listed on any of the documentation." Ian sighed. "It appears that Brandon may have never had his papers updated after the divorce. It's something we'll have to look into. We'll have to make sure there's not another will out there somewhere."

"So what are you going to do?"

He shrugged. "I have to discuss this whole thing with Donna and our lawyers. Find out if there's anything we don't know." He checked his watch. "Speaking of, I have to meet with Donna soon. I should get going."

Adam and I returned to the restaurant, standing outside the doors. He looked down at me; his neck and face were flushed. "I can never say that any of my encounters with you are dull."

"That's a good thing, right?" I cringed at the hopefulness in my voice.

He chuckled. "I suppose it is."

That night when I was getting ready to sleep, I paced around my bed, thinking about everything that had been going on. Maybe Megan was right; maybe I was trying to convince myself that I wanted to stay out of the investigation. I did, didn't I?

But how could I, I argued with myself. I stared at my mattress. Kikko watched me with anticipation. She could sense I was up to something.

I lifted the edge of the mattress, and Kikko sprang up, jumping to the floor.

I pulled out a spiral notebook with worn edges. It was my "detective" notebook. I had used it to help me sort my thoughts during the Mr. Feng ordeal.

Rifling through the notes I'd made at that time made the whole thing seem surreal. When I'd begun, I had no idea how much I would uncover and where it would lead me.

Before going to bed, I turned to a fresh section in the notebook and wrote out the details of what I knew so far, which wasn't a lot. I made notes about the murders and it being staged as a murder/suicide. After that, I jotted down my feelings about Constance Yeoh and what I thought her involvement might be. So far all I could come up with was either jealousy or greed. She seemed to want that property pretty badly; I just couldn't figure out why. A woman of her means should be able to attain anything she wanted . . . so why *that* store?

Lastly, I wrote a brief description of my mystery man . . . Captain Kirk. As far as I knew, he was the last person seen with Brandon. Did that have any significance?

When I was satisfied, I stashed the notebook back under my mattress and curled up underneath my blankets, Kikko burrowed behind my knees.

As I fell asleep, I started to think about how I could hear Megan saying, *I told you so.*

CHAPTER

9

"Laaaaa-na," my mother yelled into my ear.

My phone had rung when I was in that place right between consciousness and sleep. I was beginning to think I would never have another solid night of sleep again. The first call to let me know that they made it safely was fine, but was she planning on calling me this early the entire time they were gone?

"Mom!" I yelled back.

Kikko popped her head out from under the blanket and snorted. I guess she didn't like her sleep being disturbed, either.

"Ai-ya! Why did you not tell me about what happened next door?"

"What do you mean?" I asked, sitting up in bed. My heart began to race.

"About the Yeohs." By the tone in her voice, I could tell that she was losing her patience.

"Oh . . . that." I shifted under the covers.

"Yeah, 'oh that,'" my mother spat. "What happened?"

I went through the story, explaining the new developments Adam had informed us of earlier that day. Every couple of minutes she gasped. I ended with, "I didn't want you and Dad to worry. We have everything under control at the restaurant. And the police are almost finished there, so everything's pretty much back to normal." Except the killer was still on the loose. But I wasn't going to point that out to her.

"I told you. I told Mr. Feng. I told Mr. Sung. I told your daddy. That store is not lucky."

"Mom," I whined. "Don't be so superstitious. That could have happened anyplace."

"But it happened next door. Nothing stays there, nothing is good there." My mother started screaming in Mandarin. I couldn't make out what she was saying, but I caught the words "fish" and "taxi."

"What's going on over there?" I asked. "What are you talking about?"

"Your a-ma wants to go shopping for fish. She is making fish stew today."

"Ew." I crinkled up my face as if she could see me. "Are you going to leave the head on, too?"

My mother grumbled. "Do not change the subject, Lana. You need to be careful. If I did not talk to Anna May, I would not know anything. What if you were in trouble? How can I help you when you don't tell Mommy everything that is happening there?"

So Anna May had ratted me out after all. I'd have to remember to give her a good scolding. "Mom, we're fine. There's no trouble to get into. Adam has been stopping by and he won't let anything happen to me. Plus, the Mahjong Matrons gave me a jade bracelet for good luck. Everything will be fine. And don't forget, Peter is with me all day . . . and wait a second . . . I thought A-ma was having problems. She's making stew now?"

My mother paused before answering. "Everything here is okay. We will take care of her. You worry about you."

"Yeah, yeah, I know."

"Is the policeman your boyfriend now?"

"No, I told you, we just had dinner a few times. It's no big deal."

"Policemen are okay, but I wish you would meet a doctor . . . or a lawyer. Someone who can take care of you."

"Mother . . ."

"Okay, okay, you go to sleep, I will call you later this week. If something happens, you call Mommy right away, okay?"

"Yes, Mother, I will call you if anything else happens."

Unable to relax after our phone call, I stared at the ceiling, trying to clear my mind. I tried counting sheep, singing the alphabet . . . twirling my hair, but nothing worked. I was starting to feel hopeless. Or even worse . . . cursed. Every time I thought things were getting better, something else happened. And not just small, silly things.

I reached for the jade bracelet on my nightstand and slipped it on my wrist. Evil spirits, begone.

I woke up a minute before the alarm went off, but I didn't bother getting up. I wasn't looking forward to the employee meeting or another day at the plaza in general. Who knew what the day might bring?

I trudged through my morning routine, stalling at the coffeemaker for longer than necessary. Megan was still asleep since she'd worked the late shift the night before, and I could hear her snoring through the door.

Snowfall had been nonexistent overnight and temperatures remained below zero, as promised. I listened to the weather report on the way to work as the newscaster talked with enthusiasm about breaking winter records. I was not equally amused.

More important, at what point in my life had I started listening to the weather report?

When I arrived at Asia Village, the lot was filled with cars and the plaza was buzzing with employees. Everyone was gathered near the entrance of the property office in small huddles. A few folding chairs had been set out for the elderly employees to sit during the meeting. Mr. Zhang from Wild Sage sat front and center, his head nodding back and forth in a slow rhythm. Esther sat next to him, chattering in his ear, and I questioned if she counted as one of the elderly.

News had traveled fast about the recent update to the investigation, and the whole room was abuzz with gossip. As I passed the Yi sisters, I overheard them rambling off something about what had been reported on the six o'clock news the previous day.

Ian and Donna were whispering between themselves off to the side, and I sighed with relief knowing that the meeting hadn't started yet.

Someone tugged on my arm, and I turned to find Kimmy staring back at me.

"They've been arguing like that for fifteen minutes," she huffed. "I have to pee and I know the minute I go to the bathroom, they're going to start the meeting. I wish they would hurry up already."

"Have you seen Peter?"

She threw her hands up. "Why does everyone automatically assume that I've seen Peter? I'm not his keeper, you know."

I raised a brow at her. "What are you talking about? All I asked was if you've seen him. I don't know if he's here yet." I stood on my tiptoes and searched the crowd.

"Oh, well . . . no, I haven't seen him."

I gave her a sideways glance. "Everything okay? You seem a little on edge this morning."

She brushed a strand of hair from her face. "Yeah, fine. I'm just tired of everyone asking what's going on with me and Peter. We're just friends."

"I'll keep that in mind."

"It's like . . . I don't know. If people keep saying stuff, then he's gonna pull the guy card and disappear or whatever."

"What are they saying?" I asked.

"Just . . . stuff."

"Are you interested in him?"

She turned away. "I don't know. He's okay, I guess."

The crowd began to quiet, and when I turned to face the front, Donna was shooing Ian off to the side. She took her place at the head of the crowd, looking elegant yet professional in her cream-colored pant suit.

She smiled, taking in the group that formed, and waited for all attention to be on her. When everyone was silent and facing her, she took a step forward, the flower pattern on her suit jacket shimmering with the movement. "Good morning, everyone. Thank you for joining us on such short notice."

"Good morning!" we replied in unison.

"As you know, we have had yet another tragic incident at Asia Village. And so soon after the loss of my husband."

The crowd nodded, some bowing their heads in respect.

Donna, known for her articulate manner of speaking, took a moment to choose her next words. "While we transition through this difficult time, I must ask that all of you refrain from any type of unsavory gossip. If you know anything of importance, please pass this along to the police. Our point of contact for this situation is Detective Adam Trudeau. I'm sure all of you are familiar with him as he's been in and out of our lovely plaza quite a bit."

"I bet they're not as familiar with him as you are," Kimmy whispered to me.

Without turning my attention away from Donna, I elbowed Kimmy.

Donna continued. "The loss of this young couple is, without a doubt, tragic. And I'm sure that we are all equally surprised by these . . . developments. But we must remain respectful to the passing of Isabelle and Brandon. The media may want to talk to you about what kind of people they were or if they had any associations that might bring this type of danger into our workplace. I would like for everyone to stay away from those associated with the media as a courtesy to their families. This is a very difficult time for them, as you can imagine." Her eyes slid in Ian's direction.

A hand went up in the crowd. "Is the plaza going to shut down?"

Donna shook her head. "No, there will not be any changes in business. The plaza will remain open and we hope business will continue to thrive. Especially with Chinese New Year right around the corner."

Another hand shot up. "What will happen to the Yeohs' store?"

Donna glanced at Ian. "That is still to be decided. It will most likely be put on hold until after the Lunar New Year."

"I think the store should stay empty! That spot is bad luck!" someone yelled from the back.

Murmured speech flowed through the crowd as people agreed and disagreed with this statement.

Ian, who had been standing behind Donna to give her the spotlight, stepped up next to her and clapped his hands together. "Let's save that topic for another time. We can discuss things with the empty property as they come up, but for right now, we want to pass along that the funeral services will begin on Monday and the plaza will be closed for the duration of the ceremonies so we may all pay our respects. We have posted the details and information outside the community center." He stepped back, returning the floor to Donna.

"I'll be around for the next hour if you have anything you'd like to discuss. Otherwise, you are all free to go about your day," Donna said. "Thank you for taking time out of your morning to meet with us."

More than half the group stayed to talk with one another. With a break in the crowd, I spotted Peter, who'd been sitting on the floor outside the public restrooms. I waved him over and he responded with a nod, heading in our direction.

When Kimmy saw him coming, she ducked behind me and sneaked off to her store.

"Was that Kimmy?" Peter asked as he approached me. "Where's she running off to?"

"Uh, yeah, she had to pee."

He laughed. "She's going in the wrong direction."

Esther came up behind him, her face filled with worry. "Lana, I talked with your mommy this morning. She is very concerned about you."

I sighed. "I know, I talked to her, too. I'm fine, really. Just a little sad, is all."

She nodded in understanding. "Those two were very young people. They are too young to die."

I felt that rock in the pit of my stomach again. "Yeah . . . way too young."

"Me and your mommy saw Brandon at the casino the night before she left," Esther said. "He was so happy; he said that he had won a lot of money that day. No one would think he would die the next day."

Peter and I glanced at each other.

"Did you tell that to the police?" I asked.

Esther studied my face. "Do you think this is important?"

"Maybe. It could help them figure out what he was doing before . . . before what happened."

"Okay, I will tell them." She let out a deep breath, shaking her head. "Well, I will go open my store now. You call me if you need anything, yah?"

"I will, thanks."

She gave me a once-over, and before she walked

away, she said, "Stand up straight." Peter and I headed to the restaurant while I fished the keys out of my purse.

"He was at the casino . . . I thought he was running errands that night?"

He shook his head. "Man, that's so shady leavin' his lady to fit in some gambling. I was hoping he would be a better guy than that."

"I agree." Even though I hadn't liked Brandon to begin with, I had always held out hope that his errands were at least something of worth. That night he'd said he needed to run somewhere important before it was too late. Had he really ditched his wife at the store to spend time at the casino? And if so, what could have possibly been so dire?

And he'd run off with the mystery man. He had to be involved somehow. If he wasn't involved directly, he would at least know where Brandon went next. I needed to find him.

CHAPTER
10

- - - - - - - - - - - - - - -

Anna May came rushing through the door. Her cheeks were rosy and she was gasping to catch her breath. It was one fifteen and she was well past late. "Sorry, sorry, my criminal defense class ran over and traffic was a mess . . . I swear, you'd think these people never saw snow in their life. It's Cleveland, people."

I rested a hand on the podium. "It's fine, I'll just add it to the list . . ."

"List of what?" Anna May asked, taking off her hat and smoothing her hair down. "We're making lists of something now?"

"Why did you tell Mom about what happened next door? I thought we agreed that you weren't going to mention it."

"You said that, I didn't," Anna May shot back. "I told you I wouldn't say anything unless the plaza came up in conversation. And it did."

"I told you I didn't want them to worry about this.

They just left and they don't need to add more to their plates while they're trying to deal with A-ma."

Anna May rolled her eyes. "Oh please. The only reason you didn't want to tell them is because you don't want them to know that disaster follows you everywhere you go."

I gasped. "It does not!"

So the pleasantries were over, then.

"It's starting to seem that way, little sister," she said in a smug tone.

"Whatever, what do you know about me?" I went behind the hostess station and straightened the menus, tapping them on the counter.

"What I *do* know is that they should have left me in charge."

"Is that what this is about? You told them to get back at me?" I slapped the menus on the counter. "You can't even get here on time!"

"That's beside the point. I'm the oldest . . . and way more responsible than you are."

The door chimes tinkled and we stopped bickering before our conversation was overheard by a potential customer. A petite woman with a round face and even rounder curls smiled at us as she approached the hostess booth. Immediately, I recognized her, but I couldn't place her.

Shaking off the agitation that Anna May had boosted into high gear, I got my smile ready, returning hers as best I could. Anna May slipped away to the kitchen.

"Hello, how can I help you?" I asked.

"I'd like a table for one, please."

"Follow me." I grabbed a menu and lead her to a booth. "Would you like some tea?"

"Yes, please." The same expression was on her face, and I started to wonder if that was how she looked all the time. She was so familiar, but where had I seen her before?

I scurried into the kitchen, almost smacking Anna May in the face with the door.

"Watch it!" she yelled. "You're going break my nose one of these days."

"Who stands by the door like that? It's a door, people, open it."

"You're impossible, you know that?" Anna May said, shaking a finger at me. "You just want to fight with me all the time over nothing."

"Me? You're the one who starts the arguments all the time." I went to fill up a teakettle, turning my back to my sister.

Peter clanked around in the background pretending we weren't there. He'd known us long enough to know it was best to avoid contact when we were squabbling.

"That's so typical of you," my sister said to my back. "Walk away while we're arguing. An argument you started, by the way."

I whipped around with the teakettle in hand. "I don't have time for this conversation. I have to get this tea out and then you need to take over that woman's table so I can go to the bank. We can fight about this later if you want."

Anna May lifted her chin. "Fine . . . where's Nancy?"

"On lunch," I spat. "Now, if you'll excuse me." I left her stewing in the kitchen.

When I returned to the woman's table, she was scanning the menu with a pleased look on her face. She nodded to herself as her eyes went up and down the menu page.

I placed the tea on the table along with a glass of ice water. "Your server will be over in a few minutes."

She held up a hand to stop me. "Actually, I was hoping I could speak to one of the owners if they're available?"

I studied her features more closely, trying to place her. Now I knew who she was—she was the woman that Peter and I ran into the other day. The woman with the amazing cheekbones. Of course! "I remember you from the other day. You were here asking about Brandon and Isabelle. I knew you were familiar when you walked in."

She blushed. "Yes, I wasn't sure if you'd remember me."

"The owners are on a . . . business trip at the moment. But I'm handling things while they're away. Is there something that I can help you with?"

She closed her menu and gestured to the empty seat across from her. "Please, have a seat with me."

"Okay . . ." I hesitated for a minute before sitting. What on earth could this woman possibly want to talk to my parents about?

She poured herself a cup of tea. "Would you like some?"

I shook my head, finally deciding to sit. "I'm okay, thanks."

She nodded. "Well, I'll just get right to it, then." She stopped, eyes focused intently on her teacup, and smirked. "I'm sorry, how rude of me. I'm Marcia."

"Lana," I replied.

"I was wondering what you could tell me about what's

been happening with the store." She pointed at the wall that separated us from City Charm.

"The souvenir shop?"

"Yes, I understand there was an incident that happened the other day . . ."

"Are you a reporter?" I gave her another once-over.

"No, definitely not," she laughed. "I've tried leaving the property manager a few messages, but he hasn't returned my calls. That's why I thought I'd stop by. I figured since you were right next to it, you might know something that could help me. I'm very eager to get all my affairs in order."

"Your affairs?"

"Yes, you see, that souvenir store technically belongs to me now, and I'd like to get everything situated as soon as possible before I have to drive back to New York."

I shook my head, trying to clear my brain. Who the heck was this woman? "Wait, I'm sorry, did you say the store belongs to *you*?"

Her eyes shifted down to her hands. "I should have mentioned that upfront. I'm Brandon Yeoh's ex-wife."

I'd excused myself to the kitchen and paced the length of it while Peter and Anna May watched. "How many wives can this guy have?" I asked, incredulous. "He was what, thirty?"

"So, wait," Peter said. "You mean that hot woman from the other day was Brandon's wife, too? Man, that guy . . ."

Anna May leaned against the stainless-steel sink with her elbows propped on the edge. "I don't see how any of this is our problem. Just call Ian and have him deal with her. Why did she come here? She should have gone straight to the property office."

"I don't know. She said she was having a hard time getting ahold of Ian. But if she really did call Ian, why would he not mention that another ex-wife had surfaced?" I asked, directing my question to both of them. "What if she's not who she says she is and that's why she came here first? Maybe she's trying to feel out what we know before talking to anyone else."

Peter's eyes widened. "She could be like a secret reporter trying to get the inside scoop or whatever."

"But she showed up before any of us knew what happened to Isabelle and Brandon . . . so she had to originally show up for something else."

"Unless . . ." Peter started.

We stared at each other, both of our imaginations getting the better of us without another word being exchanged.

Anna May groaned. "Who cares? It's not our problem, Lana. Plus, it probably *is* his ex-wife. That guy was a complete jerk; he probably had ten ex-wives for all we know."

I continued to pace. Something was bugging me. This guy had been married two other times—that we knew of—and Isabelle had never mentioned it. And both exes now claimed to have rights to the souvenir shop. How was that even possible? And more important, why them?

Anna May stood up straight. "Forget this, I'm going out there and taking her order. Call Ian already. He can handle this and we can move on with our lives. Didn't you say something about getting to the bank?"

I nodded.

"Well, okay then. Go to the bank already."

Ian didn't answer his office line so I called his cell phone, which he picked up on the first ring. I told him the situation and he said he'd be by in a few minutes. In the meantime, I counted the cash in the safe and got the overnight bag ready to drop at the bank. A thought skipped through my brain—should I call Adam and tell him another ex-wife had popped up?—but I decided to wait and see what happened after Ian talked with her. Besides, he probably already knew about this one, too.

A few minutes later, there was a knock on the office door.

"Come in!" I yelled.

Ian poked his head in. "Lana, I'd like you to accompany me while I talk with . . . Ms. Yeoh."

"Why?"

"If she's anything like the last one, I need a buffer."

"Why me? Anna May can chaperone. She's already out there."

"Your sister is a little off-putting." He grimaced. "Please, Lana, don't make me sit this one by myself. You have that gentleness about you that puts people at ease. I could really use that right now."

"Fine." With an exaggerated huff, I locked the money bag back in the safe and followed Ian out into the dining room.

Nancy was back from lunch, and I waved at her while she served a family of four. She gave me a curious glance when she saw me with Ian. I shrugged as I led him to Marcia's table.

"Marcia, this is Ian Sung, our property manager," I said, stepping to the side.

Ian straightened the lapels on his suit jacket. "Pleasure to meet you," he said.

She extended a hand. "Oh, I'm so glad that you were able to meet with me on such short notice. Please, have a seat."

Ian sat down across from her, sliding in the booth to allow me enough room. I hesitated before I sat.

Marcia crinkled her brows. "Are you joining us?" She looked between me and Ian.

Ian smiled apologetically. "I'm sorry, I should have explained. Lana is my right-hand man, so to speak. She sits on the board of directors with me and usually helps with this sort of thing. I hope that's not a problem."

I smiled as if in perfect agreement.

Marcia gave a slow nod. "No, that's quite all right." She moved her soup bowl off to the side.

Ian folded his hands on the tabletop. "How can I help you? Lana mentioned something about you claiming to own the souvenir shop next door."

"Yes, I'm afraid that my attorney was not able to come with me today. He's in the middle of a big court case. But I have all the documentation to pass along to you. I thought you could review it with your legal staff." She sifted around in the oversized purse next to her and dug out a manila envelope. "Everything you need is in here."

He took the envelope from her and removed the clasp from the back, taking the papers out to examine them. "I see," he said to himself.

Marcia directed the conversation to me while Ian skimmed the documents. "You see, Brandon was a bit irresponsible with his finances, and he needed a little help with start-up money. When he found this place, he contacted me with a proposition."

"A proposition?" I asked.

"Yes. I would front him the money for the store and he would pay me back over time. If anything were to happen to him and he couldn't pay me back, then I would take over the store for him."

Ian looked up from the documents. "And I'm guessing that he didn't finish paying you back?"

Marcia's laugh was gentle, almost apologetic. "No, I'm afraid not. He's only had this store for what . . . maybe a month or so at most? And I haven't received any payment from him at all. That's why I was here the other day," she explained, looking at me. "It's not like him to not contact me, and I came to check on things."

"These documents will need to be assessed further. Unfortunately, I don't have a lot of knowledge in this particular department," Ian said, straightening the papers and putting them back in the envelope.

"Do you think you can meet with your attorney soon? I was hoping to have this whole thing straightened out before I head back home."

He sucked in his cheeks, and his chest puffed underneath his expensive suit. "We actually have a meeting set up for next week . . . we have another matter to discuss. I'm afraid we can't schedule anything with them any sooner."

"Oh, how unfortunate, I'll be gone by then. I suppose I can make another trip out this way after the New Year."

Ian shifted in the booth. I hadn't seen Ian squirm this much since his bomb of a speech at Mr. Feng's memorial. His foot tapped mine under the table. "If you don't mind me asking, what are your intentions with the property?"

"I'd like to liquidate everything within the store and put this whole thing behind me. I'm not interested in keeping it. My life is in New York. Besides, the souvenir idea was Brandon's thing. It wouldn't feel right to continue it without him."

"I see." Ian gave me a sideways glance.

"I still can't believe what's happened." She shook her head. "I don't know what kind of trouble he could have been in that would bring this tragedy into their lives. And to be staged that way . . . sounds like organized crime to me, don't you think? I just keep thinking . . . it could have been me in there."

My mouthed dropped. Did she really just say that?

Ian cleared his throat. "Yes, we were all taken aback by this."

She slipped her hand back in her purse and produced a card. "Please contact me once your lawyer has reviewed these documents. I'll be driving back to New York after the funeral for a couple of days to handle some business. But I can make arrangements to come back once everything is straightened out."

We said our pleasantries and excused ourselves from the table while she waited for her lunch. Ian asked me to follow him out into the plaza, and I gave Nancy a heads-up that I was stepping out.

When we were out of the restaurant, he turned to me, a frown on his face. "Lana, something is not right with this whole picture."

"I know," I agreed. "I got that feeling right after she told me who she was."

"After meeting these two ex-wives, and knowing Isabelle, I am almost positive that we're being duped."

"Duped?"

"I don't think the first Mrs. Yeoh is who she says she is."

I cocked my head at him. Okay, I hadn't expected him to take it that direction. "You think she's a fake? But Trudeau said Brandon's parents told them about Constance."

He held up a finger. "Ah, but he said that his parents told him about an ex-wife, but there was nothing specific about who she was. Just that an ex-wife was the executor of the estate and that her name was Constance. But do we know what she really looks like? It can't possibly be the woman we met. It just can't be. Look at these three women. Marcia reminds you of Isabelle, doesn't she?"

"Maybe a little."

He held out a hand, palm up. "You have one woman who is completely heartless and her only concern is taking over the property. She couldn't care less about anything else that's going on. She can't be bothered. Even if they had a bad marriage, Brandon is still a human being, and she doesn't seem the least bit affected by his death."

Holding up his other hand, palm up, he raised it a little higher than the other. "Then you have this other woman, who is gentle, pleasant, and civilized, who is clearly devastated. All she wants is to wrap up this ugly business and move on with her life so she can begin her healing process."

"That's what you took from our meeting?"

"And furthermore," Ian said, ignoring my question, "I can't imagine Brandon being married to that tyrant . . . no, Constance Yeoh is definitely the odd woman out."

"So you think that Constance Yeoh is a real person, just not the person we met?"

"Exactly! Now we just have to figure out how to prove it."

Ian resolved this without asking my opinion. He walked away, leaving me dumbfounded in front of the restaurant. I suppose if he'd asked for my thoughts, I couldn't have told him anyway. I didn't know if his theories were right or wrong, but one thing was for sure: There was way more to this story than any of us knew.

CHAPTER
11

"So wait, let me get this straight," Megan said as she wiped down the bar. "The first wife has a will that says she's in charge of this guy's stuff, and the second wife has an agreement that says if he can't take care of the store, it goes to her?"

I nodded. "You got it."

After work, I stopped by the Zodiac, Megan's long-standing place of employment, to fill her in on the latest drama at the plaza. Besides, having a drink after the day I'd had couldn't hurt.

The Zodiac, known for its astrological wall art, had been our stomping ground since our college days. Shortly after we graduated, Megan started bartending in the hope of someday managing the place.

"But doesn't one agreement trump the other?" she asked.

"I don't know how these legal things work. You know that. That's Anna May's specialty."

"Can't you ask her or something?"

"Yeah right, she wants nothing to do with this whole thing. She said it's none of our business. Every time I bring it up, she gives me a lecture. I didn't even bother telling her about the conversation. Plus, I'm still mad at her for telling our parents about what happened."

She shook her head in reply. "This is nuts. Who knew Brandon had all this baggage? As if one ex-wife wasn't enough, now there are two! What if there's more? There could be a whole slew of women out there!"

"What's worse is that Ian thinks the woman who showed up as Brandon's first ex-wife is a fraud."

"A fraud?" Megan threw the bar towel under the counter and wiped her hands on her jeans. "Who would she be then?"

I shrugged. "Someone who wants to take over the property? Or the murderer?"

A husky voice from behind me said, "I didn't hear you say 'murderer,' did I?"

Jumping, I spun in my seat to look behind me.

Adam stared back at me, his green eyes sparkling with subtle amusement at my shock.

My heart thudded in my chest. "Do you always sneak up on people this way?"

His lips curved into a tiny smile as he sat down on the stool next to me. "Only you."

"What are you doing here?"

"Not happy to see me?" He nudged me with his elbow.

"Of course I am. Just surprised is all."

He lifted his shoulders. "I saw your car in the parking lot, and figured I'd stop in and say hi. We've barely gotten a chance to see each other these past few weeks."

Megan returned with an open beer bottle and placed

it in front of him. "You better watch it, Lana. You have a detective stalking your every move."

Adam sighed. "Twisting my intentions around again, I see."

Megan held up her hands in defense. "I just call 'em how I see 'em." She winked at me before walking away to tend to the other customers.

He took a sip of beer and then swiveled in his stool to face me. "Seriously, you mentioned a murderer. What's that all about?"

Despite my better judgment, I told him the story about the second Mrs. Yeoh showing up at Ho-Lee Noodle House and her meeting with Ian that I was forced to attend. I went through the details of the story she'd told us with the borrowed money and the conversation that Ian and I had outside of the restaurant about the first Mrs. Yeoh.

"That guy bugs me," was his only response.

I gawked at him. "That's all you have to say?"

"Well, he can't help himself, can he? He has to drag you around with him all the time."

"Do I sense a little bit of jealousy?"

He snorted. "Hardly. It's just an observation."

"Uh-huh."

"And on top of that, he has to put these ridiculous ideas in your head. Constance Yeoh is not a murderer," he said, tipping his beer bottle toward me. "And she's not a fraud, either. You need to stay out of it. Both of you," he added, giving Megan a glance. "Don't let Ian drag you down his rabbit hole. He's making up problems that don't need to be there."

"But what about this other woman?"

"Brandon's parents told me he was briefly married to

someone else, but she wasn't anyone crucial in his life. We're still digging into his background. You need to relax, we've got things under control."

"I'm just speculating," I said, waving away his concern.

Adam frowned at me. "That's what got you into trouble last time. Stay out of this, okay?"

"Fine, whatever." I skulked into my drink. "I won't speculate."

"I'm going to hold you to that, Miss Lee," he said, lightening his tone. "I'm also going to hold you to something else."

"Oh yeah?"

"Yeah . . . have dinner with me."

I perked up. "Oh? When were you thinking?"

"How about next Friday? After everything is said and done with the funeral services and you've had a few days to recoup, of course."

I smiled. "I think I'd like that very much."

That night, I went home with lifted spirits for the first time in days. It had been a while since Adam had asked me out. My calculations totaled at a little over two weeks . . . not that I was counting. Even though he had agreed to the double date, it wasn't the same.

Regardless of everything else going on, I couldn't help but feel a tinge of happiness soak through. I only wished that Isabelle were around to tell.

In a mixture of emotions, Kikko and I stood in front of my closet skimming the row of color-coordinated clothing that hung before us. My closet was organized in a rainbow format. I don't know what possessed me to do it, but it made one thing abundantly clear to me. I owned more black clothes than anything else.

That made picking out something for the funeral pretty easy.

I rifled through my options, holding things up in the mirror, trying to find something that was respectable and warm. Dressing up for formal events in Cleveland winters could be a tricky business.

Studying my reflection, I began to regret my decision to streak my hair with such a bright and unnatural color. Then again, I hadn't known I'd need to attend a funeral.

While I was debating over black or gray dress pants, my cell phone rang, and another long string of numbers appeared on the screen. This time it was my dad.

"Hey, Goober! Just calling to check in on you. Your mother told me about the whole business with the Yeohs next door. I'm so sorry. I know this must be hard for you. How are you holding up?"

"Yeah, it's such a shame. I was just getting to know Isabelle," I said, the sadness creeping back in. "I'm doing okay, though . . . the best I can be right now."

"They were too young," my dad replied. "I can't imagine what their parents must be going through."

"It has to be terrible," I agreed. "Especially with how it happened."

"That reminds me . . ." my dad started.

"Reminds you of what?"

"I had a feeling you would think this whole thing was strange. And I called to tell you to put away any Nancy Drew fantasies you may be having."

I sighed. "Why does everybody assume that I'm going to get involved? You sound just like Adam."

"Because you're my daughter, and I know how you think," my dad replied. "Adam? Who's Adam?"

"You know Adam, Dad. Detective Trudeau."

"Is this your new cop boyfriend your mom was tell-ing me about? The one you were going on about at dim sum?"

"Dad . . . come on." Even at this age, it was still weird to talk to my dad about dating. "And I wasn't going on about him at dim sum."

"Okay, sorry." My dad paused. "But is he?"

"He's not my boyfriend." I said, a little too firm. "We're only going on our fourth date."

"You're going on a fourth date with this man?"

Trying not to sound annoyed, I gave him my most level and adult, "Yes, Dad."

"Wonderful," my dad said. "Your mother is going to be so happy. When we get home you'll have to officially introduce us. You can't start dating this guy without in-troducing him to your old man. I have to check him out and make sure he isn't some kind of weirdo."

Without giving me a chance to object, my dad moved on to the details of their trip thus far. He went on for a little bit about my grandmother and told me that her mood had improved since they'd first gotten there. I guess she'd only thrown a few fits since their arrival, which was an improvement according to my uncle. I didn't understand what was going on with her, but I hoped that my parents being there would help alleviate the situation. We hung up after he made me promise to mind my own business.

Even though I was happy to hear from him, my father's call had dampened my mood, leaving me both sad and grumpy. I looked down at Kikko, who'd brought her stuffed duck to entertain herself. "Why does every-one naturally assume I'm going to get involved in this? I mean, they act like I can't help myself."

Ignoring my complaint, Kikko licked the duck's head and then gave it a good chomp.

I flopped backward on the bed and stared at the ceiling. Kikko hopped up on the bed with her duck, plopping it on my chest. "I am perfectly capable of minding my own business," I said, throwing her stuffed animal across the room. "I'm just not going to."

CHAPTER
12

I'm not ashamed to say that I spent the weekend moping and contemplating everything that had taken place since the beginning of the week. It was a lot to process.

Anna May was in charge of the restaurant all weekend, and I was relieved to have some time away. Keeping it together all week had worn me out more than I realized.

In an attempt to relieve some of my stress, I prepped the bathroom to be painted with the new color that Megan had picked out. Making sure the painter's tape was straight against the trim and tiles kept me preoccupied for a good part of Saturday afternoon, but after I was done, I found myself staring at the carpet with the same thoughts swirling around in my head.

I busied myself for a little while updating my notebook with the appearance of Marcia Yeoh and her involvement in the souvenir shop. If Brandon had borrowed money from her and the store wasn't doing so well, maybe he was going to the casino to win money to pay her back. But where was he getting the extra money to go the casino to begin with? And did Isabelle know any of this?

Even though Ian thought she was innocent, I didn't buy it totally. We'd just met her and I guaranteed her looks got her out of a lot of trouble. I added her to my suspect list.

Megan had to work most of the weekend and tried convincing me that I should loiter at the bar to keep her company. But really, I didn't feel like being around people or putting on a fake smile. Instead, I found myself going deep into a *Gilmore Girls* marathon. Nothing like a little fictional drama to take you away from the real stuff.

I stayed up late, letting the lives of Stars Hollow citizens remove me from my reality. And because of it, I slept away half of Sunday without giving it much effort. When I finally woke up, I drank a pot's worth of coffee and started painting the bathroom. And that was my total contribution to Sunday.

On Monday morning, we opened the restaurant for a few hours, closing the doors at noon along with the rest of the plaza. The first set of calling hours started at three o'clock. Anna May decided we should go together instead of meeting up, so she picked me up half an hour before we had to be there.

I'd spent a lot of time fidgeting with my clothes. I hated funerals, wakes, and anything that had to do with death.

The funeral home was an exquisite building made of light brick with white awnings and white matching pillars. We parked in the rear lot and made our way up the wooden ramp to the back entrance where a funeral home attendant in a black suit and tie stood waiting to direct visitors to their appropriate rooms. With a solemn expression, he gestured to his right where a door was propped open. Muted sounds of chatter could be heard from the lobby.

My sister and I gave polite nods as we walked by, heading toward the viewing room. It was a tranquil space with midnight-blue carpeting swirled with light-blue patterns that resembled flowers. The walls were cream-colored with little speckles of dark brown accented by oak trim, complementing a carved wood ceiling. It reminded me of a boat turned upside down.

Folding chairs filled the room, and an aisle split them into two sides. Quite a few people had already shown up, and they milled around in various clumps talking in soft voices. I spotted a group of Asia Village shop owners off to the side. Those sitting closest to the door turned as we walked in.

"There's Peter and Kimmy," my sister said, jerking a chin toward our left. "Let's go say hi."

As we greeted the two, my eyes sneaked a peek toward the front where two caskets were positioned side by side. I had heard through the plaza grapevine that after the news of Brandon's innocence had been released, his parents had offered to foot the bill for the entire ceremony. Apparently, Isabelle's parents didn't have a lot of money and could barely afford the casket.

They were set to be buried together. I had never been to a double funeral before, and my mind wandered places I didn't want it to go.

The Mahjong Matrons had weighed in on the subject earlier in the morning, claiming that the Yeoh family had done this to atone for the guilty feelings they had. Regardless of Brandon's innocence, there were some who felt that Brandon had brought the tragedy upon them.

With the little I knew about Brandon, it was hard for me to say either way. All I could say for sure was that I didn't like him and he was up to something. But did that "up to something" directly result in what had happened? Time would tell.

Kimmy noticed the expression on my face. "You want to get some water or something?"

I nodded. "Sure . . . yeah. I could use some water."

"They have a little beverage station set up in the hallway." She thrust her purse at Peter. "Hold this, we'll be right back."

I followed Kimmy out into the hallway, spotting the table she was referencing. There were two coffee urns and a pitcher of water placed next to stacks of Styrofoam cups.

"I figured you had to get out of there. I know how you hate this kind of stuff," Kimmy said as we made our way to the table.

I reached for a cup. "Yeah, seeing the . . . them . . . there—it makes it more real, I guess."

"For cripe's sake, Lana, we've already seen more than most in this situation. It can't get much more real than that." Kimmy blew out a puff of air. "At least here, the caskets are closed."

I filled my cup with water and took a healthy swallow. "I know, but this is . . . more permanent."

"Okay, let me take your mind off the whole thing." Kimmy sneaked a look back at the doors to the viewing room. "Peter and I were the first ones here outside of family, and we happened to overhear some of the drama going on between a few of them."

"Kimmy, this isn't really the place—"

"The hell it isn't! What else are we going to talk about? The weather?" Kimmy asked with a challenging look.

"It's disrespectful," I whispered, looking around. No one was in earshot, but I still felt our conversation was inappropriate.

"Oh please." Kimmy waved her hand, dismissing me. "Anyway, so the ex-wife is here, that one from the other day with the chubby lawyer, and she got into it with Brandon's parents because they went and did everything without consulting her first. She told them it was her responsibility and they should have stayed out of it."

"Constance Yeoh started a scene already?" I shook my head. That woman was unbelievable.

Kimmy nodded with satisfaction. "Hell yeah she did. And what's worse is that Isabelle's family heard about it and her sister came over and yelled at all of them saying that it was totally inappropriate for them to have this conversation."

"Sister?" I asked. "Isabelle has a sister?"

"Yeah, and it's super creepy because they look so much alike. You can't miss her. She's sitting right up in the front row if you want to have a look."

"Uh, maybe later . . ." Tugging at the collar on my dress, I sipped my water.

"Oh right." Kimmy said, nodding. "So anyway, none of them have said a word since the sister put them in their place. They're all just staring straight ahead like

they're mannequins or something." She gasped. "Oh!
And, I heard something else!"

"Kimmy!" I hissed. "Lower your voice!"

"Sorry, sorry." She hopped from foot to foot. "Okay,
so anyhow, I heard that Constance Yeoh's sister is here.
And she supposedly had an affair with Brandon and
that's why Constance and Brandon split up."

"Where did you hear this?" I asked, already knowing
the answer.

"The Mahjong Matrons."

"Of course."

When Kimmy was satisfied with the gossip she'd
passed along, I refilled my water cup and we headed
back to the viewing room.

People were starting to meander up front, chatting
with the family. I stayed toward the back, hunkering
down behind Anna May who was talking with Peter
about law school. The look on his face told me that he
wasn't listening and wouldn't have understood what she
was talking about if he were.

My eyes traveled up front, avoiding the two caskets
that were larger than life. They had been centered in the
front of the room, and I managed to let my eyes drift
past them, focusing on the floral sprays that stood on
either side.

I noticed Constance sitting up front behind an older
couple that must have been Brandon's parents. I tried to
pick out which one was her sister, but I couldn't guess.
I was afraid asking Kimmy might draw attention to us,
so I decided to wait it out.

I hadn't gotten a chance to tell Ian about Adam telling
me that Constance was the real deal, but he'd find out

today on his own. Where was he? I looked around the room but couldn't see him anywhere.

I also skimmed the room for Marcia, wondering what her interactions with the families and Constance would be like, but she, too, was nowhere to be found. And I kept an eye out for the mysterious Captain Kirk, but so far, he was a no-show.

On the right side of the room, Isabelle's family sat in the front row, nodding at those who walked by. That's when I caught sight of Isabelle's sister. From the back, I would have mistaken the two, and even when she turned ever so slightly to greet another group of people, I had to look really hard to notice the subtle features that made them different.

While I waited in the last row by myself, Anna May, Peter, and Kimmy went up front and knelt down by the caskets, stopping to say a few brief words to the family. Everyone nodded politely, shaking hands as they moved from person to person. Feeling disrespectful, I decided it was a good time to use the ladies' room and escape for a few minutes. Maybe when everyone was done talking with the family, we could go.

The bathroom was at the end of the hall near the beverage station, and I was contemplating more water when I ran right into Isabelle's sister. I gasped, taking a quick step back. "I'm so sorry. I wasn't paying attention to where I was going."

Her smile was the same as Isabelle's, and a pang jolted my heart. "It's okay; everyone's a little preoccupied today."

"You're Isabelle's sister, right?" I asked.

"Yes, I'm Rina," she answered, brushing the bangs

away her eyes. "Actually, Catrina, but I hate it . . . sounds so formal. And you are?"

I couldn't help staring at her. She looked so much like her sister it was unreal. "Oh, right," I extended my hand. "I'm Lana, Lana Lee."

She took my hand with a firm grip. "Nice to meet you, Lana."

"I'm so sorry for your loss." My eyes shifted to my water cup to avoid staring further. "I didn't know Isabelle long, but she was a great person. I'll miss her very much."

"Thank you. It's hard to lose a little sister." Her sigh was heavy. "How did you two know each other?"

"We met in the bookstore at Asia Village. Your sister was standing next to me in the Mystery aisle and we both reached for the same book." I smiled at the memory. "We got to talking about books and became instant friends. After that, we went to the bookstore every Tuesday without fail."

Rina returned the smile. "I'm happy that my sister had someone to do those types of things with. I worried that moving away from home, and our parents, would be hard on her."

"I'm guessing she was close with them."

She nodded, her eyes drifting to the room where her parents stood grieving the loss of their youngest. "Incredibly close. They're taking it pretty hard. You're not supposed to see your kids die."

"I can't imagine what that would be like."

Rina turned back toward me, her face sadder than before. "Do you have a sister?"

"Yeah, one older sister."

"Being an older sister is tough, I'll tell you that. There are so many things I didn't get to say, you know?" She appeared thoughtful as if she were reciting all of those unspoken words in her head and I wondered if she would always carry that around with her. "We left on bad terms. The last time I saw her, I told her off."

That explained at least why Isabelle had never mentioned her. "I'm sorry to hear that. I'm sure she knew that you didn't mean it . . . whatever it was about."

"No, I meant it." She shook her head with disappointment. "I didn't approve of Isabelle's choice of husband, and it put a rift between us. But she was head over heels for the guy. And look where it landed her."

"Not a fan of Brandon, huh?" I asked.

"Actually, no one in my family liked him. My dad isn't the happiest man about them being buried together. But my mother insisted that it be done this way because they were husband and wife and it was the right thing to do, especially since the police found out that he was murdered."

"Your dad doesn't think he's innocent, does he?" I asked.

"Not in the least. He thinks it's Brandon's fault that any of this happened to begin with. And I can't say that I blame him. They say never to speak ill of the dead, but he was not a good person. He had this weird past with that terrible ex-wife of his, and a gambling problem that was probably the basis for Gamblers Anonymous to start their group."

Ah, so Brandon had a gambling problem. Maybe his reasons for going to the casino were not what I'd originally thought. Maybe that's why the store wasn't making any money. He was spending it all.

"Wow, I had no idea. I didn't even know he was married before. They never mentioned it."

Rina smirked. "Isabelle was a little embarrassed about it, but mostly she just wanted to brush it under the rug. I don't think she liked the fact that he had been with other women before her."

"I met both of them this week," I told her.

"Really? You met the other ex-wife?" Rina asked with surprise. "I was starting to think she was a myth. No one in my family has ever met her or even knows what she looks like. Not even Isabelle. The last thing we knew about her was that she lived in Nevada."

"Nevada?" My eyebrows furrowed. "She mentioned living in New York."

She shrugged. "She might have moved for all we know. It's not like we kept tabs on these people."

I tucked that away in my memory to research later.

"Brandon was born with a silver spoon in his mouth, and I think it rotted him from the inside out. He was a good actor, though. Had Isabelle fooled, that's for sure. But the rest of us could see all of his problems like he had them out on display. He was forced into marrying that snake in there. And yes, I said snake. She's just as awful as he is."

"I have to agree. She didn't seem very nice when I met her."

"Well, in my opinion they were probably perfect for each other. But he didn't want to live that life, I guess. After cheating on her several times, she finally ended it. He left and latched on to some other poor woman . . . I'm guessing that's the other woman you met. I don't know what happened with them, but soon after he found my little sister and they moved out to Ohio."

"Do you know why they came out here?"

"I'm guessing the economy was something they could afford. I know Isabelle always wanted to move to Chicago when she was younger. We went to visit some family there when we were little kids and she fell in love with the architecture. I'll never forget the expression on her face when we went to the Sears Tower. But with the little money they had, it wasn't going to happen."

Confused, I asked, "I thought you said he came from money?"

"He did until he decided to marry my sister. His family treated us like peasants and they were not happy with his decision at all. So they took away his trust fund and told him he could have it back if he decided to leave her, but not a minute sooner."

"Then why did they arrange all of this?" I asked, gesturing to our surroundings.

"Guilt, maybe? If there was any trouble in their lives, I think they know it came from Brandon. They may not like us, but they know what kind of people we are. We're honest and keep our heads down. We've never had any trouble, and I don't think I could name you one enemy. Now, Brandon on the other hand . . . he made problems for himself left and right."

Like the Matrons, Rina had suspected guilt from the parents. Without knowing what exactly had happened to them, everyone seemed to agree on one thing: It was Brandon's fault. I contemplated that for a moment while Rina filled a Styrofoam cup with coffee.

"Sorry to go on like this with you. You're the first person I've talked to since this whole thing happened that isn't family."

"Don't mention it," I said, with reassurance. "Sometimes it's easier to talk to someone you don't know."

"I can agree with you on that." She smiled. "I really have enjoyed talking with you, but I should probably get back in there. My parents are going to wonder where I've been."

"I completely understand. It was so nice getting to meet you."

"Hey, I'm going to be in town for a little while after the funeral to tie up some loose ends for my parents. Would you want to get coffee or something? Maybe you could tell me a little more about how Isabelle was doing and what her life was like here. It's been a while since I knew what was really going on with her. I feel like she hid so much from us."

"Sure . . ." I slid a hand into my purse and pulled out one of my business cards from the restaurant. "You can reach me here. I'm running my family's restaurant for my parents while they're in Taiwan. I'm there mostly all day." I took out a pen and scribbled my cell number on the back. "If I'm not there, you can reach me at this number."

She took the card and gave a little laugh. "Ho-Lee Noodle House. How cute."

I chuckled. "Yeah, it worked out well."

"I'll give you a call in a few days. See you at the funeral tomorrow." She raised her cup to me and then headed back into the viewing room.

On our way back from the funeral home, Anna May and I drove without speaking much. I was exhausted and my mind was going back and forth between my conversation with Rina and what Kimmy had told me about the outburst with Constance and Brandon's parents.

When we pulled into the parking lot of my complex, I turned to Anna May. "Do you approve of Adam?"

"What do you mean?" she asked, putting the car in park. We had reached my building and I took off my seat belt, keeping an eye on my sister's facial expressions. Much like me, her face gave her away.

"Do you think he's okay for me to date?"

My sister snickered. "Lana, if he can put up with all your weirdness, and that crazy blue hair of yours, I think he's the perfect guy for you."

CHAPTER

13

The next morning, Anna May and I attended the church services and followed the procession to the cemetery, where I stayed in the back behind the mass of people that had gathered. The group shielded the caskets from view, and I made it a point to study the intricacies of my shoes along with everyone else's.

The sermon at the church had been difficult enough. While the priest talked about the precious state of life and how wonderful these two young people had been, my eyes couldn't help falling back on the caskets every time he mentioned them by name.

Neither Isabelle nor Brandon had been religious, and from what I heard, the ceremonies were the wishes of Brandon's parents. I was impressed with the ease and familiarity the priest used to speak of them.

After the service was over, the families had invited the attendees to have refreshments in the lounge in the basement of the funeral home. I had wanted to skip the whole thing, but Anna May insisted that it would show bad character.

By the time we got there, the low-ceilinged room was packed with people wandering from group to group, catching up with one another or giving condolences.

Kimmy and Peter were standing awkwardly in the middle of the room, huddled closely to each other and eyeballing their surroundings. After Anna May and I got coffee, we decided to join them.

Peter gave us a nod of acknowledgment.

"What are you two doing?" Anna May asked. "You look like you're up to something."

Kimmy nodded. "We're watching the show."

I groaned.

"Don't get like that, Lana," Kimmy said with a nudge to my arm. "I have to do something to take away this depression."

Peter remained silent.

"So what's the show?" Anna asked, peering around the room. "I don't see anything."

Kimmy leaned in. "You see that woman over there?" Discreetly, Kimmy pointed to a woman standing by the banquet table that held various finger foods. She was a thin woman with shoulder-length hair, apple cheeks, and a very tiny waist. "That is Constance Yeoh's little sister."

I whipped around trying to get a better look. "Where?"

Kimmy pinched my side. "Don't look!"

Anna May huffed. "What's the big deal with that?"

Kimmy filled in Anna May on the same information she had told me the day prior.

"Figures," Anna May said, her jaw clenching. "The little sister is always causing problems."

I elbowed my sister in the rib.

"Ow!"

Kimmy ignored the exchange and went on with her story. "Well, they've been mean, mugging each other ever since they walked in the door, and Constance mumbled something under her breath as they passed each other. The younger sister stopped and stared, but didn't say anything . . . but I'm waiting for something to happen. I can feel it. Between the parents, and now the sisters—and you two—there is so much tension in this room, you could cut it with a knife!"

"You are getting way too excited about this, Kimmy." I said with a shake of my head. "This is a time for grieving."

She turned to me, free hand on her hip, the other waving a half-empty coffee cup at my chest. "Yeah, I know about the grieving already, can you just—"

"You need to leave . . . you . . . you harlot!"

A collective gasp filled the room. Constance had approached her sister and they stood head-to-head in front of the banquet table.

"Why should I leave?" the sister shot back. "I have as much right to be here as anybody else!"

"How dare you!" Constance said, her face inches away from her sister. "After what you did to my marriage . . . and you think you can just waltz in here like you had a place in his life?"

"I had more a place in his life than you did!" As she said it, she took the tips of her fingers and pushed Constance's shoulder, making her stumble back.

Constance huffed audibly, straightened herself, took a step forward, and slapped her sister across the cheek. Hard.

Brandon's family rushed over and his father grabbed Constance by her arms, pulling her away from her sister. She jerked her hands free. "Don't you *dare* touch me!"

The sister held a hand to her face, rubbing the spot where she had just been smacked. "This is so typical of you, Constance. Everything is about you. Show some damn respect." And with that, she stormed away.

Kimmy turned back around to face me. "Told you."

I watched Constance's sister storm up the stairs. My brain was one step ahead of me. "Hold my coffee," I said, thrusting the cup at Anna May.

"Where are you going?"

"I'll be right back." I pushed my way through people who were all a-chatter after the show that Constance and her sister had put on. I took the stairs two at a time—which was a lot considering I was wearing high heels.

As I stepped outside, I spotted Constance's sister ready to get in a red car at the other end of the lot. "Hey!" I yelled. "Wait up!"

She whipped around and gave me a curious look, no doubt wondering who I was. She shut the door and stood waiting for me to catch up to her.

"Hey," I said, attempting to catch my breath.

"I'm sorry about in there. I didn't mean to disrupt anything. I hope you could pass along my apologies to their families."

"Oh, that's not why I came out here."

"It's not?"

"No, I wanted to see if you were okay."

She folded her arms and leaned against the car. Her face was red where Constance had smacked her, and part of her eyeliner had smeared near the corner of her eye. "Yeah, I'll survive."

"I'm Lana, by the way." I extended a hand.

"Nice to meet you, I'm Victoria." She returned the gesture, and I noticed how bony and cold her hand was in mine. "Sorry my sister is such a jerk."

"Hey, I know the feeling," I said with a chuckle. Okay, I knew that Anna May was nowhere near that bad, but relating to her as much as possible would work to my benefit. "I'm a little sister, too."

"Ugh, so you know my pain."

"Your sister is an interesting person."

"You know Constance?"

"Sort of." I filled her in on my encounters.

"Ah . . ."

"I was wondering if you could tell me about Brandon. Everyone seems to think what happened to them is his fault. Do you know of any . . ." I paused, trying to think of an appropriate word. ". . . shady dealings?"

She thought for a moment, her eyes traveling back to the funeral home. "Unfortunately, I don't think I can be of much help. I haven't seen Brandon in years. After the whole incident with him and my sister, Constance forbid me to go anywhere near him. Shortly after that, I moved upstate. Best to stay as far away from both of them as humanly possible." Her eyes shifted back to me. "By the way, you *do* know about the incident I'm talking about, right?"

"I heard a little bit," I admitted. "I don't know any details, but I bet there were a lot of hard feelings."

"Only on her end, I'm afraid. Everything worked to her benefit, so I don't know why she's so upset with me. If anything, I did her a favor."

"What do you mean?"

"The agreement in their prenups stated that any type

of cheating would result in a clean break. If she could prove he was having an affair, she could walk away payment-free. But if she just up and broke off the marriage without any concrete proof of him cheating, she'd have to pay him spousal support, and she hated him too much for that."

"I hate to ask, but were you his only affair?"

"I can't say that I was." She hugged herself tighter as she said it. "He was a little bit of a ladies' man. And she did try to do something about it. But she had a hell of a time proving it. He was pretty good at covering things up and making it seem like she was taking the whole thing out of context. So she kept her mouth shut and her head down until she could figure something else out. I don't know why she didn't hire a private investigator. She could have gotten rid of him a lot sooner."

"And you were the solid proof that she needed?"

"You guessed it," she said with a little pride. "Brandon and I really loved each other. I know that sounds hard to believe because he was known for sleeping around. But we really had something. It's possible we wouldn't have been right for each other in the long run, but as far as young love goes . . . well . . ." She drifted off. "Anyway, my sister had no business marrying him to begin with. The whole thing was a disaster. They were both incredibly unhappy. Personally, I don't think Constance is the type of person to be married. She's too independent and stubborn for that. Then, when she accused us of our indiscretion, I figured I was doing her a favor. So I came out with it. I shared some photos and text messages with her that she used to show her lawyer and present in court. Gave her times and dates and everything. Brandon wasn't very happy with me, but if neither one of them was going to do anything about it, I had to step up."

"I take it that's when the feud started?"

She replied with a nod. "We haven't talked since the divorce. I'm okay with it really; we never got along to begin with. We talked more out of obligation . . . family appearances and whatnot."

I felt a little bold for asking my next question, but since she didn't seem to care much for her sister, I figured I'd take the gamble. "Do you think your sister would be capable of revenge?"

"Meaning what exactly?" she asked.

"Truthfully?"

"I'm not going to rat you out if that's what you're worried about. This conversation stays between us."

I took a deep breath. I didn't know if I could trust this woman, but I had to take the chance. "Do you think she would hurt Brandon or his new wife in any way? You know, to get back at him for things that happened in the past? Maybe even accidentally . . ."

"Are you asking me if my sister had something to do with Brandon and Isabelle's death?"

I could feel my face turning red. "Well, if you say it like that, I sound like a crazy person, don't I?"

"Not at all," she said, reassuring me. "Look, my sister is definitely high-strung, and she's got her mental problems, but she's no killer. She's too proper for that. I don't think she'd want to dirty her hands. Plus, a woman like her . . . well, she finds other ways to make your life miserable. She's highly resourceful. Trust me."

"Do you think she'd hire someone to do the dirty work for her?" I thought about the mystery man I had seen with Brandon on that last day.

Victoria turned away from me, her eyes focusing again on the funeral home. "I'm not sure . . . she has the money, I suppose."

"Sorry if I offended you," I said. "It's been an odd time around here."

"No need to apologize," she said. "I just wish I could help you more. I can tell you old college-days stories, but that's about it."

"It's okay; I'm not sure where I'm going with this whole thing. I was hoping you'd be able to tell me something since you were so intimate with him. I thought there was a slim possibility that you would have kept in touch . . . as friends."

"No . . . things got pretty ugly after the divorce with my sister. I didn't want that kind of negativity in my life. And I knew that I wanted more than what Brandon had to offer in the long run. He was a great guy, but he had a lot to learn about being in a committed relationship. I know this probably sounds weird to you, but I loved him as a person. Deep down, there was something good there; he just had to find it. I couldn't wait around anymore . . . a girl's got to live, you know?"

She was right about one thing. I didn't get it. All I could see about Brandon was that he was a horrible person. I had yet to find a redeeming quality about his character.

"You know, if you want to talk to someone who knows Brandon better than anyone, you should look up Jay Coleman," Victoria said.

I pulled out my phone and opened the Notes app, typing in the name. "Who's that?"

"Jay and Brandon go way back, like to kindergarten days. They still kept in touch until recently as far as I know, although I didn't see him here today. But give him a shot; he may know something."

"Thanks so much, Victoria. I really appreciate all of this," I said. I pulled out a business card and gave it to her. "If you think of anything at all, call me."

She took the card and nodded. "No problem, and good luck, Lana. If there's anything to be found, I hope you find it. Even if it *is* my sister who's guilty."

CHAPTER
14

Anna May dropped me back off at my apartment. I ran in, made a few notes in my notebook, and changed my clothes before hopping into my car. Even though I didn't have to open the restaurant at all today, I wanted to. I couldn't take another day sitting at home with nothing to do but think. I needed normalcy.

Ian and Donna had closed Asia Village for the duration of the ceremonies, allowing everyone the chance to attend. But Donna, knowing that a lot of people—including herself—like to work through their grief by keeping busy, decided to amend the original scheduled closing to an optional half day.

The streets were decent—barring slush—and traffic had picked up its pace with the excitement of an ice-free drive.

I parked, sitting in my toasty car and dreading the walk inside. Before long, a red Mustang pulled up next to me and honked. It was my stylist and good friend, Jasmine Ming. She waved at me through the window, her big, ebony curls dancing around her face as she bounced in the driver's seat.

I waved back and got out of my car, careful to avoid the slush puddle that was forming outside my door. "Good morning."

"Hey, woman." She removed her large-framed sunglasses and placed them on top of her head. "Did you happen to catch that wild nonsense after the funeral?"

I nodded. "I did, indeed."

"As if everything isn't messed up enough as it is." She slung an arm over my shoulder and ushered me toward the doors with her. "Rough stuff, for sure. Especially since you knew her better than anyone else here."

I sighed. Funny that everyone kept saying that: I had begun to think I didn't know her at all. "I'm not so sure anymore . . ."

"Why do you say that?"

"Just a feeling, I guess." We entered the plaza and I stamped the snow from my boots. "Let me ask you something."

"Sure thing, chickadee."

"Did you ever notice anything strange about Brandon? Maybe he was acting funny or suspicious?"

Jasmine tilted her head. "Are you talking about how he used to disappear all the time?"

"Yes! You noticed it, too!"

"Of course. It was practically every day. One day I was leaving for lunch and I saw him meet some guy in a fancy car out in the parking lot. Brandon got in and they sped off to who knows where."

"A guy? Did he remind you of William Shatner at all?"

She looked at me with a puzzled expression. "That's a weird way to describe someone, don't you think?"

"I know . . . but did he? Not what he looks like now, but maybe around the original *Star Trek* times?"

Jasmine teetered her head back and forth. "I guess, kinda. I've seen him more than once, too. But that was the first time I'd seen them leave together in that guy's car. Wherever they were off to, it was sure in a hurry."

My mystery man was turning out to be a repeat visitor. How come I had never noticed him before? And who was he?

Jasmine dropped off at the salon, and I made my way through the plaza to the restaurant. As I passed China Cinema and Song, I noticed that Kimmy was already open and ready for customers. I decided to pop inside and say hello.

"You got here pretty quick," I said to her.

Kimmy looked up from the cash register and gave me her version of a smile, which is a quick twitch of her lip. "Yeah, after the drama ended, I decided to bail." She assessed my appearance. "How'd it go with the sister? What'd you say to her?"

"I asked her about Constance. She didn't really offer up too much." I trusted Kimmy, but I didn't want to get her involved. The less she knew about what I was up to, the better.

"Well. At least this business is over and done with it." She sighed. "The whole thing is a lot, you know? We go here, then we go there, then we go to this other place. I told my parents, if I die before them, I don't want all of that."

I didn't say so, but I didn't want to think about what

would happen when I died. I was still holding out hope that I was going to live forever.

I said my goodbyes and headed over to the restaurant, flipping on the lights as I made my way through to the kitchen. I opened the door to my mother's office and noticed the light blinking on the answering machine my mother insisted on keeping. I had yet to win the battle of digital voice mail.

There was a message from the meat delivery guy who said he'd tried to stop by but we were closed. *Damn.* I had forgotten to call the delivery guys to let them know about our adjusted hours. I made a note to call and have them come back now that we were open again.

The second message was from Marcia Yeoh. She wanted to speak with me and asked me to call her back when I had a chance. I jotted down the number, wondering what she could possibly want to talk to me about. I hadn't seen her at the funeral and I found that to be suspicious. If she cared about Brandon at all, wouldn't she have been there?

I heard a loud banging come from the front of the restaurant. I raced up front to unlock the door. I'd forgotten about Peter!

He gave me an exasperated look. "Whoa, don't give me flashbacks or whatever. I thought maybe you were hijacked in the back or something."

I locked the door behind him. "Sorry, I was listening to the messages and forgot to check for you. By the way, we missed the meat delivery yesterday."

Peter smacked himself on the forehead. "Totally slipped my mind. Don't worry, I'll give Jack a call and let him know that we're open again."

"Thanks, I have to call back Marcia Yeoh . . . she

said she wants to talk to me about something. Do you remember seeing her at the funeral? I don't think she was there."

"Wait, that's the hot one, right?"

"Yes, Peter, that's the hot one."

He nodded in approval. "She's totally hot."

"What about Kimmy?" I asked.

His cheeks turned pink and he looked away. "She's okay sometimes."

"Uh-huh."

"I better, um, get the kitchen set up and stuff. The Matrons might surprise us with a late breakfast or something."

I followed behind him, and as we entered the kitchen he started to chuckle to himself. "What's so funny?" I asked him.

"Nothing." He glanced at me over his shoulder and I could see the smirk on his face.

"Oh come on, you can't do that. You know that drives me crazy."

"Nothing, just . . ." He stifled a chuckle. "If you put the two ex-wives together, they're kinda like hot-and-sour soup." He paused, waiting for my reaction. "Get it?"

"Yeah, Peter, I get it."

Marcia answered on the third ring. "Thank you for calling me back so fast," she said after I announced myself.

"I have to say, I didn't expect to hear from you," I admitted. "I assumed you would be at the funeral today."

There was a short pause before she answered. "There

have been a lot of bridges burned over the years. I decided it might be best if I didn't show my face."

"But he was your husband at one point; you have just as much right to show your face as anyone else. You'd think everyone could put aside their differences for one day. Especially considering the circumstances."

She chuckled. "It would be nice if things worked that way, wouldn't it? Unfortunately, not everyone is quite as civilized as you or myself."

"By 'everyone,' do you mean the other Ms. Yeoh?"

"She's just for starters." She took a deep breath, and it sounded as if she was going to say more, but she stopped herself. "Anyhow, I had called to ask a favor of you, if it wouldn't be too much trouble."

"I'm not sure how I can help, but I can try."

"I'm back in New York for a few days, and I was wondering if you wouldn't mind giving me a call if there are any changes at the shop. If something changes . . . anything at all . . . I'll come back right away."

As far as requests went, it sounded simple enough. "Sure. Should I call you at this number?"

"Yes, this is my cell phone, and I have it with me at all times."

"Okay, I'll call you if anything happens before you get back. But I'm sure that Ian will call you if anything changes."

"I'm sure he will, too, but in case it slips his mind, or if something happens there, I'd like if you'd let me know."

I frowned. "Like what kind of something?"

"Oh, you know . . . *anything* at all. Us girls have to stick together."

"Okay . . . no problem. I'll call you the minute anything changes."

"Great. Oh, and Lana . . ."

"Yeah?"

"Maybe you can keep this between you and me. I wouldn't want Ian to think I didn't trust him."

"Um . . . sure."

"Thank you so much. I feel so much better knowing that I have an extra set of eyes on this."

After we hung up, I sat in my mother's office for a few minutes staring at the wall. An extra set of eyes . . . did that mean there were other eyes on the shop as well?

CHAPTER
15

Business was picking up each day we got closer to Chinese New Year, and I spent most of the afternoon busy taking care of customers as they piled into the restaurant, one party after another. Even the Mahjong Matrons, who typically liked to lounge after they ate, were bustling in preparation for the parties and events they were planning to attend.

Nancy came in to help, giving me a chance to sneak back into my mother's office to prepare the bank deposit and handle a couple of loose ends I had been meaning to take care of. Information had to be filed into my mother's monthly budgeting system, and a vegetable order had to be placed before the end of the day. Peter had already given me an earful about his dwindling supply of ginger and shiitake mushrooms.

I was in the middle of filling in data for an expense report when Nancy came into the office. She wrung her hands together as she approached the desk. "Ms. Yeoh is here to see you . . . and she is very upset."

"She is?" I asked, surprised. "That's impossible, I just talked to her earlier today. She's in New York."

Nancy cocked her head at me. "No, she is sitting in the dining room."

Oh. Constance. *That* Ms. Yeoh. I got up from the desk and followed Nancy out into the dining area. We needed to start referencing them by their first names instead; this was getting too confusing.

Constance sat in a booth appearing both discontented and impatient. Her purse was placed in front of her and her hands lay on top of it as if the contents needed protection. She looked up at us as we made our way over.

"Nancy," I said, using my customer service voice. "Would you mind getting us some tea, please?"

"Yes, I'll get it right away," Nancy replied, practically running back into the kitchen.

"I'm a little surprised to see you." I turned my attention back to Constance. "After everything you've been through today."

She scowled at me. "I don't wish to speak of that. Frankly, none of this is your business."

Instead of fueling the fire further, I simply smiled and asked, "How can I help you?"

"Sit," she barked, pointing at the empty seat across from her.

I did as she said without hesitation.

A thin smile of satisfaction spread over her lips. "I need you to speed up the process of what's going on with my ex-husband's store."

A part of me wanted to be surprised that she would even entertain this ordeal with the store after the day she'd had, but I wasn't. She definitely didn't waste time,

I'd give her that. I shook my head in confusion. "I'm sorry; I'm not sure how I can do that. Ian—"

"Men are incompetent, don't you think?"

Nancy arrived with the tea, pouring each of us a cup. I nodded in thanks and she whisked away to tend to her other tables.

She stared at me expectantly. "Well . . . do you agree?"

"Um . . . sure." It came out as more of a question than a statement. In truth, I didn't agree with her, but I felt it was necessary for my safety that I go along with whatever she had to say.

Her smile widened. "Good, then we're on the same page." She repositioned herself in the booth, leaning in toward me. "I know that property manager of yours is a complete idiot. I asked to speak with Mrs. Feng because I've heard such great things about her, but he insisted he could handle everything."

I nodded. "Ian is technically in charge of the plaza now. Mrs. Feng acts more as a consultant these days."

"Regardless, he's an idiot, and I'm sure that detective doesn't have much for brains, either," she spat. "If he did, he would have figured out that my ex-husband wasn't the guilty party immediately. How careless!"

My stomach tightened. "I can assure you, Detective Trudeau is very good at his job."

"In any case, I've found a woman can be very persuasive when the situation calls for it, and it's clear to me this Mr. Sung has feelings for you."

"What?" I choked a little, covering it up with a cough. I sipped at my tea. "That's—"

She held up a hand. "Please, I have two eyes, I can see this myself. The way he looks at you is atrocious . . . and obvious. So unprofessional! But, we can work this to our benefit. All I need you to do is work that magic of yours and convince him to hurry up with the legal issues he's supposedly having."

"What legal issues?" I thought it was in my best interest to act like I was completely clueless. If she knew that Ian had shared the details with me, she might go on a tirade.

"He keeps muttering something about the verification process. Frankly, I don't think he's even talked to his lawyer yet. The paperwork I gave him is above standard. There shouldn't be any issues with it at all."

"Well, you know how things get hectic around this time of year."

She glared at me. "Oh please. Planning for Chinese New Year is hardly anything to get worked up over. I could have this whole place up and running within the day. It's just an excuse he's using to keep me away from what's rightfully mine." She clenched her fist and gave the table a good pound.

A few customers turned our way and I smiled apologetically at them. I was thankful the Mahjong Matrons weren't here to witness this, at least. With any luck, I might be able to stop news of this little meeting from spreading around the plaza.

"Constance," I whispered, hoping my soft tone would calm her down. "I'll try to help any way that I can, but I can't promise anything. If the situation is tied up because of legal matters, I'm not sure I can do much."

She took a deep breath, straightening herself in the seat. "I'm positive that you'll find a way. I don't want to take this whole ordeal to the media and cause more problems for your little plaza, but I'll do what I have to."

If I had any doubts, the look on her face told me she meant it.

"I'll do what I can," I told her. And I meant it. I'd do just about anything to get her the heck away from me at this particular point in time. "But can I ask you what the rush is?"

She raised a brow at me. "What do you mean?"

"Well, are you planning on keeping the store open?"

She scoffed. "Nonsense, I plan on clearing out all the inventory as soon as possible and then turning the space into a designer handbag boutique." She looked around the walls of the restaurant with disdain. "This place *could* use a little class."

I bit the insides of my cheeks. I wanted to deck her after that comment. I wanted to tell her there was nothing wrong with the way our plaza was now. But instead I asked, "So you don't intend to keep the store as it is?"

"Silly girl, of course not. A souvenir store is a bit garish, don't you think? No, I think a designer accessory boutique is exactly what this place needs." She reached for her own designer handbag and slid out of the booth. "I'll be in touch."

I'm sure it was meant to be a statement, but it came out more like a threat. And with her, well, it definitely was.

Ian sat across from me in my mother's office. I'd spent most of the day being cornered by people I didn't want to talk to, and I really wasn't interested in talking to anyone else—which I told him—but Ian refused to leave.

"That dreadful woman came to see me again," Ian said, bordering on a whine. "She insisted that I'm taking too long working out the details of her transfer . . . she called me an incompetent pig. I can't deal with her another day."

"Maybe you should speed up the process," I suggested. "Stop stalling and call the lawyer. Have him verify the paperwork and move on with it. She even came to see if I could do anything about it. The longer you take, the worse she's going to get. She threatened to go to the media . . ."

His jaw dropped. "You're kidding me."

"I wish I were." I shook my head. "Adam mentioned they were done over there. You can't exactly use the police as an excuse anymore. And your story about being tied up with legal issues isn't fooling anyone."

A line formed between his brows. "Adam?"

"Detective Trudeau, I meant."

"I didn't realize you were on a first-name basis." He cleared his throat. "When did that happen?"

I squirmed in my chair. "We've had dinner a few times."

He looked down at his hands in disappointment. "Ah, I see."

"Ian, the papers," I said, trying to bring the conversation back around to its original point.

"Oh, right, the papers," he said, waving a hand. "Well, they are with the lawyers and they're reviewing them. We have a meeting with them in a few days. I told them to take their time."

"I wouldn't delay this anymore. She's going to keep harassing us until she gets her way, and we can't afford another story in the *Plain Dealer*. How are you going to feel when they write a piece about the dictator of Asia Village?"

"Are you really that anxious to have her move in next to you?" Ian asked, desperation etched on his face. "Lana . . . you have to help me."

I leaned back in my chair. "What can I do?" I contemplated telling him about the little I'd learned from Victoria, but decided to keep it to myself.

"Find something out on this woman . . . on both of them for that matter. You agreed with me that something isn't right. Let's prove it before she can get her claws into that store."

"Ian, the only thing you suspected was that she wasn't the real Constance Yeoh. But we know that's not true. And if she has the documents to prove that City Charm is hers for the taking, then that's all she needs. I know she isn't the greatest person in the world, but what can we really do about it?"

"Documents can be falsified . . ." Ian said.

There was a sound in his voice that I couldn't quite place, but I had a feeling it might have something to do with the fact that he had lied about his own past. While Megan and I had been investigating the murder of Mr. Feng, we had uncovered secrets that Ian had been keeping. He had been lying about his job history in order to make himself seem more credible. Of course, he didn't know that I knew about it, but maybe the sound I was hearing in his voice was guilt.

"Isn't that for the lawyer to decide?" I countered.

"Couldn't you see if there's anything at all on this woman? It doesn't have to be about the store. Anything that would discredit her is just fine." He sat forward, resting his elbows on his knees. "Consider it a favor."

"Why don't you do it?"

"Lana . . ."

I sank in my seat. "Okay, fine. I'll dig around and see if I can find anything out about her. But, if I don't find anything suspicious, you have to promise to let this angle go. This shouldn't be about Constance; this should be about what happened to Brandon and Isabelle. If we waste too much time looking at one person, we could miss something really important." The mysterious William Shatner look-alike was still swirling around in my brain.

"Deal. And I know you're right about getting caught up, but I can feel in my gut that this woman is guilty of something." He stood up with a new bounce in his step. "And maybe after this whole thing is resolved, we can finally have our own dinner date."

Yeah . . . great.

That evening, when I got home from work, I searched the Internet for information on Constance Yeoh, but came up empty-handed. She didn't seem like a very interesting person. Her name popped up a few times in relation to the college she had attended and her place of employment, but aside from that, nothing sprang up as a red flag.

It was clear without researching anything at all that she had motive. She was a woman scorned . . . and scorched, for that matter, but did she have the means? I tried to imagine her in the back room of City Charm, staging the crime, but the imagery wouldn't come together. If anything, just as her own sister had said, she was an opportunist, not a murderer.

My mind played again with the idea of a hit man. She had the money to do it, and it would give her the safety of an alibi. Plus, she wouldn't have to get her hands dirty. Supposing that my mystery man was the hit man—how would that work? Clearly, he was seen with Brandon multiple times. Did Constance hire him to befriend Brandon . . . to get close to him? How do you even go about hiring a hit man? There was so much I didn't know!

I did a quick search to see if I could find anything out about Marcia and whether or not she'd ever lived in Nevada. I found a few websites that listed address information on name searches and clicked on one. Marcia's name pulled up a hefty list of previous residences: Las Vegas, Reno, Atlantic City . . . even Windsor. And her current address was New York. I didn't know much about gambling, but I did know what those cities had in common. They were all home to popular casinos. But what did it mean?

Since I was already online, I decided to go through Brandon's social media. I skimmed through the posts and comments that had come in since Brandon's death. His page had turned into a memorial wall of sorts. After that, I scoped out his friends in search of Jay Coleman, the man Victoria had mentioned.

I found him right away and was thankful something was working out. I sent him a message cooking up a story about writing a tribute article for a plaza newsletter. This newsletter didn't exist, but Jay didn't have to know that.

While I was at it, I thought it might be a good idea to reach out to a few of Brandon's other friends to see if I could get any other info. I needed to talk to people who knew Brandon outside the plaza . . . people who might know what he could be involved in. There were a few friends with connections to Marcia, so I jotted their names down on my list.

Two or three of his Cleveland friends also "liked" the casino. None of them were familiar, but I wrote their names down anyhow. Whoever these people were, they'd never come to visit at Asia Village. Outside of the Captain Kirk guy, there hadn't been any visitors at the store.

Off my list, I picked a few of his friends from both Cleveland and New York, and used the same story about the newsletter feature I had with Jay.

I felt satisfied with what I had accomplished and made some notes in my notebook while considering the recent details I had uncovered. Brandon had a gambling problem, and maybe Marcia did, too. Constance was angry, betrayed, and had a lot of money—she had resources. My mystery man had been seen by Jasmine, and by me, but who else? Was there anybody else I could ask? Were he and Brandon running off to the casino together? That had to be it. But how did the ex-wives fit in? And did they?

Collapsing face-first onto my bed, I let out a groan that I'd been holding in all day. Figuring this out was going to be impossible!

To top things off, not one but three people had reached out to me in the same day and asked me to help them with their own self-serving requests. How had their issues become my problem? Wasn't anyone besides me concerned about what had really happened to Isabelle and Brandon? And why did both of the wives trust me to do their dirty work?

I stood up and went to my closet, opening the door and peering at myself in the mirror. I smiled at myself. First with teeth, then with no teeth. Did I appear trustworthy? Is that why people kept confiding things in me? Or was I naive? Were they using me to their advantage?

I didn't know the answers to those questions. In the meantime, I was going to have to work on my "not so approachable" face.

CHAPTER

16

The next morning as I got ready for work, I gave myself the "it's a new day" speech. Whatever happened yesterday was in the past and I was ready to start fresh. I will often give myself these little pep talks, but I don't know if they do any good. Half the time I don't believe myself.

Still, I left the house with a chipper disposition and even sang along with the radio on my ride into work. I refused to listen to another morning of dreary weather advisories.

Esther and I pulled in at the same time, and I waved good morning to her as I got out of my car.

She squinted at me from her parking space. "Where is your hat?"

"I don't have one," I said, walking up to her car. "It messes up my hair."

"You will get sick this way." Esther slammed the door to her car and shooed me inside.

"I'll be fine. I never wear a hat." Truth was, I hated

things on my head. Always have. I wasn't a fan of headbands, hats, shower caps . . . anything that felt restricting.

"I will find you a hat," Esther assured me. "I can pick out something pretty to go with your new hairstyle."

Instead of arguing the point, I just nodded. It was much easier to agree with her and be done with it. Esther, much like my mother, always knew what was "best" for me, and any backtalk from me was considered a challenge of her intelligence.

We entered the plaza and circled the koi pond, stopping in front of the abandoned souvenir shop. She sighed. "This store is bad luck for so many people. Since the beginning nothing has stayed here."

"I know, but maybe the next owners will have better luck." I didn't think I should mention anything about Constance or it was bound to travel throughout the plaza before lunchtime.

She shook her head. "I thought this time things would be different. Brandon was very lucky at winning money all the time." She gave another heavy sigh and started to walk away.

I followed after her. "Wait, what do you mean he *won* money all the time? Are you sure that he was winning?" If he was winning money, then where was it going? And why didn't he pay Marcia to get her off his back?

"Your mommy and I would see Brandon at the casino almost every day, and he was very good at playing blackjack. Sometimes, me and Betty would watch him play. He would win at least one time every night."

"One time *every* night?" I asked.

"Yes, sometimes I think he was there more than me and Betty."

"And the last night you saw him, you said he won a lot of money. Did you ever tell the police that?"

"Yes, I told your boyfriend."

I blanched at "boyfriend." Was everyone referring to him that way now?

She sighed. "Brandon was so happy that night. He won so much money, he said he could pay the rent for his store for the next two years."

So he *was* intending on paying Marcia back. But what had stopped him previously? "Esther, do you remember seeing him with anybody that night? Or did he say anything strange?"

"I think he was by himself. Sometimes he had a friend come with him . . . a tall white man."

It had to be my mystery man. If Esther saw him with someone, it had to be the same guy. "Do you know this man's name?"

She tapped her chin. "I don't think so. He would never talk and he did not say hi to us. Your mommy would get very mad about this. Young people do not have manners anymore."

I laughed. My mom was a stickler about proper manners more than anything else. You could be a total jerk, but as long as you said *please* and *thank you* while doing it, you were just fine in her book.

"I have to open my store now." She started to walk away but then turned around. "Don't forget to lock the door until Peter comes to work."

"Believe me, I won't."

After I let myself in and promptly locked the door behind me, I went straight to my mother's office and took off my coat. Digging my cell phone out of my purse, I sent Megan a text asking her to stop by the res-

taurant around lunchtime to go on a little adventure
with me.

It was time to make a trip to the casino.

It was close to noon and I hid in my mother's office waiting for Megan to show up. My cover was that we were
going to the bank together to drop off a bank deposit
and then grab lunch while we were out.

I didn't want to explain to Peter or Nancy what we
were actually doing. I was sure neither of them would
approve, and if it got back to my sister, I would never
hear the end of it.

With some time to kill, I checked my Facebook messages to see if Jay had responded. There was nothing. I
told myself not to be disappointed and busied myself
with organizing a stack of sales slips from the previous
day. I was behind in my work and they needed to be entered into my mother's tracking system.

While I was sorting through the slips, my phone rang.
I didn't recognize the number on the screen. I had been
getting too many unwanted calls lately, and there was
no telling what fresh disaster this could bring. "Hello?"
I asked with caution.

"Lana?" a soft voice asked. "This is Rina . . .
Isabelle's sister."

"Oh hi." I set the sales slips down on the desk. "How
are you?"

"I'm okay. It's been a rough couple of days, but we're
surviving."

"Glad to hear it."

"Hey, I was wondering if maybe you'd like to meet
for coffee this afternoon?"

"Oh, today?"

"Are you not free?" she asked. "We can always meet a different day . . . if you're busy."

"How about tomorrow?" I suggested. "I could meet you around noon?"

"Great, I was thinking we could meet at a Starbucks somewhere? I don't think I'm ready to go to the plaza just yet."

"Believe me, I totally understand. There's one over on Lorain Road. Would that work for you?"

"That would be great. I'll look it up on my GPS and meet you there. See you then."

After we hung up, I went back to organizing the sales slips and typed everything into the system. I had just finished as Megan was walking into the office.

"You ready?" she asked, plopping down in the guest chair.

"Yup, just need my coat and purse." I grabbed my things from the coat tree. "Let me ask you something before we go."

"What's up?"

"Do you think I look like a trustworthy person?"

She cocked her head at me. "Are you asking me if your new hair makes you look like a deviant?"

"Huh? No, I mean my face . . . do I look like a person you'd trust?" I smiled at her, showing all my teeth.

"More like a crazy woman." She laughed. "What's all this about?"

I told her about the encounters I'd had the day before. When I finished, I said, "I just don't get it. I mean, why me? All three people asked me to help solve their problems on the same day. Don't you find that a little strange?"

"It's just a coincidence, Lana," Megan answered. She stood from the chair, smoothing out her top. "I wouldn't think too much about it."

"And then my parents, asking me to manage the restaurant." I pointed at the desk. "I'm clearly the irresponsible one in the family . . . why would they entrust me with the family business?"

I gasped.

"What?" Megan jumped, eyes darting around. "Spider?"

"No, it just dawned on me—I'm getting responsible looking in my old age. That has to be what it is."

Megan snorted. "Oh please, you still get carded at the bar. I wouldn't sign up for your Buckeye card just yet. I don't know why you're freaking out about this. This can't all be from what happened yesterday."

"Well, Vanessa did ask me if I was going through a midlife crisis the other day," I told her. "Because of my hair."

"Ha! That little twit." Megan turned to leave. "If anything, you're going through a quarter-life crisis . . . and if that's the case, join the club."

CHAPTER
17

- - - - - - - - - - - - - - - -

After we made it through Jack Casino security, we were welcomed into a sea of slot machines. They rang and played cheerful sounds of promising wins as people pushed buttons and pulled levers. Music and happy chatter filled the room as groups of people laughed and tried their luck.

Not being much of a gambler, I had only been to the casino a handful of times and didn't know my way around. I stood in awe as I watched people move around from game to game.

The more I thought about it, the more I wondered where Brandon was getting the money for these casino outings to begin with. From the things Isabelle had told me, I knew their finances were not the best, and with him being cut off from his parents, I couldn't imagine where he found the cash for his gambling habit. Clearly, he had been winning, but where had his start-up money been coming from? Someone couldn't possibly win all the time . . . was he losing all his winnings?

Megan tugged on my sleeve. "Blackjack is over there." She pointed to the other end of the room.

Working our way through the crowd, we headed for the blackjack tables. The area was congested and people hovered near the tables, watching their friends and significant others as they contemplated card strategies.

A girl with blond hair and glasses wearing a casino uniform walked by with a tray of drinks. I stepped in front of her. "Excuse me, have you worked here long?"

She appeared taken aback and hesitated before she answered. "Yeah, why?"

I pulled out my phone and opened my photo album, showing her a picture of Brandon I had taken from a social media page. "Have you ever seen this man before?"

She inspected the photo and then gave me a sideways glance. "Is he a famous person or something?"

"No," I laughed. "He's just a regular guy. I was wondering if you've ever seen him in here before."

She shook her head. "Nope, sorry." And she walked away without giving me time to thank her.

"Time is money around here," Megan said with a shrug.

"Everything is money around here."

She smirked. "Okay, well, what do we do? Try someone else?"

"I don't know how else to find someone who knew him. But someone had to, if he came here as much as Esther said he did." The blackjack dealers started to look our way. "Come on, let's move around. We look suspicious."

After we walked around aimlessly for a few more minutes, a petite woman with caramel-brown hair walked by, an empty tray in her hand. I had to do a double take, because when I saw her something triggered in my brain. I knew her from somewhere.

She was the reporter from the plaza!

Only not so much. Today she was dressed in a Jack Casino uniform.

Recognition set in on her face as she made eye contact with me. It was followed with a guilty head slump and a poor attempt to turn around and go the other way.

I grabbed her arm. "Um, excuse me, but I think I know you . . ."

She whipped around, jerking her arm away from me. "I'm pretty sure you have me mixed up with somebody else. I get that a lot."

Megan had moved on the other side of her, blocking her other exit route.

"No, you're the woman who claimed to be a reporter the other day," I said with confidence, taking a step closer. I noticed her name tag read CARMEN. "You were snooping around Asia Village right after my friends were—" I stopped myself. "What were you doing at the plaza? And why you were pretending to be a reporter?"

There was an awkward pause as she seemed to weigh her options: continuing with her lie or 'fessing up.

"All right, fine," she said, dropping the tray to her side. "You caught me, okay? I'm not a reporter. What are you going to do? Turn me in?"

"No, I'm not interested in getting you in trouble. For the time being, I just want to ask you a few questions about Brandon Yeoh."

"I can't tell you much." She inhaled deeply. "What do you want to know?"

I was in a tricky spot, I realized, thinking on how I

should go about this. I didn't know what type of involvement this woman had with Brandon or what she could be hiding. For all I knew, she could be the killer. "First, why were you snooping around Asia Village the day after . . . everything happened?"

"Because I wanted to know if it was true," she replied. "I wanted to see if the whole thing . . ." She stopped, rubbing the back of her neck and looked around toward the blackjack tables.

I turned around to see what had caught her attention, but I couldn't pinpoint anything in particular. "What?" I asked, turning back around. "You wanted to see what . . . ?"

"I wanted to see if the whole thing was staged, okay?" Carmen huffed, shifting her weight. "He won a lot of money that night."

"Staged?" I asked. Was she implying that she knew the murder scene was staged to begin with?

"Yeah, people do that, you know. I had to see for myself. My first thought was that he faked his death so he could take off with the money. I went to the plaza to see if the store was cleaned out. Then I would know that the whole thing was planned."

Oh, that kind of staged. I told my brain to calm down. "Well, I can tell you, firsthand, he didn't fake it."

"I don't see what any of this has to do with you," Megan said.

"It has to do with *me* because I fronted him some of the money he used and he took off with my cut," she said, sounding a tad bitter.

"This money that he won . . . how much was it?" I asked.

"Like hundreds of thousands of dollars."

Megan and I gawked at her in disbelief. "Hundreds of thousands of dollars?" I repeated. "How much did he have on him when he left the casino that night?"

"At least a hundred thousand in cash."

"Actual cash?" I tried to imagine what that kind of money would look like.

"Yes, actual cash." She pursed her lips. "My cash."

"Do you remember seeing him with someone else that night? A tall man with Captain Kirk hair?"

"What's Captain Kirk hair?" Carmen asked.

Megan groaned. "You have got to stop saying that."

"You know," I said, gesturing to my head and making a swooping motion with my hand. "Like a flip thing . . ."

Megan covered her face with her hand. "Please stop."

I clucked my tongue at her. "Well, you describe him then."

Carmen glanced between the two of us. "Is he a beefy sort of guy?" She flexed her arm. "Dark hair?"

"Yeah, that could be him," I confirmed.

"I've seen him around. But I don't think he was here that night. Before I lost track of Brandon, every time I saw him, he was alone."

"Do you know anything about this other man?"

Carmen shook her head. "Nope."

Megan looked confused. "So, wait . . . if he came with that guy, but no one saw them together . . . then where did he go? Does that mean Brandon left alone?"

Carmen turned to her and shrugged. "If he was running off with my cut of the money, he coulda ditched that guy, too . . . if they were even together."

"Maybe," I said. "But there's an even more important question here."

They both looked at me as if to say, *What?*
"Where's the money now?"

We left the casino more puzzled than when we'd come in. Why hadn't I thought about the money before? When Esther had first mentioned that he'd won at the casino that night, I hadn't given it another thought. Maybe because I hadn't known exactly how much. If Adam had found a large sum of money with the bodies, wouldn't he have mentioned that?

And despite her original unwillingness to help, Carmen had proved to be more useful than I'd thought she'd be. She'd even given me her cell phone number in case I wanted to ask her any more questions. I think part of her was holding out hope that I would somehow miraculously find her money.

Fat chance of that happening.

When we were alone in the car, Megan asked, "What do you think this means?"

I maneuvered the car out of the parking space and headed for the parking garage exit. "I don't know. But now we have this missing money to consider. Esther did say that he told her it was enough to pay rent on the store for two years. It never dawned on me how much that would actually be. It couldn't just disappear into thin air, right?"

"Do you think he was robbed? Maybe someone knew he won the money and followed him to the store. Like, this unknown man, for example. It would certainly explain why the police didn't mention finding any money at the scene."

I shrugged. "The thought had crossed my mind. But

I just have a hunch that it's personal, you know? Why stage something so elaborate if it was just about the money? Something is nagging at me, and I can't put my finger on it."

"So what do we do now?"

We drove through the parking garage exit and pulled out onto Ontario. "I'm not sure, to tell you the truth. Maybe look for someone who Brandon knew that was hard up for money? Maybe Mar—"

"Hey!" Megan yelled.

I slammed on the brakes. "What?" I looked left and right, but I was clear to pull onto the street.

"What if they're all working together?"

"Oh my God, don't do that!" I put a hand to my chest. "I thought I was going to hit someone!"

"Sorry," Megan replied sheepishly. "But seriously, what if this mystery guy and Carmen *and* her boyfriend are all working together. She could be covering for him?"

"It's a possibility." I contemplated the likelihood of this scenario.

"Now the only thing we have to figure out is how to find this guy."

"No one seems to know who he is, and even though Esther has seen him around, she doesn't know, either."

"Maybe we should question our new friend Carmen further. We should convince her to come clean before anyone beats her to it. That always works on those murder mystery shows."

I snorted. "Come on, get real, Megan."

"It's true, though. Who's going to rat out who first?"

"Let's try to find out a little more on our own before we contact her again," I suggested. "If we come at her with too much too soon, she'll probably clam up and refuse to talk to us anymore."

Megan turned to me. "But you definitely agree that she wasn't telling the whole story, right?"

"Oh absolutely. She's holding out on us for sure."

When we got home that night, Kikko and I plopped in front of my laptop with cold pizza and a notepad. Excitement followed: I had three responses from the people I had reached out to. I was a little disappointed that none of them were from Jay Coleman, but at this point, I would take what I could get. In truth, I hadn't expected to get any at all.

The first reply was from a guy named Steve who lived in Brooklyn asking if I was single. He mentioned that he'd never dated an Asian girl before. And if he kept running with that line, he never would. I clicked DELETE.

The second message was one of Brandon's friends from Cleveland, who told me he didn't know that much about him but would be willing to answer whatever questions I had. I put a checkmark next to his name on the notepad. And the last message was from a guy named Todd in New York.

I decided to give the New York friend a call. He answered on the first ring.

"Hi, this is Lana Lee," I said, using my professional phone voice. "I was the one who emailed you about Brandon."

"Oh yeah," he replied. "I was real sorry to hear about his . . . situation. I tried to make it out to Ohio for the funeral, but I couldn't get off work. The beginning of the year is a busy time for us."

"It was a nice service," I told him. "Very sad, though."

"The whole thing is a shame. He finally seemed to be getting his life together."

"What can you tell me about him?" I asked. "I'd really like to capture who he was for . . . the article I'm writing. I didn't know him that well; I was more Isabelle's friend than his."

"Well, let's see. He was super easygoing about everything, even when things weren't really going his way. He didn't seem to mind when everything around him was chaos. I think he preferred it, actually. He breezed through school while the rest of us almost went bald stressing over exams. I envied that about him."

"What did he go to school for?" I asked.

"He was a business major. A group of us were all in the same classes and we'd hang out at the bars and stuff after school. You know, a little happy-hour study session."

"And he met his first wife, Constance, when he was in college, right?" I asked, pretending I didn't know.

He chuckled. "Yeah, she was a real piece of work, that girl. So uptight. I can see why he had a thing for her sister, Victoria." There was a long pause on the other end, and it made me wonder if he was daydreaming of the good ol' days. "Man, that Vic, she was something else. Fun girl, beautiful . . . no, sexy. You wouldn't even know the two were related."

"I met her briefly at the funeral," I told him, leaving out the details. "He liked Victoria before he even married her sister?"

"Oh sure," he responded. "Vic was part of our business crew. They hung out almost every day, but his parents didn't approve of her. They thought she was too wild for him, and maybe she was. They had an arrangement with their parents to marry off their eldest or something like that."

"Hm, I see," I said, mulling this over. "That's interesting that kind of thing still happens."

"You're telling me! Needless to say, that's not something you'd want to put in your story," he said with a laugh. "Speaking ill of the dead and all."

"Of course," I replied.

"Oh, he had a thing for cards," he told me. "He loved to gamble. He'd go to the frat houses and spend all his money on game nights."

No surprise there, I thought. "Did he win?"

"I'd say it was about fifty–fifty. A lot of times he'd let his arrogance get in the way."

"I see." He didn't seem to have any information that I didn't already know myself. Aside from the fact that his and Victoria's interest went farther back than I'd originally thought. "Well, I think I have everything I need," I told him. "Thanks for taking the time to talk to me."

"Hey, sure, no problem. If you have any other questions, just let me know."

Feeling disappointed that I had learned nothing new, I did another search through Brandon's list of friends on various social media accounts. My hope was to find the elusive Captain Kirk.

No dice.

Maybe this guy didn't exist online. And if he was a hit man, he definitely wouldn't be advertising himself on the Internet.

Even though it bothered me to do it, I clicked on Isabelle's name. This would be the first time since she'd been gone that I'd visited her page. Much like Brandon's, her wall had turned into a memorial. Family and friends left post upon post filled with memories and prayers.

I chomped on the pizza crust, trying to push back the tears that were welling in my eyes.

To torture myself even further, I went through her pictures. Her smiling face stared back at me as I scrolled through the happy images. What a tragedy for such a young life to be taken. And on top of that, she had been such a good person. She didn't deserve for things to end this way.

Ugh, I couldn't look anymore! I was driving myself crazy with this. It was time to call it a night.

Sitting there going through her pictures made me realize just how much this meant to me. I was going to figure this whole thing out and find their killer. I would find justice for them no matter what I had to do. Whoever was responsible for this wasn't going to walk away.

Before I closed the page, I typed a message. It read: *Miss you, dear friend.*

CHAPTER
18

Asia Village was hopping with customers rushing in and out of stores purchasing last-minute items or getting their hair done at Asian Accents. The breakfast rush continued until eleven. I had never served so many steamed buns in my life. The brief moment I had to look out into the plaza, I even saw a line coming out of the grocery store.

Nancy and I worked the tables as fast as we could, but it was hard to keep up. I was actually looking forward to my sister coming in for the day. If that wasn't a sign of the apocalypse, I didn't know what was.

There was a lull in the traffic coming into the restaurant and a flow of people ready to cash out at once. Nancy cleared the emptying tables while I worked on getting customers paid up and on their way. Anna May strolled in while I was cashing out a family of three at the register.

She scanned the restaurant. "Wow, this place is packed today. I almost couldn't find a parking space."

I gave the family in front of me their change and wished them a good day. "It has been nonstop since we opened," I said to my sister. "Since you're here now, I'm going to hurry and get the bank deposit ready and head out. I have a lunch appointment, too, so I might be gone for a little longer than normal."

"You're going to leave me and Nancy to handle this rush?"

I surveyed the now half-empty restaurant. "You'll be fine. We had it way worse than this most of the morning."

"You know, I think you're taking this 'in charge' thing a little too far. You can't just run off every day because you're the boss. You're not Mom."

"Oh whatever. You need to get over the fact that Mom and Dad left me in charge already. It's been a week since they left. And besides, I've been working ten-hour days and the only day I've cut out early was yesterday. So just calm down and go help Nancy."

We stood staring at each other in defiance until Nancy came up to see what was going on. "Is everything okay?" she asked, looking at my sister and me. She had that tone in her voice that said things better be okay, or else we'd have to deal with one of her lectures on sisterhood.

"Fine," I said, keeping my icy stare on my sister. "Anna May is just about to take over. I'm going to lunch."

Without saying anything, Anna May stormed off into the kitchen.

I got to Starbucks a little after noon; Rina was already there, sitting at a table by the window. She waved at me as I walked in. I returned the wave and pointed toward the line, letting her know I was going to place my order.

After I had my coffee and cranberry-orange scone, I made my way over to the table she'd gotten by the window. "I hope you weren't waiting long. I had to drop a deposit off at the bank and it took me a little longer than I thought."

"No problem, I kept myself busy with this *Scene* magazine." She pointed to the free local magazine spread out in front of her. "I've never been to Cleveland before. There's so much to do here, I had no idea."

"Never?"

"No. Even though Izzy and I sort of kept in touch, she never invited me to come see her. We were never right again after I gave her such a hard time about Brandon. Our relationship had become very . . . civil. Of course there were the regular check-ins with each other, but we didn't get too detailed. We sounded more like old acquaintances than sisters."

"It's too bad their marriage took such a toll on you guys." I took a bite of my scone. "I don't blame you, by the way."

"What do you mean?"

"Well, I didn't really care for him, either. I mean, he was never rude to me personally or anything, it's just . . . I don't know, I didn't like the way he treated her most of the time. It was almost like she was his maid or something," I said, putting down my scone. "But I've also been known to be a bit of a feminist at times. Maybe I'm not the right person to judge."

She slapped the table. "Yes! Oh my God, he always treated her like a servant. I saw it, too, and I couldn't stand it. She didn't seem to mind his demands, but every once in a while she'd get this look on her face, almost like she was going to snap. She never did, but I was always waiting for it to happen."

I thought back to her face on the night that Brandon told her he needed to leave again. I wondered if that was the same expression Rina was thinking about. "Did you ever notice anything else strange about him?" I prodded.

"Like what?" She sipped her tea, peering at me over the mug.

"Did he happen to disappear a lot when they lived in New York?"

She nodded. "Oh yeah, absolutely. He'd run off constantly. And sometimes he wouldn't come home all night."

I shifted to the edge of my seat. "Do you know where he'd go when he didn't come home?"

She rolled her eyes. "To the casino, of course. He'd gamble all night long. I don't want to know how much money he lost in the process."

"So this gambling problem has been long standing?"

"He swore to Isabelle up and down that he quit cold turkey, but—" She shook her head. "—someone like him doesn't just stop on the drop of a dime. Gambling is a serious addiction for some people. He had it too bad to just give it up completely without seeking some kind of professional help. He would win thousands of dollars a night and then lose it all before he came home. At that point, you're just doing it for the adrenaline rush."

Losing all of his money . . . it lined up. It would explain his nightly disappearances and why he had nothing to show for himself. He must have lost all the money he should have been paying to Marcia. But what was different about that last night? He'd told Esther his plans for the money. Something must have changed for him. "Do you think it could be possible that's what got them . . ." I paused, looking down at my coffee. ". . . into this mess?"

"What do you mean? His gambling got them killed?"

"Maybe . . . ?"

Rina tilted her head. "Why would you think that specifically?"

I informed her on my trip to the casino and running into Carmen.

She sat back in her seat and spread her hands out on the table as if to steady herself. "Do you think it could have been this woman from the casino?"

I shook my head. "I don't think so. She seemed sincere when she was telling me her story. I'm not completely convinced she's telling the whole truth. But either way, Brandon could have been involved in something that led to him and Isabelle getting killed."

She drummed her fingers on the tabletop, staring at the magazine in front of her but not really looking at it. She was off somewhere and I wanted to know what she was thinking. She started to say something but then stopped herself, focusing her attention out the window instead.

"Rina . . . if this is too upsetting to discuss, we can talk about something else. I know you wanted to catch up on what was going on with your sister's life since you last saw her. We don't have to talk about this."

"No, it's okay, it's not that. I'm just thinking if this is plausible or not."

"I know, I'm sorry to spring this on you."

"I'm glad you brought it up actually. It gives me

something to think about rather than just feeling sorry for myself. I've tried to avoid thinking about the details of the murder. But maybe that's been a mistake. Maybe I *should* be thinking about what really happened."

I leaned forward. "What can you tell me about Constance?"

"Constance?" She laughed. "Like if she's capable of murder?"

I nodded.

"It's possible, I suppose. If she was pushed enough that it would be justified . . . at least to someone like her."

I leaned in. "After Constance's outburst at the memorial reception, I had a few words with her sister, Victoria. She admitted to the affair and that Brandon was involved with other women. Did Isabelle know about all of this? I'm assuming someone tried to warn her?"

With a sigh she said, "Yes, I did. Numerous times. Izzy never wanted to believe it. Anytime I brought it up, she'd tell me that we didn't know the whole story and that it should be left in the past. People deserve second chances and all that."

"How bad was it? I mean, how many women are we talking?"

"More than I care to think about. Brandon was a womanizer, through and through." She took a deep breath. "Like I told you the other day, he was forced to marry Constance, and I think that made everything worse. His parents thought she could straighten him out, and they offered him a considerable inheritance if he agreed to it. So naturally, he did. He probably thought it would get his parents off his back, and he could have an unlimited source of money in the process. But he couldn't help himself. He had a thing for Victoria, and

those two ended up having an affair within months of
him and Constance tying the knot. I don't know how
differently things would have turned out had he just
been allowed to marry whoever he wanted to begin
with."

I leaned back in my chair and mulled this over. How
could Isabelle marry someone with such a terrible track
record with women? What could have been his redeeming quality? If it were me, I wouldn't have been able to
look past it all.

Rina rested her head in her hands, shaking her head
back and forth. "I still can't believe that my little sister
is gone. All because of that good-for-nothing jerk. I
know we don't know anything for sure, but I feel like it
was his fault. It had to be."

"How are you holding up, by the way?" I asked.

"As you'd expect. Some moments are harder than
others. Like I said, I've been trying not to think about
it. I've been keep myself busy with as many distractions
as I can find. My parents asked me if I would clean out
Izzy's things from their apartment. Constance called
them and asked if someone would take care of my
sister's things, which I was really surprised by. I thought
we'd have to fight to get her stuff back. So I told them
to head back to New York and I'd take care of any loose
ends around here."

"That was really nice of you," I said. "I'm sure your
parents appreciate it."

She sipped her tea. "I think staying in this city was
making things harder for them. It's better for them to
be back in New York . . . somewhere familiar."

I shimmied in my seat, thinking about what I wanted
to ask, and I hated to even bring it up.

Rina seemed to pick up on my uneasiness. "Lana, what is it?" she asked in a gentle voice that reminded me so much of her sister. It was amazing to me how much they were alike and how different Anna May and I were.

"When you go to clear out her things from the apartment . . . if you find anything that might be suspicious, would you mind letting me know?"

She contemplated my question and slowly began to nod. "Of course. Anything I can do to help."

For a while after, we switched our conversation to her sister and how life had really been for her in Cleveland. I told her about the pride that Isabelle had in running the store, and how her cheerful demeanor spread to everyone who came in contact with her. I told her about our weekly bookstore trips and casual dinners at the Bamboo Lounge. And despite the secrets that were beginning to surface, I told her that Isabelle had seemed truly happy, finding the good in every day.

We should all be so lucky.

As we left Starbucks and said our goodbyes, I felt a tinge of guilt flow through me. I hated to involve Rina in my suspicions, but I wanted her to know about the possibilities. She promised that she wouldn't share what I'd told her with anyone. And even though I didn't know her that well, I knew I could trust her.

When I got back to the restaurant, most of the tables were filled. Nancy and Anna May wove in between tables, dropping off platters of food and pots of tea. I fell right back into work and didn't stop moving until almost four o'clock.

The busy environment kept my mind off everything else in my life. Which, for once, was a welcome relief. Matter of fact, it wasn't until I was totaling receipts in my mother's office that the outside world came back into existence.

My cell phone chirped, jolting me from my accounting zone. It was Adam, and seeing his name light up on my screen sent my stomach into roller-coaster mode.

"How's my little restaurant manager holding up?"

I laughed. "Oh, fine. Just adding up receipts from today's day shift. It's been nonstop all day."

"Glad to hear that business is good and it's keeping you out of trouble."

My face went flat. "So good to know that you have confidence in me."

"Oh, don't be sensitive, I'm teasing you . . . you know, like you tease me."

"That's fair," I said, not wanting to admit that he was right. I did like to tease him. It was too easy.

"Anyway, I just called to make sure we're still on for our date tomorrow night? You're usually done with work around five or six, so I was thinking we'd head to dinner around eight if that works."

"Tomorrow night?"

"You didn't forget, did you?" he asked, sounding disappointed.

"No, no, definitely not."

"Great, I'll pick you up at eight then."

Truth was, with everything going on, I *had* forgotten. The days were meshing together and I didn't know which way was up.

I scrambled to finish the receipts and pack up for the

day. My next priority was to find something suitable to wear that would be sure to catch Adam's attention. Our dates—and me out of my work uniform—had been few and far between. I had to make every night count.

CHAPTER
19

Friday morning, I got to sleep in. Anna May had an afternoon class and needed to work the morning shift. I gladly complied. Not only because I wanted some extra sleep, but also because Lou was working that morning. Peter needed the day shift off so he could attend some painting seminar they were having at a local community college. It was one of those specialty adult classes where you show up three times and pay a reasonable fee.

Peter had been spending a lot more time on his art since he'd found out that Mr. Feng had been his real father. He had gone his whole life not knowing about his mother's affair with someone else's husband. Being creative with his art was a good way for him to deal with the emotions that came with learning the truth. He'd been to two of the three classes so far, and both times he had returned seeming a little more at ease.

When I finally stumbled out of bed, I took my time walking Kikko and lounged over morning coffee.

Megan had worked the late shift at the bar the night before, so I had the kitchen all to myself. I squeezed in a chapter of my new book before heading into the shower.

In true Betty Lee style, I strolled into the restaurant at eleven a.m., my face crunched up in scrutiny as I walked in. Anna May was perched at the hostess station, and Nancy was at a table taking someone's order.

"How's business today?" I asked, imitating my mother.

Anna May spread out an arm. "Take a look for yourself. The lunch rush is starting early."

I noted that the dining room was getting full and nodded in approval as my mother would. "I'll be in the back handling the books until you leave."

My sister gave me a flat stare and I broke character, beaming back at her with satisfaction, before heading to my mother's office.

Lou was busy at the grill when I walked into the kitchen. He was so enthralled by the shrimp he was sautéing that he almost didn't notice me walk by. Almost.

"Hey there, boss!" Lou bellowed from the grill, waving a metal spatula in my direction. Unlike Peter, he wore a proper chef's hat, which he straightened as he waddled over. "How've you been? I feel like we haven't worked together in a long time." He knelt down to my height and nudged me with his elbow. "The team is back together."

Lou is not my favorite. There's something about a person who is always smiling that unnerves me. Like clowns—you never know what they're really feeling behind that painted face. I forced a tight-lipped smile in return. "Yeah, it's been a few weeks. How's everything going back here? Good?" I asked, inspecting the kitchen. He did a good job of keeping it clean, but not quite as immaculate as Peter.

"Absolutely," he said with a wide smile. "Everything is in tip-top shape." He gave me a salute and then hustled back to the grill to tend to his shrimp.

"Great, I'll be in the office if you need me," I said, and shuffled off before he could say anything else.

I flipped the light on in my mother's office and slid behind the desk, where I got to work knowing that I had limited time before Anna May left for class. Since I had my date with Adam tonight, I wanted to make sure everything was finished so I could leave right at five. As long as I left as scheduled, I'd have plenty of time to get ready. I still hadn't settled on an outfit, and my nails could use a good painting.

While I waited for the computer to boot up, I pulled out the accordion file with the sales slips from the previous evening and sorted through the receipts. I would get everything organized as best I could, and put it back in the safe. If business slowed down, I could run to the bank at some point before I went home for the night.

Anna May popped her head into the office. "Hey, I'm getting ready to take off. The restaurant is about a third full and Nancy needs to take her lunch. Are you done in here?"

"Just about." I stuffed the receipts back into the accordion file and placed it back in the drawer.

My sister watched me. "It would appear to me that you're trying to get this done awfully fast. Are you eager to rush off tonight and do all that stuff you supposedly do?"

"I have a date with Adam later."

"Ah, another date . . . should I be waiting on that wedding invitation, little sister?"

"Would you stop? I wish you wouldn't make such a big deal about this. This is weird for me after . . . you know." I zipped up the deposit bag and stuffed it in the safe.

My sister turned her gaze away from me, staring at the desk. "You're right, I'm sorry. I shouldn't make you feel so uncomfortable about this whole thing. After all, this is the first guy you've dated since . . ."

I stood up from the safe, waiting for the next dreaded words to come out of her mouth. Just to jab me where she knew it counted. But the words never came, and for a brief second, we shared a moment of understanding. For those few seconds, we were just two sisters who, despite their constant bickering, were able to put aside their pettiness and live on the same page, rooting for each other.

"But just promise me one thing?" Anna May said, a small smile forming on her lips.

"What?"

"Please consult me on wedding theme colors before you make any rash decisions." She broke out into a wry grin. "I mean . . . just look at your hair."

Leave it to Anna May to ruin a good moment.

Eight o'clock was fast approaching and I had changed my outfit five times, feeling odd and less than stellar in the fashion choices I experimented with. It wasn't my ideal outfit, but I finally settled on a sparkly silver cam- isole and a long dark-gray cardigan with black leggings and heeled boots. I only hoped it would work for wherever we were going. With everything going on, I'd never thought to ask.

Megan had left for work, so it was just Kikko and me sitting on the couch with me growing more anxious by the minute. To kill some time, I paced back and forth to the bathroom, checking myself in the vanity mirror. I reapplied my lip gloss and added a silver necklace with a blue stone that matched my hair. Then I added a jade ring and a cuff bracelet. If he didn't get here soon, I'd start digging through my earrings.

After what seemed like an eternity, my cell phone chimed and without looking at who it was, I rushed to the door. But, when I checked the parking lot, Adam was nowhere to be found.

The text turned out to be from Ian instead. He wanted to let me know he was calling a last-minute board meeting for Monday evening. Great, I could hardly contain myself.

Back on the couch I went. My palms were starting to sweat. You'd think after a couple of dates, I wouldn't be quite so nervous. But in all honesty, they weren't exactly what I'd call the most successful of dates. Not that the dates were *bad*, but I could tell both of us were holding back.

The first one was what I like to refer to as the "safe" date. You see a movie and then have dinner after, thereby giving you something to talk about while you eat. Which worked out pretty well, but there wasn't much substance to conversations like those. After we talked about the movie, we then talked about other movies we'd seen in the recent past and how they stood up in comparison with the one we'd just seen. After that, we resorted to the "list of favorites" portion of the evening. This usually entailed talking about favorite colors, TV shows, restaurants, and maybe hobbies, if you're so inclined.

In case you're wondering, his favorite color is blue, he's addicted to *The Walking Dead*, and he's a huge fan of steak houses. As far as hobbies go, he isn't much of a sports guy, but he does enjoy a good car show here and there.

But it was the things he wasn't saying that I wanted to know. On the outside, he appeared to be a simple man, but I knew that behind the professional facade he maintained so well there was a complex man with a wealth of secrets. Whether those secrets were good or bad was another mystery I wanted to solve.

The next date had been a little better. Coffee and the art museum. He'd seemed more comfortable during this second go-round, but still there was a lot of filler talk about Monet, Renoir, Degas, and who the truly best Impressionist was.

I had high hopes I would learn more about him during our third date, but it was cut short due to him being called in to work. It turned out to be a big case, and that, of course, had kept us from having the chance to get together since. The times that he'd been available didn't work for me and vice versa. And now here I was feeling like it was the first date all over again.

My lucky number has always been eight, but I had my fingers crossed that it didn't take that many dates to figure out whether he was actually interested or just killing time.

There was a light knock at my door, and I jumped up again, the butterflies in my stomach springing to life. By the time I left the house tonight, I was going to be a nervous wreck.

When I opened the door, Adam barreled in, flustered and flushed. Kikko bounced to action from the couch, making a beeline for Adam, her wrinkled nose plastered to his shoes.

"Sorry I'm late," he apologized, running a hand through his hair. "Geez, I got stuck at the gas station . . . the line was twelve people long, you'd think they'd get some more help around that place. All I wanted was a pack of gum." He pulled the gum packet out of his pocket to show me it existed. "If I'd known it would take that long, I wouldn't have bothered."

"No problem," I said as I shut the door. "I didn't even notice the time."

When his eyes finally settled on me, they crinkled with his smile, and the hardened lines on his face softened. "Did I mention that you look beautiful?"

I blushed. "That might have slipped your mind."

He pulled me to him. "I hate being late, especially when a beautiful woman is waiting for me."

I batted his chest. "Really, it's no big deal."

Kikko whined, lifting her paw up and swatting Adam's leg.

"What's she doing?" Adam asked, looking down at the dog.

"She's going to do that until you pay attention to her."

He laughed to himself and knelt down to pet her. "Are you feeling left out, little one?"

"I just have to get my coat and we can go," I said, moving to the hall closet.

I gave Kikko her customary "be good" treat, locked up the apartment, and we were on our way.

The streets were clear of snow and ice, and the weather was behaving itself. Traffic wasn't too heavy as we drove toward downtown Cleveland, and we made it to the city in less than twenty minutes.

We turned onto the apron of East Fourth Street and he stopped the car, turning it over to a valet attendant. The sidewalk and street—which was closed off to traffic—were crammed with people bustling in and out of the bars and restaurants. Adam put an arm around my waist and guided me to the entrance of Pickwick & Frolic.

At the podium, he told the man standing behind it that we had reservations and we were immediately whisked to an intimate two-seater table along the far wall, away from the main aisle.

"I hope this is okay," Adam said, peeking at me over his menu.

"This is great," I assured him. "The last time I was here was for a comedy show downstairs. I really wanted to try the restaurant, but we didn't have reservations—and this place is always packed."

"I considered getting us tickets for the show tonight, too, but I thought this would give us more of a chance to chat." He skimmed his menu as he talked to me.

Okay, this was good: We were on the same page about wanting more quality date time. Most of the time Adam was ambiguous with his emotions, and I couldn't tell if our interest in each other was on the same level.

Our server, a curly redhead with bright-red lipstick, stopped to take our drink order and zipped off so fast I wasn't sure she'd heard what we said.

"So how's that big case?" I asked.

He raised an eyebrow. "Which case?"

"The one that interrupted our last date."

"Oh, that one." He focused back on his menu. "It's finished."

I looked down at my own menu with a sigh.

While we perused the menu, the server came back with our drinks. Adam ordered some calamari for the both of us, and the server zipped away again.

Adam shut his menu and placed it on the table. "So how's it been at the restaurant without your parents there? Everything running smoothly?"

I peeked up from my menu. *Fantastic*, I thought, *more filler talk*. Both of us were starting conversations with our work. "So far, so good. I'll be glad when they get back, though."

"Not much for the managerial life, huh?"

"Not much for the restaurant life is more like it," I replied.

He sipped his drink. "Is there something else you'd rather be doing?"

The server came back around, ready for our order. Adam ordered a crusted salmon something or other, and despite the pep talk I'd given myself about not ordering messy foods on dates, I went with the Cajun chicken fettuccine. What can I say? I love noodles.

When the server left, I answered Adam's question. "I've been trying to find a decent office job, and I thought I'd found one that was perfect for me. But I lost my chance. They needed someone to start right away and with my parents gone, I had to decline their offer."

"What was the job for?"

"An office manager position at a metal company in Solon."

Adam cocked his head. "An office manager position?"

"Yeah, what's wrong with that?"

The waitress dropped off the calamari and Adam scooped some onto his plate. "Nothing. It doesn't sound like you, is all."

"It doesn't?"

"Not really," he replied. "I picture you more as working with the public. You have that kind of face . . ."

"Ah-ha!" I said, filling my own plate.

He laughed. "Ah-ha what?"

"I knew it. I knew I had that kind of face." I pointed at my face. "The kind of 'come tell me your troubles' face."

He looked confused, and an inner battle began on whether I should tell him some of what was going on. If we were going to date, honesty needed to be a factor. Even if it was about things he didn't want to hear.

In a hurried explanation, I told him about the interactions I'd had with each of the three people.

His jaw clenched. "I thought you promised me that you were going to stay out of it?"

I jabbed a calamari with my fork. "I'm not the one trying to get into anything," I reminded him. "It's these people . . ." I gestured toward the window like they were standing outside.

He shuffled the squid around on his plate. "You send them to me, and I'll take care of it. I don't want you in the middle of this."

"I'm not some fragile little girl that can't take care of herself, you know. I did help with the Feng case."

His eyes bulged. "That's your argument? You were held at gunpoint and if I hadn't gotten your message when I did, we might not be sitting here together right now."

Trying to hide the cringe that thought induced, I replied as calmly as possible, "Well, it all worked out."

He snorted. "It all worked out? I can't be saving your life every five minutes, Lana."

"Every five minutes?" I retorted. "Dramatic much?"

"You know what I mean," he said with a sigh. "Hey, let's not argue about this right now, okay? Let's just have a nice evening and enjoy each other's company. We can always talk about this another time."

"Fine," I replied, stabbing another squid with my fork.

"Anytime a woman says 'fine,' she doesn't mean it."

I looked up at him, studying his face. He had me there. "Okay, you're right . . . on both counts. I won't get involved, and we shouldn't argue while we're out. Is that better?"

He laughed. "You're a sassy one, Lana Lee, and I like it."

After dinner, we stayed for one last drink before heading home. The car ride was a tad awkward since I was still carrying a partial chip on my shoulder. I didn't know why I was getting so defensive when I'd known exactly how he was going to react. His feelings on my getting involved were nothing new or surprising. And I couldn't expect him to understand the responsibility I felt to find out what had really happened to Isabelle and Brandon.

Especially since I hadn't mentioned my meeting with Carmen and what Brandon had been up to. After the way he reacted about what I had told him, I figured it was best that I kept those details to myself.

Okay, so the honesty wasn't there 100 percent, but I was working up to it.

When we got off the freeway and back to North Olmsted, thoughts about my lost job opportunity sprang up again as we passed a few office buildings. It got me thinking about the comment Adam had made earlier in the night about me and my job choices. Cindy from the bookstore had made similar statements. I wondered what made both of them feel that I was making a mistake in my job quest.

"Adam . . ."

"Hmm?"

"How did you know you wanted to be a cop?" I asked.

Silence.

I went on. "Earlier you said that I didn't seem like the office type. But how do you know what type you are? Did you always know that you wanted to be a cop?"

He stared straight ahead, and I wasn't sure if he'd heard me or was purposely ignoring my question.

When we stopped at a light, he turned to me with a grave expression on his face. "It's a long story . . ."

"Well, what better time to tell a story than on a date?" I asked.

The light turned green and we were moving again, but not talking. I made a mental note that this wasn't the first time he'd avoided telling me why he'd become a cop. I didn't know if that actually meant anything or I was trying to read into something that wasn't there. Not that I did that sort of thing . . . ever.

We pulled into my apartment complex in silence. Adam turned into the parking lot and put the car in park. We sat staring ahead at the apartment building. The quiet was suffocating and I urged him with my thoughts to say something. Anything.

I sneaked a peek at him from the corner of my eye.

"Do you want to come in?" I whispered, feeling unsure of myself.

He let out a long sigh. "I should be getting home."

"Okay," I said, trying to hide my disappointment.

He leaned over and gave me a quick peck on the cheek. "I'll stop by the restaurant for lunch sometime next week."

I nodded without saying a word and got out of the car. Instead of turning around to wave goodbye, I watched the lights beaming off the apartment building slowly fade as he backed out. At this point, I wasn't so sure we'd make it long enough to see a date number eight.

CHAPTER
20

I woke up the next morning discouraged from my night with Adam. With Anna May running the show at the restaurant, and fully covered shifts, I opted to hibernate.

I stayed in bed until well past ten, and just contemplated. I thought about how my previous night's date hadn't gone as well as I'd hoped, how the solving of Brandon and Isabelle's murder was going nowhere except for in circles, and my current life situation, in general.

Maybe Megan was right. Maybe I was going through some sort of quarter-life crisis. And that irritated me. Was it really fair that we had to have one of those, too? I mean, first you go through puberty, and that's a hot mess. You break out, become somewhat awkward looking, and get stuck with all kinds of weird emotions and bodily changes that you have zero control over. Then you mellow out for a little while, the world seems like it has gone back to normal and growth has just become a normal part of life. But now we're throwing in this supposed quarter-life crisis deal, too? How much time do we get to actually be normal human beings?

As my thoughts spiraled more and more into that shadowy abyss of panic, I must have stirred Kikko. She popped her head out of the blanket and waddled up to me, plopping down in front of my face. In one movement, she rolled onto her back and put her paws in the air—the universal signal for a belly rub.

There was a knock at the door and Kikko flipped over, hopped off the bed, and gave the crack under the door a long sniff.

"Are you up in there?" Megan's voice mumbled through the door.

"No, go away," I said, putting a pillow over my face.

The door opened. "It's Saturday, we should do something fun. We could go shopping or get breakfast . . . or get breakfast and then go shopping. Oooh, maybe we could catch a movie, too. You can't sleep all day."

"Says who?"

I felt Megan jump onto the bed, Kikko following suit. Megan lay next to me and tugged the pillow away from my face. "Did your date with Detective Hottie Pants not go well?"

"Would you stop calling him that?" I jerked my pillow away from her.

"No. It irritates you and that amuses me. I have to do something with my time."

"It was awful," I admitted, hugging the pillow to my chest. "We got into a disagreement about the case, and that put a funk in the air all night. I tried, but I couldn't shake it. Then on the way home, I asked him about being a cop and he clammed up like he did the last time I asked."

"Maybe it's a sore subject?" Megan offered.

"And the worst part . . . the worst part is that he kissed me on the cheek . . . like a grandma kiss." I hugged my pillow tighter remembering the feeling of his lips hitting my cheek like a bird peck.

Megan scrunched up her face. "Really? He doesn't seem like the timid type. And he's kissed you before, right?"

"Maybe he's not into me anymore. He said he can't worry about saving my life every five minutes. He probably thinks I'm some busybody and doesn't want to put up with it."

"No way," she said with resolution, hoisting herself up on her elbows. "Detective Hottie Pants is way into you. I can tell by the way he looks at you. And . . ."

"And what?" I asked.

"Well, I wasn't going to tell you, but he's been coming into the bar more often. I sorta think it's because he's trying to casually run into you."

"Really?" I didn't want to get hopeful, but a glimmer of excitement found its way in.

"Swear on my life," she replied with a nod. "Just give it some time. You're always so impatient with these things. You know all this stuff takes time to develop and grow. Before you know it, you won't be able to get rid of the guy."

Before long Megan convinced me to get out of bed, then lured me into the kitchen with promises of coffee. She'd also run out and grabbed half a dozen doughnuts, which now sat waiting for me at the table. If she'd led with that, I probably would have gotten up a lot sooner.

While I savored my Boston crème doughnut, Rina's number popped up on my cell phone screen. When I'd told her to call me if she found out anything useful, I didn't really think I'd get that lucky.

"Hi Rina," I said, answering the phone.

"Lana! It's Rina," she said in a panicked voice. She hesitated. "Oh, you already said that . . ."

I laughed. "It's okay, what—"

"Someone broke into the apartment. The whole place is trashed!"

"What?" The doughnut I was holding dropped onto the table.

"I showed up around ten this morning to meet Constance and pick up Izzy's things. When we got here and she opened the door . . ." She paused, huffing into the phone. "When we got here, the whole place was trashed."

"You're kidding? When did this happen?"

"I'm not sure. Constance went over to the neighbors and asked them if they heard anything, and they said they thought they heard something going on last night, but they weren't sure. The door wasn't broken, but the window by the fire escape was wide open. I don't think Brandon or Isabelle kept them locked."

"Have you called the cops?"

"Yeah, they're on their way now. We don't even know what to tell them is missing. It's not like either one of us has ever been here before."

"Well, it's okay, they'll do whatever it is they do, and then . . . well, I don't know. Maybe the person left fingerprints behind or something."

There was silence on the phone. I had no idea what else to say to her.

Rina gasped. "The apartment buzzer just went off. The cops are here, I better go, okay?"

"Okay, call me later if you need to," I said, feeling helpless.

"I probably will," she said. "Oh, and Lana . . ."

"Yeah?"

"I think you were right after all." And she hung up.

I sat staring at my phone. What the heck was going on?

Megan came and sat across the table from me, grabbing a glazed doughnut from the box. "What was all that about?"

"Someone broke into Brandon and Isabelle's apartment." I picked up my dropped doughnut and set it on a napkin. Since I'd dropped it, Kikko had been circling my feet like a shark hunting its prey.

She paused mid-bite. "What? Just now?"

"According to the neighbors, potentially last night. One of them told Constance they might have heard something."

"Wow," Megan said, biting into her doughnut. "That's insane."

"I know, talk about timing." I scrolled through my phone, searching my address book.

"What do you mean?"

"It's just a coincidence that their apartment gets broken into after we talk to Carmen?"

"You think it was her?" Megan got up, bringing the coffeepot to the table and filling both of our mugs.

"Yeah, I do. She's probably still searching for her money. And since we told her that there wasn't any money found on him when he was killed, she probably assumed he stashed it in his apartment somewhere." I found Carmen's number and typed a text message asking when she would be available to talk. I didn't say anything about the broken-in apartment just yet. "Who else would it be? The ex-wives are out of the picture. Marcia's in New York, and if Constance has an all-access pass to get in on her own, why would she bother breaking in?"

"True. So what are you going to do now?"

I hit SEND and looked up at Megan. "We're going to call Carmen out on it."

Within the hour, Carmen texted back that she would be at work and I could meet her at the casino before her shift started. Megan agreed to come with me, and I hurried to get dressed so we'd make it in time.

Carmen told me I could find her in the food court area near where we'd met last time. Sure enough, when we showed up an hour and a half later, she was sitting at one of the tables with a plate full of food and a jumbo pop.

I sat across from her without greeting. Megan sat in the chair next to me.

She eyeballed me dumbfounded, lettuce hanging from the corner of her mouth. "You're an intense person, aren't you?"

"If I'm passionate about something . . ."

"And what's her deal?" Carmen asked, nodding toward Megan. "She your bodyguard or something?"

Megan leaned forward. "Maybe I am."

"Okay . . . so what's this about?" she asked, chomping on her burger and ignoring Megan's response. "More questions for me?"

"Just one," I replied. "Do anything interesting last night?"

"You mean besides work my dream job?" She held up a hand as if to display the casino. "No, I don't tend to do much after work these days. You know, money trouble and all."

"So you weren't at Brandon's last night looking for your money?"

"What?" She dropped her burger on the plate and gawked at me, her eyes shifting to Megan. "Are you flippin' kidding me? You guys came here to ask if I was rummaging around in some dead guy's apartment?"

A few people sitting around us turned to see what was going on.

"Shhhh, lower your voice," I rasped at her. "Someone's going to hear you."

She grunted. "I don't care. We would never do something like that."

"'We'?" Megan asked.

She stared at her plate. "I mean, I . . . *I* would never do that." She said this last part as a half mumble that did not sound convincing in the least.

"Too late, Carmen, you screwed up," I said, pointing a finger at her. "I knew you were hiding something from us the other day. Whatever it is . . . out with it."

"I don't know what it matters, the money is gone. You don't need to know anything more from me." She picked her burger back up and took a bite.

"Yes, I do. Two people are dead; it has something to do with that money . . . it has to."

"And why is that my problem?"

"Because the person you were working with could be the killer and if they can't find the money, either, they might think you have it."

She seemed to contemplate this for a minute, taking extra time to chew. "No way, he would never do that."

I felt like I was talking to a broken record. "Just tell me who it is. If you and he are so innocent, then it doesn't matter who he is, right?"

"I suppose." She mulled it over for another minute, chomping on a fry. "My boyfriend is a blackjack dealer at one of the high-stakes tables. Brandon would win lots of games at his table . . . matter of fact, he was playing at Ryan's table the night he won his huge payout."

A creaky wheel started to turn in my brain. "Your boyfriend is a blackjack dealer?"

"Yeah," she said, watching my reaction.

"So this all ties together how exactly?"

She huffed, leaning toward me over the table. "Ryan came up with a plan to double our money, but we needed someone that could play the game who had no ties to us whatsoever . . . you know, just in case the casino started to get suspicious."

"Let me guess. That's how you met Brandon?"

"Yeah. My job was to scout the casino and find someone who won a lot. I noticed Brandon because he came in so often. He'd come in here and spend tons of money, and most of the time he'd win. But lately, he wasn't having very much luck. You could tell by the look on his face that he was hurtin'. So one night, I followed him out and proposed this deal to him. At first, he turned me down and called me crazy. But then, about a week later, he shows up outta nowhere and tells me that he wants to take me up on my offer after all."

"What changed his mind?" Megan asked.

She shrugged. "The hell if I know. I wasn't about to

ask questions. I just introduced him to Ryan and they went through the rest of the details from there."

"Okay, then what?" I urged her to continue.

"With our plan, Ryan would make sure Brandon won every time. He came to the casino at designated times with his own money, plus mine and Ryan's. Then he wins, doubling our original pot. We wait a little while and then we meet up to split the money. We even let Brandon take a larger chunk since he had to claim the winnings on his taxes."

"How thoughtful of you."

She scowled at me. "Do you want to hear the rest or not?"

"Yeah, go on."

"Well, in the past few weeks, there'd been another regular at the table when Ryan and Brandon were running the scam. Some rich, old guy who would put down more than I make in a year. He lost quite a bit to Brandon, and I think he was starting to get suspicious. He tried asking Ryan for his name, but he would just say he didn't know him. Then we saw that same guy harassing Brandon outside the guys' bathroom. He seemed really pissed about something. We figured it had to do with his losses, but Brandon told us it was no big deal. But now he's dead, so it might have been more than he was letting on."

I took a minute to think over the prospect of this other blackjack player, and what the implications might be had this man figured out what Brandon and Ryan were doing. I also took the time to assess Carmen. I didn't know her well enough to tell if she was lying, but she appeared to be telling the truth. "And how do you know that Ryan didn't go behind your back and go to Brandon's apartment last night?" I asked her.

"Because he was with me all night," she said plainly. "And I'm telling you, we wouldn't do that."

I studied her face. She looked at me head-on and kept eye contact. "Oddly enough, I believe you."

"Well, you should," she said, wiping her hands with a napkin. "I wouldn't be sitting here eating fast food if I had my damn money."

"Good point," I said, looking at the empty greasy plate. "But I'd like to meet this boyfriend of yours. See if his story checks out."

"Why? He's just going to tell you what I did. It's better if you leave him out of it."

"It's better us than the cops, right?" I was hoping that the mention of police getting involved would be enough to get her to agree.

Carmen drummed her fingers on the table, staring at her empty plate.

Megan shifted in her seat, turning to face me. "Cops, good point, Lana. Or if she's not willing to introduce us, I'm sure we can find a way to meet him on our own. Name is Ryan . . . blackjack dealer. Shouldn't be hard to find."

Carmen rolled her eyes. "Calm down, princess." She groaned, pushing the food tray away from her. "Give me a little time to figure out how to approach him about it. He's going to be mad that I told you guys anything at all."

"Are you afraid of your boyfriend?" I asked. "I thought you said he was harmless."

"He is. But we're not exactly running a fund-raiser

here, ladies. I'm not supposed to be sharing all our secrets."

"Fine . . . figure it out. You have my number."

"Right." She stood up. "This has been fun and all, but I gotta get to work. Okay if I go now, Detectives?"

"Just one more question," I said, holding up a finger.

"What?"

"Do you happen to know the name of the older man who comes in every week? The one who you think might be a problem?"

"No, but I can find out and let you know." She started to walk away, but stopped herself and turned around. "Funny thing, though. Now that I think about it, we haven't seen him since the night before Brandon died."

CHAPTER
21

By the time we got back from the casino, it was nearly five o'clock, and I had no Saturday-night plans to speak of. Part of me wanted to change that. Megan had to work until close, and before leaving the house she suggested I visit her at the Zodiac, so I did have that option. But there was still a part of me that didn't want to deal with this day anymore. And that part won the inner battle. After a short walk with Kikko, I rummaged around my room for my pajamas instead. I decided tonight was going to be another *Gilmore Girls* marathon. It was just the thing to get me out of this funk that had followed me around since my date.

I needed popcorn or something. I dug around in the kitchen cupboards for something suitable to snack on. All that I found were old cookies and a jar of peanuts. We really had to go shopping.

A half-full bag of tortilla chips sat on top of the freezer. And as luck would have it, there was salsa in the fridge. Good enough.

I plopped down on the couch and opened the bag of chips, sending Kikko into a fit of spins and mini jumps.

About half an hour into the first episode, I must have passed out. When I woke up again, Kikko was barking furiously at the door, and the TV's screensaver danced around in square formation.

I checked my cell phone. It was already eleven thirty. How had I slept so long?

While sleeping, I had five missed messages. All from Megan.

Come to the bar, I'm here and it's dead. I'm bored.
Where are you? Come hang out with me.
Hello?
Lana.
Hey pay attention to me, your boyfriend is here and I'm going to steal him for myself.

I rolled my eyes. With a sigh, I got up from the couch. Kikko had stopped barking and watched me expectantly. Her food dish was empty.

"Is that why you're so grumpy?" I got the dog food out of the cupboard and filled her bowl.

After that, I paced the length of the apartment and thought about starting my marathon over again.

I wasn't feeling it.

It was early enough and I was too restless to sit around. I could still visit Megan at the bar . . . not that Adam being there sparked my interest at all.

Nope.

I texted Megan back, letting her know I had been napping and was getting ready to head up there. I dug through my closet for a clean pair of jeans and found a teal sweater with a low neckline.

I let Kikko out for a quick tinkle and said my good-byes. Thankfully my car wasn't covered in snow, just a little ice on the windshield. I'd sit it out in the warm car.

There was a piece of paper under my windshield wiper blade. Great. More flyers for Avon, I'm sure.

But when I picked it up, I realized it was most certainly not from Avon. Scrawled in sloppy writing, it read: *Stop snooping around. Mind your own business. Or else!*

A prickly sensation trickled down my spine and I whipped around, feeling as if I were being watched. The parking lot was quiet except for the sound of my engine fighting against the cold. As far as I could tell, no one was in the parking lot with me. I rushed into the car and locked the door, peering out the window in search of any sudden movements. The note rattled in my hand as I double-checked for moving shadows between the cars directly behind me. Nothing.

I turned the heat on full blast and waited for the ice to thaw. My eyes were pinned to the note. Was this a message from Carmen? Or from her boyfriend? Had she told him we wanted to meet with him and this was his way of saying no? Did someone follow us home from the casino? Was that what Kikko had been barking at earlier?

My mind went in circles. If I were a smoker, I would have smoked a whole pack of cigarettes right then and there.

Five minutes later, the car was warmed up and I put the gearshift in reverse. My car struggled to back up, and the movement I made felt like I was stuck on something. I put the car back in park and got out to see what the problem was.

My back tire was flat! I swore a string of profanities that would make any sailor proud as I rounded the car. Correction, all four tires were flat! When I bent down to do a closer inspection of the tires, I noticed long slash marks in each of them. My finger traced the slash mark for a minute before reality set in.

With renewed fear, I got back in the car and turned it off, rushing inside, still clutching the note in my hand.

I called the police department and told them about the note I'd found and the state of my tires. The dispatcher asked if I was in immediate danger.

"No, I don't think so," I replied, my voice shaky. "I'm in my apartment and the door is locked. I think the person already left."

"Okay, ma'am, someone will be out right away. Just hang tight and stay inside."

Kikko, sensing my tension, came over and put a paw on my leg. A tiny whine escaped her throat. I leaned down and gave her a pat on the head. "It's okay, we're okay," I told her . . . more for my benefit than for hers.

I inspected the note again.

Then I remembered Megan. She was expecting me. I sent a text letting her know what had happened. *Tires slashed. Cops coming. Can't make it to the bar. Don't tell Adam.*

I paced.

A few minutes later, there was a knock at my door. I looked out the peephole before opening it. I could see a uniformed officer standing there looking around. He was dressed in a bomber jacket and a black beanie hat covering his head.

I opened the door. He was a little bit older than me and had a chubby face with a five o'clock shadow. He was not amused.

"You called about the tires?" His facial muscles barely moved as he talked.

"Yes, come in, Officer," I said, stepping to the side.

"Can you tell me what happened?" he asked, glancing around the apartment. Soundlessly, Kikko came up to him and sniffed his boot. The cop glanced down at the dog. "Does he bite?"

"No . . . and it's a *she*."

"Right," he said. "Go on."

"I was heading to the bar to meet some friends, and when I got to my car, there was this note on my windshield." I handed the slip of paper to him. "And all four of my tires were slashed. I didn't notice the tires right away, I tried putting the car in reverse and that's when I realized something was wrong."

"I see," he said, with little emotion. He removed his leather gloves and whipped out a small notebook. Pulling a pen from his breast pocket, he jotted down some notes.

There was a strong knock at the door. The sound made me jump and Kikko howled, circling around my legs.

The cop eyeballed me. "Are you expecting anybody?"

"No." I went for the door.

He held up a hand to stop me. "I'll answer." He stuffed his notebook and pen back in his pocket.

When he opened the door, Adam stood staring back at us. The expression on his face was familiar and I knew that somehow, *I* was the one in trouble.

"Detective," the cop said with surprise. "I didn't realize you were on duty tonight."

"I'm not," he said, his eyes traveling past him and landing on me. "I found out about this through a mutual friend." He was talking to me, not the cop.

I groaned. Megan.

"Did you . . . did you want to take over?" the cop asked with apprehension. His eyes shifted between Adam and me, unclear what was going on.

"No, you go ahead and pretend like I'm not even here," he said coolly. "I'll be sitting over here on the couch, keeping Kikko entertained."

After the cop left, Adam and I sat speechless for a few minutes, the dog in between us on the couch.

I couldn't take it anymore. The only sound was the dog panting, and it was driving me nuts. "I'm the victim here," I blurted out.

He clenched his jaw. "We just had a discussion about this yesterday. Are you snooping again?"

"What would give you that idea?"

"The note . . . you know, the note that someone left on your car right after they slashed all four of your tires."

I sat back on the couch, putting my head back and closing my eyes. "That is gonna cost me a fortune."

"That's what you're worried about?" he asked, his voice climbing an octave. "How much the damn tires are going to cost?"

"Well, yeah," I replied. "I don't have the money for that. I'm going to have to put it on my credit card and it's almost maxed out."

He snorted, throwing his hands in the air. "Unbelievable. Someone leaves a threatening note on your car and you're worried about your credit card bill."

"Hey, if you owed as much as I do on your Master-Card, you'd understand."

"Lana . . ." He pinched the bridge of his nose. "I need you to take this seriously. This isn't a joke."

"Okay, fine," I folded my arms over my chest, tantrum-style. "Are you happy now?"

"No," he said firmly. "And I don't feel comfortable leaving you here by yourself. When does Megan get home from work?"

"Usually around three a.m.," I said.

"Well, we have some time then, don't we?" he said, settling back down on the couch.

"Wanna watch *Gilmore Girls* with me?" I asked innocently. "I have half a bag of chips and some salsa . . . we could—"

He glared at me. "No, I do not want to watch *Gilmore Girls*. What I want is for you to tell me what you've been up to."

"But I'm at the part where Rory and—"

"Lana."

He had his detective voice, and I knew that I'd pushed too far. But I couldn't tell him everything. If I told him about Carmen, then he would look into it right away and she might freak out and clam up. I needed to stall until I had a chance to meet her boyfriend, Ryan. Then once I had more info, I could turn her and her slimy boyfriend in to the cops. "Fine . . . I'll tell you . . . but only if you answer some questions for me."

"You're not exactly in a position to make a deal."

I crossed my arms. "We can sit here all night in

silence if you want. I don't mind." He wasn't the only one who could be stubborn.

A few minutes went by. I inspected my cuticles while I waited. He shifted uncomfortably next to me, shaking his leg as he weighed his options. "All right, I'll give in just this once."

Once I started talking, his leg had stopped shaking and he remained absolutely still, listening carefully to everything I had to say.

I went through the story about running into Carmen, but left out her name and any info about the missing money. For the purposes of my story, she was just some girl with brown hair that I had failed to get any information on. I did admit to asking her about Brandon and recognizing her from snooping around the plaza.

When I was finished, I expected a lecture about the dangers of approaching random people about the case, but instead, he asked, "What do you want to know?"

"Do you think this has something to do with the casino? It has to, right?"

"Possibly. We've investigated the casino angle. I'm assuming that you sent Esther Chin to me."

I nodded.

"We've been tracing Brandon's whereabouts and now that we know he came into a considerable amount of money that night, it adds a different angle to the investigation."

"Do you think this woman could be involved?"

"Hard to say. I'd definitely like to talk with her if I can find out who she is."

My hands started to sweat as I thought about it. Hopefully Carmen would get in touch with me soon so I could tell Adam the real story.

He continued without me having to prompt it. "Also, from what I've learned so far, your friend Isabelle wasn't aware that he was gambling away their life savings."

"No," I confirmed. "She had no idea where he was running off to all the time. She thought maybe there was someone else."

"She may not have been far off."

I gasped. Could he really have been cheating on her on top of everything else?

"We're still tracking down some leads on that subject. As far as the money is concerned, we haven't found it yet, but we don't think it was stolen so much as Brandon may have hidden it somewhere. The money being missing and the murder might just be a coincidence."

"What do you think happened then?"

"Your friend fell . . . which means it either happened on its own, or she was pushed. Now, if you ask me, I say she was pushed. At the force she hit her head, I doubt it happened without help."

"And . . ."

"And I don't know, Lana," he said with frustration. "They were killed together. His ex-wife Constance, whom he cheated on multiple times, is awfully adamant about getting her hands on that store. The legal documents . . . well, I just wonder why exactly nothing was updated. Then you have his second wife, Marcia . . . she seems to be a very . . . passionate soul, doesn't she? Almost a little too much considering her circumstances."

Passionate. What did he mean by that?

"All of this leads me to wonder . . . what did this guy have on these women to make them so . . ."

"Passionate?" I spat.

He squeezed my leg. "Lana . . . I didn't mean it like that . . ."

"Then how did you mean it?" I asked, moving my leg.

Adam sighed. He rubbed the caps of his knees with his hands. "Well, Marcia was still willing to stick her neck out for him with a considerable amount of money. Don't you think that's a little strange considering he married another woman so quickly?"

"You think she did it then?"

He shook his head. "Not necessarily. We're waiting on tollbooth footage so we can compare her timing on the road with the timing of the murders. It's taking a little while for them to get back to us with the photos."

"But if you had the photos, then you would know whether she was guilty or not?"

"She drove to Cleveland . . . but so did Constance." He put an arm around me, pulling me toward him. He kissed the top of my head. "I don't want you to think about this anymore, okay? Don't go back to the casino searching for this woman . . . whoever she is. Give me a better description of her and I'll have one of the guys look into it."

I had to stall on the description. I mean, brown hair, brown eyes, and short was pretty vague anyway, but I didn't want him to start drilling me on specifics. I pouted. "It's been a really long night, can we go over it tomorrow?" I pointed at the TV. "Can we please just watch one episode?"

He sighed in defeat. "Fine. Just one. But don't tell the guys."

CHAPTER

22

Adam ended up staying the night . . . on the couch. After our long discussion, neither of us was able to keep our eyes open any longer, and I suggested he just crash at my place. Having a detective in the house also seemed like a bonus.

When I woke up in the morning, I could hear Megan and Adam chatting away in the dining nook. I also heard the clinking of cups and spoons. And coffee . . . I smelled coffee.

I checked myself in the mirror and found my hair to be akin to that of a troll doll. I tried to flatten my crown the best I could, threw on a hooded sweatshirt, and headed out to see what was going on, Kikko dancing around my heels.

They both turned and stopped talking when I entered the room.

I looked between the two of them. "Am I interrupting something?" I could feel a chip forming on my shoulder.

Megan laughed. "Nope, just talking about our little Lana." She turned her back to me, facing the coffee-maker, and poured me a cup. She brought it over to the table and placed a spoon in front of me.

"Thanks," I mumbled. I sat down, sliding the mug closer.

Adam snickered. "Is this how you are every morning?"

I sucked in my cheeks. "I didn't sleep well."

"Good thing you're off today," Megan replied, sitting down with us. "You can go back to sleep if you want."

"I'm fine," I said as I put cream and sugar in my coffee.

Adam raised his eyebrows. "Here she goes with her 'fine' stuff again."

I sipped my coffee, ignoring his comment.

"Well, I'd better get going. I have to stop by the precinct today." He chugged the rest of his coffee. "Can you manage to stay out of trouble for one day?"

"Yeah," I murmured.

He got up and kissed me on the forehead. "Great. Now try to find someone who can deal with your tires on a Sunday. We can talk about that woman's description later."

After he left, Megan asked. "What woman's description?"

I glared at her, ignoring her question. "What was all that about?"

"What was what?"

"What were you two talking about?"

"Oh stop," she said, waving a hand at me. "We were *really* talking about you."

"And . . ."

"And he was telling me how much he likes you . . ."

"I see." Tapping my nails on the side of my mug, I scrutinized her as she looked at me innocently. "What did he say specifically?"

Megan pursed her lips. "Specifically he said that he cares for you a great deal and doesn't want anything to happen to you. Then he called you stubborn, and I agreed with him, and that's when you walked in."

"I'm not stubborn."

"So other than being cranky, what are you going to do today?" Megan asked, changing the subject. "Want me to help you find someone to tow your car?"

I groaned. "I can't believe they slashed all four tires. Don't you think that's a bit overkill? They could have slashed one and it would have been just fine."

"Who do you think it was?"

"Well, we were at the casino yesterday." I said, letting that statement hang in the air.

"You think it was our new informant? Or maybe an angry boyfriend?" Megan got up and put some bagels in the toaster. "You want one?"

"Sure." All I'd eaten the night before were the tortilla chips. The tire slashing kind of put a cramp in my night.

While we waited for the bagels, I filled Megan in on my conversation with Adam, including the Carmen cover-up, which I was still feeling guilty about.

Megan chewed on her bagel, thinking it over. "You know," she said, waving the bagel at me. "What if it *was* the boyfriend guy? Maybe she told him about you questioning her and he got mad."

"I had the same thought, but I felt like that might be too obvious. I mean, is she that stupid? Is he? We were just talking to her earlier that day. She would have to know that I would suspect one of them."

"We've both seen dumber things happen."

"True. And she swore that he's not that kind of person." I made sarcastic air quotes as I said it. "But people are always capable of surprising you and she may not know him as well as she thinks. I mean, take for instance what Brandon was hiding from Isabelle. She had no idea that he was involved in this gambling scam. And who knows what else she didn't know." I was thinking specifically about Adam making references to Brandon possibly being involved with other women.

"Well, whoever it was, they're a little on the crazy side. Do you think maybe you should back off? What if this person comes after you personally next time? I think you should have told him the truth about Carmen, at least."

"Not a chance. I can't just let this person go free. If I walked away now, I couldn't live with myself . . . not if there's something I can do about it. And besides, Carmen doesn't strike me as the type of person to come clean with the cops. If he goes after her, the boyfriend could take off, and then we'll never know if she was telling us the truth."

"Well, whatever happens, I've got your back."

My cell phone rang, making both of us jump. The number on the screen told me it was Rina. "I wonder what she wants."

"Hey, Lana, I hope I'm not disturbing your Sunday," Rina said when I answered.

"No, I'm just lounging around. What's up?"

"I'm back at Izzy's apartment, and I wondered if you could come by and keep me company while I finish packing up her things. Constance left already, and to be honest with you, this place kind of creeps me out." She paused. "I don't mind doing all the work myself, but having you here would make me feel better."

"Yeah, I'd love to keep you company. It's not a problem. Can you give me an hour?"

"Sure. I'll text you the address," she said. "See you soon."

"What's going on?" Megan asked.

"Rina asked if I would come hang out with her at the apartment while she packs up Isabelle's things. Do you mind if I borrow your car?"

"No, go ahead. It'll give me a chance to work on my blanket. But hold on." She ran into her room and came back out carrying a Home Depot bag. "Can you put this in my car? I keep forgetting to bring it with me."

I peeked in the bag and found the new metallic-blue flashlight and mini tool kit that she'd purchased on our last trip to the store. "Are you going to buy everything in blue now?"

"What can I say? Your hair inspires me."

"Great," I said, getting up from the table. "I'm gonna call a tow truck place to take my car before I go."

The tow truck guy said to give him about an hour. So I got ready and walked the dog while I waited. As promised, a tow truck with a flatbed pulled into our parking lot an hour after I'd made the call. I threw on a coat and ran outside.

I waved the truck driver down and he stopped and got out.

"My car is the black one," I told him, pointing.

He went over and examined the car. After walking around the entire vehicle and crouching by the tires a few times, he gave a long whistle. "Wow, someone really did you good, didn't they?"

"Is this going to cost me a fortune?"

"Hmm, I'll see if I can find you some decent used tires, but it won't get done today. I could probably have you finished up in a day or two. Does that work?"

I sighed. "It'll have to. I'm sure I can find a ride to work until I get it back."

He tipped his hat and got back in the truck, maneuvering around my car so he could tow it out. I watched him pull away with it and all I could see were dollar signs trailing after the truck. Whoever this person was, they were really getting on my bad side.

Half an hour later, I was standing in front of an unexceptional brick building that overlooked the East Bank of the Flats, Cleveland's riverfront district. There was a small, gated parking area on the back side of the building. Rina had given me the code, and I pressed the cold metal numbers in the order she'd given me. The gate screeched open and I pulled my car into the only available spot.

The lot maybe had eight parking spaces, and they were all filled with high-end model cars. I parked in between a Mercedes and a Corvette. *One day, Lana, one day.*

I had passed this building so many times on my way into the Flats, but I'd never known what was inside, always mistaking it for an old office building of some sort.

Rina was standing in the entryway waiting for me, and gave me an eager wave as I came into view. She nudged the door open. "I can't thank you enough for helping me so last-minute like this." She gestured to the stairs, and I followed her up two flights.

"It's no problem, really." I said. "Sorry I'm a little later than I told you I'd be. I had to call a tow truck."

"Oh no! What happened?"

"Long story." I decided to spare her the details. She had enough to worry about already.

She pulled out a ring of keys, found the right one, and stuck it in the lock. "I don't expect to finish today. She had more stuff than I realized . . . everything is different than I thought, actually. Yesterday, we spent more time cleaning up broken glass than anything else. I hardly had a chance to go through her things."

"Broken glass? I thought you said the fire escape window was open?"

"Oh, it was, but whoever did this managed to shatter every vase, picture frame, and breakable object they could find."

"Unbelievable! The timing can't be a coincidence."

"Tell me about it. And there's no way to tell what they were searching for because we don't know what was here to begin with." She put her hands on her hips and scanned the room. "Anyhow, I thought today I could at least go through some of her personal effects . . . I have no idea what we'll do with all this furniture. I'm looking for some places that will come pick it up for free. Constance asked if I wanted it, but I don't have a use for any of it."

"What about Brandon's family?" I asked, following her in. "Don't they want anything?"

I would have heard her answer, but I was too in awe of the apartment that we walked into. I don't know what I thought their living situation was; I guess I figured it would be similar to my own. I imagined they would live in a reasonable two-bedroom apartment with that same dreadful carpet and bland eggshell wall. Boy, was I wrong.

What I stepped into was Cleveland luxury at its finest. The hardwood floors gleamed in the rays of light coming in from the giant picture windows facing the Flats. The living space was wide open with an exposed kitchen entirely composed of stainless-steel appliances and marble countertops. The bedrooms and bathroom were at the far end of the room with no hallway separating them from the common area.

Even with the recent break-in, the place was incredible.

"Wow . . ." I said, my eyes traveling over the art adorning the walls. "I never thought . . ."

"I know," Rina said, dropping the keys into a dish on the table. "It's not Izzy's style at all, it's Brandon's. His New York apartment was very similar to this one."

I stepped farther into the apartment, absorbing the surroundings. It definitely felt "big city." "I can't imagine how much they were paying for this place," I said, my hand running along the exposed brick walls. "This had to cost a fortune."

"I have no idea where they got the money for this. With the way their finances were, this place was totally out of their budget. Constance met with the landlord to discuss the break-in, and I overheard them talking prices. Let's just say you and I couldn't afford this if we put our incomes together." Rina headed to one of the doors. "This one was their bedroom. I figured I'd start packing up her clothes. Do you know of a charity I could donate them to?"

"Yeah, I can drop them off for you if you want. Save you the trouble."

"That'd be great."

She disappeared into the bedroom and I moved into the kitchen, inspecting all of the appliances. They were a far cry from our beat-up little kitchen with its old fixtures. How on earth would the two of them be able to afford an apartment like this with the money they made at the souvenir shop—a struggling new business no less? Add in Brandon's gambling problem, and it was a miracle they'd been paying rent at all.

Rina clanked around in the bedroom, focused on the project she was starting. Since she wasn't paying me any attention, I decided to check out what was behind door number two.

Turned out to be a home office. There was a desktop computer and a printer, with several books stacked in two neat rows next to the keyboard. On top of one pile, there was a Post-it that read *TBR* . . . and my heart dropped thinking about how Isabelle would never get the chance to conquer her to-be-read pile.

I couldn't help but rifle through the pile. The books she had stacked were from one of our recent book outings. I remembered helping her choose between the next Sue Grafton and a new Michael Connelly. Unable to decide, she'd bought both.

I flipped through the pages of the top book and a blue slip of paper flew out, landing underneath the desk. I got down on my hands and knees, hunting for the paper. It read *Bobby* and was in Isabelle's handwriting. It had a local phone number on it.

Hm, who was Bobby? I couldn't remember her mentioning anyone by that name, and she'd told me several times over that she didn't have a lot of friends in the area. Between being a newlywed and running the store, her life revolved around Brandon and the plaza. Everyone she knew or met had some association with Asia Village.

I flipped through the rest of the book pages but found no other notes. My eyes traveled to the bookcases that lined the wall next to the desk. One note in a book did not justify anything exciting, but if Isabelle was anything like me there were more things to be found.

I flipped through several paperbacks but came up empty-handed.

"Hey, are you doing okay in there?" Rina yelled from the other room. "Are you bored?"

I stuffed the paper in my pant pocket and went to join Rina in the bedroom. "No, I'm fine, just digging through some of Isabelle's books."

"I've never met anyone who has as many books as my sister." Rina laughed. "That girl loved to read."

"That's because you hadn't met me yet," I said with a chuckle. "I'm just as bad, if not worse."

"Do you want her books? I'm just planning on donating them anyhow. You could go through them and see if there's anything you want. I'm sure she'd want you to have them."

"Maybe . . . I'm not sure I would be able to read them knowing they were hers. I don't do well with sentimental things like that."

She nodded in agreement. "I'm the same way. My parents asked me if I wanted any of her things . . . I've put aside some stuff, but it's hard to look at any of it right now."

"One day you'll be glad you kept those things."

"True enough. Also—you know what's strange to me? Everyone around here calls her Isabelle." She closed up a box and taped it shut. "She's always been Izzy to me."

"Maybe she thought it sounded more mature for a business owner?"

"It's possible . . . I'm starting to feel like I didn't even know her anymore."

I looked around their bedroom while Rina fumbled around in the closet with shoes. There were a few wedding photos and some pictures of family hanging on the wall. They were all pictures of Isabelle and her family, and nothing with Brandon or his. "What did you say about Brandon's family earlier?"

"Oh . . . they weren't interested in his things. They told Constance and me to throw it all away. They agreed to pay for whatever rent was left on the apartment, but they didn't want any of his things."

"Don't you think that's weird? Wouldn't his parents want some kind of memento of his?"

"Not really." Rina started a new box, filling them with shoes. "I think they were embarrassed by him at this point."

"But he was their only son."

She shrugged. "If you met them, you'd know that type of thing doesn't matter to them. Personally, I think they had a kid because that's the thing you're supposed to do after you get married. They're not exactly what you'd call parenting types."

After another hour of packing up clothing, shoes, and random accessories, Rina and I packed up the cars.

I took all of the clothing bags and told her I would drop them off at a Salvation Army.

"Thanks again for your help," she said before getting into her car. "After yesterday, I didn't want to be in there alone. What if that person who broke in decided to come back? And why did they break in to begin with? Do you think they were looking for that missing money?"

I shrugged. "It's possible. It's also possible there was some kind of evidence in the apartment that tied them to Brandon and Isabelle that they wanted to get rid of." I thought about the slip of paper in my pocket and the mysterious Bobby.

Rina shivered. "Either way, that apartment doesn't sit well with me."

"I don't blame you," I said, looking up at the building. "I can't imagine what it would feel like to clean out my sister's apartment."

"Just hope you never have to."

On my way home, I dropped the clothes off at a Salvation Army bin in a grocery store parking lot. While I was there, I searched around for a pay phone. Without thinking, I had almost called the number I'd found from my own phone. Thankfully I had thought twice about that.

I was a little surprised to find a pay phone near the entrance of the grocery store. Fifty cents to make a call—when the heck did that happen? I dug around in my car for some change and dialed the numbers carefully onto the keypad.

I waited. But there was no answer. After it rang for what felt like an eternity, a computerized voice repeated the number and told me to leave a message. When the beep sounded, I stared at the receiver, my mind blank. I quickly hung up. I could try again later.

When I got to the apartment, Megan was on the couch working on her blanket. Kikko lay next to her chewing on a bone. She was so enthralled that she didn't even get up to greet me. Traitor.

"What happened at the apartment?" Megan asked, shifting her eyes back and forth between me and the blanket.

"Not a whole lot. You should have seen this place, though." I filled Megan in on the lavish apartment I hadn't expected to be visiting.

"Wow. So, wait . . . if Brandon was cut off from his family, and Isabelle knew that, wouldn't she wonder where the money came from to get that apartment?"

I shrugged. "I don't know. And it's not like we can ask her anything. Maybe he lied about having money stashed away? Maybe he did have money stashed away. Adam does seem to think that the money he won that night is being hidden somewhere."

"Well, did you find anything interesting while you were there?"

I showed her the slip of paper. "This number . . . it could be something, or it could be nothing."

She squinted to read the handwriting. "Bobby? Did you try calling it?"

"Yeah, no answer . . . and no personalized voice mail."

Feeling semi-defeated by a bust of an afternoon, I decided to check my Facebook messages and see if anyone had gotten back to me. I had to do a double take when I realized that Jay Coleman had finally responded to me. Success!

He'd left a number and told me I could call him any-time. And since I was in this whole "the time is now" thing, I dialed his number without hesitation.

"Nice to hear from you, Lana," Jay said after I intro-duced myself. "It's always good to hear from one of Brandon's friends. He told me that you and his wife were quite the pair."

"Yeah, I suppose we were," I replied. "I loved Isabelle, she was a great gal."

"She was indeed," he answered. "Especially after that nightmare of an ex-wife."

"Yeah, I've witnessed the wrath of Constance a few times so far. Not the most pleasant of people."

He snorted. "Ha! Constance was a saint compared with the other one."

"I'm sorry?" I replied with confusion. "The other one?"

"You know, Marcia . . . or as we liked to call her, Manic Marcia." Jay laughed. "Now, *she* is a real piece of work."

CHAPTER

23

"I thought for sure she'd be at the funeral," Jay admitted. "No one was more surprised than me that she didn't show. I even bet money with one of my friends that she would be flailing over the casket before the day was over."

"You were there? I don't remember seeing you."

"I had a business trip I could not get out of . . . which is why I couldn't get back to you right away. Sorry about that, by the way. Anyhow, I was there for the wake and then had to fly out that evening."

"Marcia told me she stayed away because of Constance. She didn't want to create waves."

"Ha! That would have more likely gone the other way," Jay told me. "Constance is big and scary when she's got her lawyer with her, but she's got nothing when it comes to battling a crazy person. She's way too civilized for that."

"She did slap her sister at the funeral . . ." I relayed

the story about Constance and Victoria hashing it out after the burial.

Jay whistled. "That surprises me. It's not like Constance to get physical."

I was floored by all of this. I hadn't seen any of it coming. The whole time I had been focusing more on everything and everyone but her. "So tell me more about Marcia."

"I might as well fly back to Cleveland for that," he joked. "How much time do you have?"

For the next thirty minutes, Jay went through his rendition of the "quick version" of Brandon and Marcia's whirlwind relationship. It turned out that Brandon had gone for Marcia completely for her money, and used her to live the lifestyle he'd become accustomed to while married to Constance. And apparently, he hadn't hidden his intentions very well.

Eventually, he tired of the "too easy" relationship and sent Marcia packing. Unfortunately for him, she didn't want to let go so easily. She'd kept in close contact with him after their divorce and even tried winning him back a few times. All to no avail.

By the time he'd met Isabelle, it was too late. He was smitten with her and talked about turning his life around. You would have thought that Marcia would get the clue, but instead, to keep herself in the picture she'd played the supportive card and helped the newlywed couple any way that she could. She claimed to only be interested in Brandon for friendship, continuously going on about how her main wish was to see him happy. She'd even gone as far as paying for their living arrangements and their move to Cleveland—and of course she'd loaned the money for the souvenir shop. All of this had taken place without Isabelle having a single clue. Brandon had worried that if Isabelle knew how much financial help he'd taken from his ex-wife, she might not stick around.

My heart ached for my unknowing friend. If she'd known any of the secrets going on behind her back, things might have turned out differently. But that's something you can never know. There was no sense in me going down the road of "what if."

"So that about sums it up," Jay said.

"Wow," I said, still dumbfounded. "I don't really know what to say."

He chuckled. "That's most people's reaction. You don't come across someone like Marcia every day."

"Something to be thankful for. It explains a lot, though. I just saw their apartment earlier this afternoon and I couldn't figure out where the money came from to pay for it."

"I hope you're not planning on adding this to your story. It's a little too colorful for a memorial dedication in my opinion."

"Huh?"

"The Marcia and Brandon situation . . . I hope you're not going to put that in your little newsletter. It wouldn't make Brandon look the best. And Marcia would know that I was the one who squealed. I wouldn't put it past her to come after me."

"Oh, right," I said. I'd forgotten for a moment what he was talking about. "No, of course not. I'll keep that part between you and me."

"If you think of it, send me a copy. I'd really love to read it."

"Sure thing." Yeah right. Hopefully he'd forget about it in a few days.

"Is there anything else you'd like to know?" he asked.

I couldn't think of anything else to ask so I suggested he tell me anything he thought might be helpful for my fake article.

He went on a little bit about Brandon's life in New York, which I hardly paid attention to. I made the appropriate "uh-huh" and "oh yeah" sounds when they seemed fitting. But I couldn't help thinking about how Marcia had played us all. She was good. She had successfully convinced all of us that she was the good one by lying about her entire relationship with Brandon. And who were we to know the difference?

Before we hung up, he extended the same offer that Victoria had about contacting him with further questions. He wished me well on my article and I thanked him for his time.

I sat back in my chair and took a minute to absorb this new information. There was something in this whole mess. I just had to figure out what it was.

CHAPTER
24

Monday morning came before I knew what happened. I stood in front of my closet with my eyes half closed, searching for something decent and clean to wear. With all the commotion over the weekend, I'd forgotten to do laundry.

Snow had reappeared overnight. I stared out my apartment window at the three feet that had accumulated since I'd gone to bed as I waited for Peter's headlights to appear. He showed up at seven thirty on the dot. He grunted at me as I got in the car. Neither one of us was a chipper morning person, so we drove together in comfortable silence. I hugged my coffee to my chest as he drove us down Center Ridge at a slow pace. Not a single snowplow was in sight, and the roads were slick and caked with slush.

The plaza parking lot was clear and we were among the first to arrive. Peter found the closest spot to the entrance, and we hurried to get out of the cold.

Ian stood outside Ho-Lee Noodle House with his

hands behind his back, tapping his foot. "Where have you been?" he asked as we approached. He unfolded his arms and pointed at his watch. "I've been waiting for twenty minutes. You're normally here by now."

"There's some serious snow out there," Peter answered. "We had to go slow and stuff."

Avoiding eye contact with Ian, I pulled the restaurant keys from my pocket and sidestepped him to unlock the door. "What he said."

Ian followed behind Peter as we entered the restaurant. "We need to talk."

I continued on into the kitchen, talking over my shoulder. "I know, the board meeting is today, I remembered. I'll be there, I already told you that."

"That's not what I'm talking about," he said, his voice sounding more stern than usual.

"Okay, then about what?"

Peter dropped off at the kitchen and Ian followed me into my mother's office. He stood in the doorway watching me take off my coat.

I turned around to face him, pursing my lips to show him I was agitated. "As you mentioned, I'm already running late, so I don't have a lot of time."

"Have you made any progress on our . . . situation?" He gave me a pointed look.

Instead of acknowledging the question, I shimmied past him back into the kitchen. Grabbing a tray off the counter, I busied myself lining it with soy sauce bottles. "There is nothing out of the ordinary about Constance. I checked her out online and couldn't find anything remotely interesting. There's nothing more that can be done about her at the moment. The end."

His eyes slid to Peter, whom I could guarantee wasn't paying us any attention. Ian didn't continue speaking until we were in the dining room.

"Constance contacted Donna over the weekend," he started to say.

"I had a feeling that was going to happen."

"She complained that we're taking too long."

"What did Donna say to that?" I asked.

"She pretended to be furious that it hadn't been brought to her attention sooner. She figured that would appease her most."

"Smart woman."

"But now the meeting with Constance and our attorneys to discuss the paperwork and terms of transfer has been expedited."

"When?" I continued through the dining room, setting down soy sauce bottles on any table that needed one. My eyes skimmed over each surface, ensuring that they were all clean and had utensils at each place setting.

He followed me through the maze of tables, right on my heels. "We're supposed to meet with her in a few days . . . Thursday, maybe. Donna is confirming with the lawyers."

I stopped. "Thursday? I thought this whole thing was going to at least be put off until after Chinese New Year."

"Not anymore. She told Donna she didn't want to wait that long. She went on and on about how it's her right to take over the property as soon as possible and we can't keep stalling. She keeps throwing the living trust in our face." He paused. "We have to do something,

Lana. I don't want that woman moving in here. She's going to make my life a living hell, I know it. I can feel it with every conversation we have. She's a nightmare."

"But if the papers are legit," I said, "there's really nothing that we can do about it."

"I thought you said you wanted to help figure things out?"

"I said I would try, and I did. It's not my fault I couldn't find anything. Besides, my main concern is to figure out what really happened to Brandon and Isabelle. And we agreed that might not have anything to do with Constance. If you're not happy with my results, then hire a real private detective."

"Oh come on, Lana, you know it as much as I do. That woman is no good, private detective or not."

I moved on to the next table. "Look, I don't know what you want me to do about her specifically. Like I said, what's important to me is finding out what really happened to Isabelle and Brandon. I don't know if Constance is involved or not. But I can't make something happen if she's innocent just because we don't like her."

"I'd be a little more concerned about her if I were you," he spat. "Because she is going to be your next-door neighbor and I'm not going to be the only one that has to deal with her."

I huffed. I was fed up with this man. I felt like a tape recorder stuck on repeat. How many times did I have to tell him that the object was truth, not convenience? I took a deep breath. *Patience, Lana, you talked about practicing patience.* "Ian, as a nonprofessional, what do you want me to do? I can only search the Internet so many times and find nothing before it feels like a complete waste of time."

"Find something. Anything. And make it happen fast," he snapped. He turned and marched out the door.

I let out a deep sigh as the door shut behind him. If Constance really was the guilty party, and we couldn't find a way to prove it, she would be my next-door neighbor at the plaza. And that was a little too close for comfort in my book.

The restaurant was packed all day and I hardly had any time to think or worry about my conversation with Ian earlier that morning. Nancy hustled around the restaurant taking orders and dropping off food while I bused tables, filled teakettles, and greeted new customers at the door.

The preparation for Chinese New Year continued at a steady pace as the final days ticked by. I hadn't heard anything more from my parents and I wondered what was going on with them. I made a mental note to check on them when I had a free moment.

Close to noon, I sent Nancy off to lunch while I staffed the dining room alone. Anna May was scheduled to come in within the next half hour, and she could help pick up the slack until Nancy got back.

While I was busy serving tables, Megan popped in. She stood at the hostess booth waiting for me, and waved me over when I noticed her.

"Wow, this place is really busy," she commented after realizing how packed the restaurant was. "You're running the show all by yourself?"

"I sent Nancy on lunch," I explained. "What brings you by?"

She dangled her car keys in front of me. "I'm dropping off my car so you can leave here whenever you need to. You know, in case anything comes up."

I took the keys from her. "Thanks, but how are you going to get to work?"

"Nikki's in the parking lot, waiting for me. She's coming down to the bar with me for lunch. She's absolutely obsessed with our new panini sandwiches, so I bribed her to take me to work in exchange for one on the house."

Nikki was a mutual friend of ours from college. I didn't get to see her much these days, but she did manage to visit Megan quite a bit at the bar. I laughed. "Tell her I said hi."

"You got it." Megan turned to walk away. "Oh, and pick me up at nine. I'm not closing tonight."

After Megan left, I went back to working the tables by myself until Anna May showed up. We worked in rhythm until Nancy came back. We were so busy all afternoon, we didn't even have the chance to bicker. Not even once.

At four thirty, I escaped into the back room to tie up a few loose ends in my mother's office. I had to make the meeting by five o'clock. On my way back through the restaurant, I saw that Vanessa had shown up and Nancy was wrapping up with the few tables she had left.

I signaled them to meet me at the hostess podium. "If you guys need me, I'll be at the Bamboo Lounge in a board meeting. I should be done in an hour or so."

"Are you going to talk about what's going to happen with City Charm?" Vanessa jerked a finger in the direction of the abandoned store.

"I don't know," I said, not wanting to discuss it with her. Vanessa had a big mouth, and if I said anything at all, it'd be all over the plaza before the meeting was over.

"Well, maybe you should bring it up," she said. "You know, since you're a big-shot board member and all. It's way creepy just leaving it there like that. People keep coming by and gawking at it. I even caught some people taking pictures of it."

"Pictures?" I asked. "When did you see that?"

"There was a guy and some woman out there yesterday, taking a bunch of pictures."

"Reporters?"

She shrugged. "They didn't look like it, but maybe . . ."

"I'll bring it up to the board, but it's not my call," I told her as I slung my purse over my shoulder. "I'll be back to check up on you guys after the meeting is over."

So far, our meetings had been held in the community center next to the property office. However, the space was in the middle of a spruce-up per Ian's instructions. To say that it was plain was giving it too much credit. I'd seen hospital rooms with more character.

Outside of housing mahjong tournaments once a month, it became a place to put pamphlets and calling cards from local Asian entrepreneurs or businessmen. Ian planned to change all of that and turn it into a hub for event planning and community building. But with the recent ordeal, progress had been put on the back burner.

That meant today's meeting would be held in the Bamboo Lounge's private karaoke room, which could be reserved by special request. I'd never even been inside it yet. I'm not a singer. At all. If there's one thing you never want me to do, it's sing. Not if you appreciate the ability to hear.

Muffled karaoke music made its way through the closed door. I pulled on the wooden handle and the sound came at me full blast. A petite, older woman with thick-rimmed glasses sang a Chinese song I recognized called "Dancing Girl." She tapped her foot to the beat of the music with her eyes closed and her hands on her hips. She wasn't half bad.

Penny Cho, proprietor and karaoke aficionado, stood behind the bar drying glasses and mouthing the words to the song. Her head bobbed along with the music, making her blue-black hair sway back and forth. When she lifted her head and brushed the hair away from her face, she caught my stare and waved me over to the bar. "Hey, Lana, what can I get you?"

I hopped up on the plastic-covered bar stool and set my cell phone in front of me. Giving the bottles on the shelf a quick scan, I shifted my eyes up to the chalkboard hanging above them, listing the specials of the day. "What's a Shanghai Shimmer?"

"Let's see, it's got three kinds of liquors. We've got whiskey, apricot brandy, mango vodka," she said, ticking the ingredients off on her fingers. "Then a touch of passion fruit juice and a splash of champagne. It's my most recent concoction, and it's delicious . . . you're gonna love it."

I was so used to Megan drumming up new drinks for me to try, I figured, why not keep it going? "Okay, I'll try one. I'm probably going to need it." I glanced toward the party room. "Is Ian here already?"

Penny laughed. "He's been holed up in there for the past half hour. I don't know what he's so anxious about."

She mixed the drink contents together in a glass shaker. "This whole City Charm thing has him worked up more than normal."

"Tell me about it. He actually snapped at me this morning."

"Wow, you're kidding? You're his favorite."

I blushed.

"I wish something would happen with the store already. I hate walking past it every day. It's depressing." She poured the mixture into a tall, skinny glass. She shook a small bottle of juice and filled up a little more of the glass. Then she added the champagne and threw a cherry on top. "There," she beamed, passing me the glass.

I took a sip and my cheeks puckered. "A little stronger than I thought."

"That's the whiskey," she giggled. "Hits you in the soul, doesn't it?"

I nodded as I tried to swallow. "Something like that."

"Anyhow," Penny continued. "I think I'm going to ask him to take the sign down or put tarps up in the window or something. This place has got to get back to normal at some point. We are still recovering from what happened to Mr. Feng."

"You don't think things have been normal?" I asked. Maybe I had been so preoccupied with everything else that I hadn't really noticed the state of the plaza.

She busied her hands with cleaning glasses as she talked. "Most of the shop owners are unhappy. They're complaining that it's a constant reminder of the murder. Everyone feels unsafe."

"But do they really think they're in danger?"

"With the killer still out there, I'd say so."

Kimmy and Jasmine showed up next, flanking me at the bar. Jasmine flashed a bright smile as she sat down next to me, swinging an arm around my shoulder. "Hey girl, starting the party without us, I see."

I smirked. "I've had a total of one sip."

Kimmy sat on the other side of me and grabbed the glass from my hand. "Let me have a taste." She took a sip and her face puckered just like mine had. "Whoa." She looked at me and then at Penny. "I'll have one of whatever that is."

"Me too." Jasmine laughed. "It's going to be an interesting meeting with all this liquor around."

As Kimmy passed my drink back over, I noticed that my phone was lit up with a notification. I had a missed call.

The number belonged to Carmen. "Can you guys excuse me for a second? I'll be right back." Without waiting for a reply, I stepped out into the plaza where I could hear the message better.

Her message was brief but stated that Ryan was willing to meet with me. It had to be now before he changed his mind, she warned. The timing couldn't have been better. So far, I had managed to dodge Adam and his request for descriptions. Once I talked with Ryan and Carmen, I'd be able to give Adam any information he wanted.

I threw my phone back in my purse and dug around for my car keys.

"Hey," Kimmy's voice said from behind me. "It's showtime."

"I can't make the meeting," I told her. "I need you to cover for me. Say I got sick or something."

"Ian's going to blow a gasket," she said. A tiny smile peeked through.

"I'm sure you'll enjoy it thoroughly. I gotta go." I rushed back to the restaurant to grab my coat before heading to the casino. I didn't have any time to waste.

CHAPTER
25

- - - - - - - - - - - - - - -

I called Megan on the way to the casino to let her know that Carmen had contacted me. Disappointed that she couldn't join me, she insisted that I call her as soon as I left to give her an update.

Carmen was sitting at a table with a husky blond man who had his back turned to me. They were both leaned over the table, having what appeared to be a very heated discussion. I tried to walk a little slower to the table to see if I could sneak up on them and catch wind of anything they were saying, but Carmen noticed me and shushed Ryan.

"Where's your bodyguard?" Carmen asked, glancing around for Megan.

"She couldn't make it today. And she's not my bodyguard."

"Whatever." She gestured to the empty chair next to Ryan. "Are you going to sit down or what?"

I pulled the chair out and moved it so that I sat at the edge of the table with the ability to face both of them straight-on. "You're Ryan?" I acknowledged him with a head nod. He didn't seem like the type of guy who'd want to shake my hand.

"Yeah . . . what's all this about? You have my girlfriend in a foul mood." He rested a hand on the table and shifted in his seat. "You think you're some kind of detective?"

"No, I'm a concerned friend. I'm assuming by now that your girlfriend has told you who these people were to me." I kept my focus on him, pretending Carmen wasn't there.

"Regardless, you should learn to mind your own business." Ryan held my gaze, his watered-down blue eyes narrowing, making me feel like I was being challenged to a staring contest.

I tried my best not to blink. "I either make it my business or turn whatever I know over to the cops."

Carmen slapped the table. "You see? She keeps saying that! We're gonna get busted, Ryan. Just tell her what you know so we can get on with our lives."

He was the first to break eye contact, turning to glare at Carmen. "Chill, woman."

Shifting back to me, he asked, "How do we know that you haven't gone to the police already? You could be wearing a wire for all we know."

I gave him my best eye roll. "What do you think this is? A movie? Plus, do you think the cops would trust *me* with a wire?" Never mind that my maybe boyfriend was a police detective. They didn't have to know that.

He seemed to weigh the validity of my statement. "I find it odd that you haven't turned us in yet . . . you being such a justice seeker and all."

I slumped my head into my hand, laying on the

theatrics to show just how agitated I was. "This is unbelievable. I come here to try to get answers . . . straight
answers. Do you think I want to work with the cops on
this? They take too long with all their paperwork . . .
and their procedures . . ." I lifted my head and waved
my hands around.

Ryan gave me a sideways glance, tapping his fingers
on the table. "Okay, fine . . . maybe. I guess I could see
it." He started to nod to himself.

Anxious to hear what he would say next, I inched to
the edge of my seat. "What can you tell me about the
older man who was at the blackjack tables while you and
Brandon were working your scam?"

"Not a lot really. He's a regular, he's got money . . ."
He held up his hands. "That's about it."

"You don't know his name?"

"I'm a card dealer, we're not friends."

"Can you find it out for me? Someone has to know
who he is."

His eyes darted to Carmen, who was watching him
intently. "I'll see what I can do. But you might want to
know about the woman he'd show up with from time to
time. Brandon never saw her . . . but I did."

In my head, I imagined Marcia . . . the man being her
new gambling partner. Maybe a sugar daddy. Or maybe
she was using him to track down Brandon. Jay Coleman
did mention that she was always keeping tabs on him.
"What did she look like? Pretty . . . great cheekbones?"

Ryan cocked his head at me. "She was kind of old-
fashioned . . . and you could tell she comes from money.
Dressed real nice . . . fur coat."

"Fur coat?" I asked. "A black fur coat?"

"Yeah . . . how'd you know?"

"That's Brandon's ex-wife . . . Constance Yeoh. We've met."

"She doesn't come around anymore . . . hasn't for a while."

I found it strange that Constance was spending this extra time in Cleveland. I wondered how far back Adam would search into someone's past. If there was proof that Constance was here a lot leading up to Brandon and Isabelle's murders, maybe it could be used to tie her to something.

"So you got what you came for. Can we go now?" Carmen asked.

"I have a few more questions."

"Hurry it up," Ryan said, gesturing with his hands. "We have things to do."

I described my mystery man to him as best I could, leaving out any references to William Shatner since no one appeared to get it besides me. "Do you know anybody like that?"

"I don't know . . . could be some guy that Brandon came around with. Could be a lot of people."

"Okay . . . what about someone named Bobby? Does that name sound familiar at all?"

"Nope."

"How about Marcia? Brandon had another ex-wife and I think she liked to gamble just as much as he did. Did you ever see him with any women?"

The couple glanced at each other and seemed to exchange some kind of unspoken message between themselves.

"No . . ." Ryan finally answered. "Doesn't ring a bell."

I let out a heavy sigh. "I guess that's it then."

They both stood up. Carmen stormed off without saying anything else. Ryan stopped, his hands resting on the back of the chair he'd just been sitting in. His gaze was fixed on the seat. "This ex-wife woman . . . the one with the fur coat . . . maybe you should be checking her out instead of hassling us."

He walked away without giving me a chance to respond. I stayed at the table a few extra minutes thinking that he might be right.

I returned to the plaza and headed straight for Ian's office. The whole drive over I had been circling back around to the Constance angle. I thought about her extreme desire to get in the souvenir store as soon as possible, the break-in at Brandon and Isabelle's apartment, and her outburst since we met.

Not only did she appear to be a woman on edge, but she seemed desperate. Of course, I couldn't actually prove that she'd broken into the apartment. Then again, what if that was staged, too?

"We need to talk about . . . the situation," I said to Ian from the door of the property office. I shut it behind me and went to stand by his desk.

"You were missed at the meeting." He stood up from his desk, giving me a once-over. "Are there any developments on our little dilemma?"

"Not really." I didn't want to tell him about the information I'd learned at the casino. Not yet anyway. "But I've been thinking. Constance has really been pushing hard to get into that store. What if there's a reason for that?"

"What do you mean? That she could be after something inside?"

"Yeah. And what if it ties her to Isabelle and Brandon's murder somehow?"

"But the police already went through everything. If there had been something in that store, they would have found it already."

"Maybe so, but perhaps they weren't looking for the right thing. Or maybe it's not something obvious right off the bat . . . you know?"

"You think you could figure out what that something is?"

"I'd like to give it a shot."

Ian mulled this over. "So . . . what is it that you need from me?"

"Can you let me into the souvenir store?"

"Sure," he agreed without hesitation. "If it means that she doesn't get to open the store, then I'll agree to anything. Just one question—what gave you this idea?"

I decided to go with the apartment angle. I told him about the break-in and my theory on that being staged, as well.

"You're kidding!"

"No, the place was turned upside down. But as far as they could tell, nothing was taken. *And* Constance waited for Rina before entering the apartment."

"So?" Ian asked, clearly confused.

"So when have you had an experience with Constance where she was being considerate of someone's feelings?"

Ian nodded. "True. So you think she staged it to make herself look innocent?"

"Well, it's plausible. At first, I thought there was no way she'd break in considering that she can go in as she pleases, but what if she got mad and trashed the place? She'd need a cover. And we've seen her temper . . ."

"Also true."

"Not only that, but it's crossed my mind that *whoever* it was might not have found what they were looking for. And that could be because it's in the store."

"Assuming they were hiding anything at all."

Telling him about Brandon's checkered past didn't seem pertinent at the moment. Like everything else, it was better if fewer people knew about it. "Just let me go into the store and have a look around. It can't hurt and the cops are done in there anyway. As you mentioned earlier today, if Constance gets her way, things are going to start happening as early as this Thursday. What do we have to lose?"

"You're right; it can't hurt to at least give it a shot. If we're going to do this, we've got to have it wrapped up before then—before it's too late." He reached for the top drawer of his desk and pulled out a set of keys. "Keep this under the radar. We don't need anyone wondering what you're up to."

After I had the keys, I went back to the restaurant to check in with everyone and waste some time. Business had mellowed out; there were only a few tables filled for dinner. I decided to piddle around in my mom's office until the plaza closed and I could go into City Charm unseen.

I called Megan to tell her about my adventure at the

casino and to let her know that I had some undercover work to take care of.

"Man, I am missing all the good stuff," Megan pouted into the phone. "Stupid job."

I laughed. "This is the good stuff?"

"You know what I mean."

I told her I'd pick her up when I was done.

A few minutes later, there was a soft knock on the office door.

"Come in," I yelled.

Figuring it was Nancy, I didn't bother taking my eyes off the report I'd started working on. "Do you need help up there?"

"I would say they have it under control," a husky voice responded.

I looked up. Adam. "Oh, I wasn't expecting to see you."

"I know," he said, shutting the door behind him. "I thought I'd stop in for a surprise visit."

Because of the information I didn't want to give him, I'd successfully avoided him up to this point. Considering the placement of that, he probably thought it was for other reasons. Remembering my manners, I asked, "Can I get you anything?"

"No, I'm good." He took a seat in the chair on the opposite side of the desk. It was too small for him and he looked like he was sitting in a chair made for little kids. "I was actually hoping I could convince you to come have a drink with me. You know, after you're done here."

"Oh . . ." I replied. Of course, he would pick tonight.

"I wanted to make up for the other night. I feel like

our date ended on the wrong foot. Then the whole thing with the tires . . . and the case."

"Well, I'd love to, but I'm going to be here for a while." I pointed to the papers in front of me. "We're off a little bit, and I want to get this fixed before I leave." *Really?* That was the best I could come up with? *Lame, Lana, so lame.*

"Is there anything that I can help with?" He craned his neck, trying to see the report.

"Oh no, I'll be fine."

He eyed me, not satisfied with that answer. "Okay, how about this? I'm going to head up to the Zodiac. And when you're all done here, you can meet me if you're up for it. I'll be there either way. No pressure."

"Sure."

He stood up from the chair, gave me a wink, and slipped out the door.

I let out a breath. Talk about timing. I'd have to speed up my snooping and make it to the Zodiac in a reasonable time. If I didn't show up he might think I wasn't interested, or—even worse—that I was up to something.

CHAPTER
26

- - - - - - - - - - - - - - -

I stood on the threshold of the back room of City Charm, peering into the darkness while the outline of stacked boxes started to form. As my eyes adjusted, I contemplated the direction my life had gone in the past few months. If you asked me a year ago what I would be doing, I wouldn't have guessed it'd be sneaking into people's offices or trying to solve crimes. Yet here I stood getting ready to snoop through someone's things . . . again.

The last time I had gone through this door, the back room had been a horrible mess. But now, the room had been returned to its normal state. Professional cleaners had scrubbed down the entire area; not a single trace was left behind showing that any type of crime had taken place. If you didn't know otherwise, you would assume everything was business as usual.

Isabelle had prided herself on being an organized person, and I found her office to be a reflection of that. It was in pristine condition. I took a minute to admire the tranquil work environment she had created. Out-side the office, the stockroom was a cluster of boxes and random inventory arranged in a maze of haphazard piles. Standing in it for a while could make you feel a bit claustrophobic. But in her office, you felt a sense of calm. The space, though small, didn't feel cramped or chaotic.

The desktop was free of clutter; the only things on it were a pencil cup and a tiered filing tray with color-coordinated folders stacked in each slot. A beach cal-endar hung above the desk with a Post-it note stuck to January's photo of a Hawaiian coast that said, *Wish I was here!*

Black filing cabinets stood on both sides of the desk. I opened one of the drawers and took a peek. Inside were past invoices and receipts from different distributors. Nothing of real interest to me.

I skimmed through another drawer but found more of the same. I opened all of the drawers just to be safe, but nothing unusual or out of the ordinary jumped out at me.

I inspected the folders that were on the desk tray. These were their current bills and appeared to be out-standing. Assuming that Constance would finally get her hands on this place, she would be in charge of mak-ing sure these got paid. I put everything back the way I'd found it.

There was nothing interesting here. I had been so sure that I'd find something . . . anything. Another slip of paper. Some incriminating note. A planner that had secret meetings in it. I guess you can't strike gold twice.

With disappointment, I flipped off the light switch and went back out into the stockroom. I stared at the piles of boxes for a minute, contemplating the likelihood that something of importance might be in one of them. The chances were slim. The police had been through everything in the room, and then the cleaning crew, which led me to believe that nothing looked or was placed exactly the way it had been that day anyway.

If Constance wanted in for something specific, it couldn't be the inventory. She'd made it pretty clear that everything sold in the store was unworthy of her attention.

I trudged back through the service hallway to Ho-Lee Noodle House. I stuffed the keys in an envelope, wrote *No Dice* on the outside of it, and slipped it through the mail slot of the property office before I left.

I wasn't very good with discouragement, and this was no exception.

Probably because I found nothing of worth, my expedition hadn't taken as long as I'd expected. I was in and out in less than thirty minutes. No one would know that I had been up to anything sneaky. And by "no one," I meant Adam.

I made my way to the Zodiac, my brain going back and forth over the lack of information. What the heck was I missing? What more was there for me to do? I could try calling the number that I'd found on that slip of paper again. When I'd tried before, I hadn't thought about what I would say. I didn't even know who I was calling. What if this Bobby person turned out to be the murderer? Even though I had found the number written in Isabelle's handwriting, it still felt relevant to Brandon. I replayed the conversation that we'd had on our last outing together when she'd mentioned how exciting it might be to be a detective. What if she had already started looking into Brandon's suspicious behavior? Had she found something she didn't want to mention to me?

I pulled into the parking lot, noticing that Adam's car was parked front and center. Good, I hadn't missed him.

Inside, he was sitting at his usual spot at the bar, his eyes fixed on the TV overhead. His blank stare told me he wasn't paying attention to what was on the screen. As I made my way over to him, Megan spotted me and went over to where Adam was sitting to greet me.

Adam following her gaze, turned around, a small smile forming on his lips. "There she is. I thought I was going to have to send a search party after you."

That comment caused a nervous laugh to escape. I turned away, pretending to be preoccupied with a loose thread on my jacket. "Oh, I just lost track of time."

"How'd it go?" Megan asked with a pointed look.

"Fine," I said, sitting down on the stool next to Adam. "Just another night of nothing out of the ordinary. Just a bunch of receipts and invoices."

Megan nodded slowly, picking up on my double speak. She pursed her lips. "I'll get you a drink then."

After Megan walked away, Adam turned toward me, giving me a once-over. "You almost sound disappointed about that. I would have thought you'd be glad."

I sighed. "No, I'm fine, I'm just tired. It's been a really long day."

He straightened in his seat. "Okay, that's the second time you said 'fine' and you haven't even been here five minutes. What gives?"

"Nothing really, I'm f—"

"Three."

"Would you stop it?"

"Is this because of the other night?" Adam asked.

"What? The whole thing after my tires were slashed? No."

"No, I meant our date. I want to make up for that." He looked down at his hands. "I know the night didn't go as well as it could have. It's hard for me to talk about my work . . ."

"It's okay, you don't have to explain," I told him.

"I'm just not ready."

A rock was starting to form in my stomach. I clutched a hand to my waist. "Ready for what, exactly?"

He shrugged. "To let someone into that part of my life, I guess."

"Oh." I didn't know what else to say since I had no idea what this was about. But what I did know was that he had doubts about letting someone get close to him. Mainly me. I squeezed my stomach.

"It's been a long time since I've had anyone close to me and . . ." He shook his head. "I swear, sometimes I forget how to be a person."

"I know how you feel," I replied. "People tell you things get easier with age, but I don't know if that's actually true."

"It sure doesn't feel like it." He took a sip of his beer, glancing up at the TV screen. "I'd like to take things slow, you know, so we don't mess things up. I'd hate for that to happen because of me. I need some time . . . to adjust. I hope you can understand that."

"Sure . . . time," I replied, attempting to act as unaffected as possible. I knew my face was giving me away. I could feel it.

Megan came back with something red and fizzy. I didn't ask what it was; I let go of my stomach, grabbed the glass from her hand, and took a big gulp. Tasted like cherries.

"Wow, someone's thirsty," Megan laughed.

"Long day, that's all," I said. "Would you two excuse me?" Without waiting for a reply, I grabbed my purse and got up, heading toward the ladies' room. My eyes fell on the pay phone that stood between the men's and ladies' bathrooms.

I had tucked the slip of paper with Bobby's name on it in my purse. I pulled it out and found some change.

I dialed the number expecting the same results. But this time the phone rang twice and a gruff-sounding man answered the phone.

"Hi, is this Bobby?" I asked in a chipper voice.

"Yeah, who's this?"

I had to think quick. "Oh, we met through a mutual friend, and you asked me out on a date, remember? It's been a few weeks, sorry I didn't call sooner."

There was a long silence and I thought he'd hung up on me. "Hello?"

"Who'd you say you were?" he finally asked.

"Katherine . . . we met through Isabelle Yeoh, don't you remember?"

"No, I don't know any Katherine . . . and I don't know any Isabelle Yeoh. Don't call this number."

Before I could get anything else out, he hung up.

I put the receiver back on its hook and stared at the phone. Clearly, whoever Bobby was, he was a big, fat liar.

I went to the bathroom as I originally intended, taking my time at the sink to think about the call. I started to wonder if this Bobby person could trace the call back to the pay phone. If some random weirdo came looking for Katherine, at least I'd know who Bobby was.

When I went back out, Megan and Adam were talking at the bar. Megan glanced up at me, noticing the perplexed look on my face.

"Is everything okay?"

"Yup, fine," I replied with a firm nod. "Everything's just fine."

Adam groaned as he took a sip of his beer.

On the way home from the Zodiac, Megan questioned me about Adam and our conversation. "What the heck is going on with you two? I could feel the tension halfway across the bar."

"Nothing, he tried to apologize for the other night."

"And?" Megan asked.

"He told me that he needed time." I focused on the road, avoiding the look I could feel her giving me.

"Time for what? Nothing has even happened yet. You've been out a few times, what's the big deal?"

"I don't know, Megan. Why don't you ask him that?"

"Because, Lana," Megan said, mimicking my tone. "I'm asking you."

I gave her a sideways glance. "Well, I don't know what to tell you. I don't have the answer to that question. He said that it's hard for him to talk about his work . . . he needs time . . . blah blah."

Megan shook her head. "This doesn't make any sense. I've been watching him come to that bar almost every night like he's waiting for someone, and that someone is you, honey. A guy doesn't just do that and then claim to need time. Something must have spooked him. Did you guys have a commitment conversation that he could have felt happened too soon? Because you know how men freak out about the *B* word. You mention the word *boyfriend* and they automatically think you're fitting their apartment for curtains or something."

I pulled into the parking lot of our complex. "No, we haven't had any conversations like that." I paused, thinking about it. "Although Kimmy did call him my boyfriend that one day we found . . . the bodies."

She threw her hands up. "Well, there you go. He probably thinks you're running around talking about him to all of your girlfriends."

"But that happened before we went out . . . so it can't be that."

"Oh . . . hmmm . . ." Megan sat back in her seat.

I parked the car and we clomped to the apartment dodging the ice patches that were beginning to form. Kikko greeted us at the door with a few spins and her floppy tongue.

I let her out for a quick tinkle, and when I came in, Megan was sitting on my bed, waiting for me. "You know what I was thinking?"

Holding up a hand, I said, "I don't want to talk about this anymore tonight. It's been a horridly long day and I want to go to sleep." I flopped on the bed, throwing the blanket over me. I didn't care if I was still in my work clothes, I just wanted to sleep.

I felt Megan's weight lift from the bed.

"Okay, but you'd better believe I'm going to find out what's going on with him, one way or another."

"You do that and I'm going to get some sleep." I said, throwing the blanket over my head. "Do me a favor in the meantime."

"What?"

"Shut off the light."

CHAPTER
27

I woke up to the sound of my phone ringing. Blindly, I grabbed for it. "Hello?" I mumbled into the phone.

"Laaaa-na," my mother sang into the phone. "It's Mommy."

"Mom." I sat up in bed. "I've been meaning to call you. What's going on? When are you coming home?"

She laughed into the phone. "That is why I'm calling you. A-ma would like us to stay here for Chinese New Year so we can go to big parties. We will come home when the New Year is over."

"What?" I yelled into the phone. "But what about the restaurant? I can't do it all alone."

"Yes, you will be okay. I talked to Esther yesterday and she told me you are doing very well. Maybe Mommy can retire early." She laughed some more.

I didn't join her.

"Mom . . ."

"Your daddy says hello. I have to go now, everybody is waiting for me. I love you."

"Love you, too." I hung up in defeat. This added potentially two more weeks' worth of running the restaurant, and a major Asian holiday was right in the middle of it.

As I got ready for work, I gave myself another one of my infamous pep talks. *I can do this*, I said to myself. I would solve Isabelle and Brandon's murder, run the restaurant, deal with Adam and whatever his issue was, and manage to remain graceful through the entire process.

Again, I wasn't totally convinced.

My car still wasn't ready. The mechanic told me it was going to at least be another day, so Peter agreed to pick me up again. When we got to the plaza, we had a surprise waiting for us.

"Wow," Peter said, taking in our first look at the front of City Charm. "That looks . . ."

The front of the store was covered by a tarp, a giant, glossy black mass of wrinkled plastic. I couldn't help but be a little disgruntled by it. Not only was it ugly, but part of it obstructed the view of Ho-Lee Noodle House as you were coming in through the main entrance. "It looks trashy, is what it looks like," I finished for him.

"Yeah, that's so not cool lookin' at all." He shook his head, and we continued on to the restaurant, glaring at the tarp as we walked by.

"Well, I hope that everyone is happy with it, because this is a terrible background for the Chinese New Year celebration," I said, getting the restaurant keys out of my purse. "This is going to be a major eyesore! How is it going to look when they record the Lion Dance and a big black tarp is flapping around in the backdrop?"

"We still have another week; maybe it'll be gone by

then. Or we could tell them to take it down that day. I wouldn't sweat it, boss."

"Easy for you to say." It was entirely possible that I was just in a bad mood due to everything else going on. The tarp felt close to the last straw. A part of me felt responsible for this outcome since I had missed the meeting.

The entire morning was spent talking to people about the tarp. I couldn't have been more annoyed. The Mahjong Matrons talked about it during their entire breakfast. Other customers who weren't regulars asked what type of construction was going on, and if we had something special planned for the coming celebration. I did my best to keep my face under control as I answered questions with the most vague of answers. It was a struggle, and by noon, I was exhausted just from keeping up appearances.

At least I wasn't alone in my agitation. Kimmy stopped by during her lunch to share her frustrations.

"And the damn thing flaps around," she said, waving her arms. "Every time someone walks by, I can hear it crinkling from the motion. At least you have closed doors. I turned up the music in the store just so I didn't have to hear it anymore."

"No offense to whoever came up with it, but this was a stupid idea," I complained. "If anything, it's raised more questions than there were before. Everyone that's been in has asked me about it and what's going on."

"It was Penny Cho. And those ridiculous Yi sisters . . . you know they had a mouthful of complaints . . . like always. I hope they enjoy the view from their tea shop.

It's not exactly a calming backdrop for their customers to enjoy while they drink their snobby tea and eat their stuck-up egg tarts."

After Kimmy let off a little more steam, she left to return to her post and relieve her mother from cashier duty.

Anna May and Nancy showed up for the day and I was relieved to see both of them. Even Anna May.

"Where's your car?" Anna May asked. "I didn't see it in the parking lot. I thought you'd left for the day."

"My car's in the shop." I left it at that. If I gave her too much information, she might end up telling my mother about that, too.

"Figures," she replied, flipping her hair. "I told you that thing is a piece of junk. You can't keep that stupid thing forever. What is it from, 1999?"

I folded my arms over my chest. "Well, Ms. Lawyer, when you start making my car payments for me, you can have a say in anything you like."

Nancy looked between the two of us as she joined us at the hostess booth. "Are you girls arguing again?"

Anna May and I scowled at each other.

"No," I lied. "I'll be in the office going over the books if you need me." I turned without another word and headed straight for the office, slamming the door shut. And here I thought I couldn't get any more annoyed.

The stack of receipts on my mother's desk needed to be handled. But the motivation to do something so mundane was lacking. I couldn't help but think about the case and all the missing pieces. The progress I had made so far only amounted to baby steps. What I needed was a bigger picture.

I needed proof on one of the following things: There

had to be something to connect Constance to Brandon and the casino, which might be the information that Ryan gave me. Or I needed to place Marcia in Cleveland at the time of the murders. I didn't know how to do that without the footage from the tollbooths that Adam was working on obtaining. My lead on this mysterious Captain Kirk look-alike was going nowhere at a steady pace, and I still didn't know who Bobby was.

I thought about all this until Vanessa showed up and the shift change was complete.

Anna May was waiting for me at the hostess station. She'd agreed to take me home. "Come on, little sister, let's go," she said, ushering me out the door.

As we walked past City Charm, I gave the tarp another dirty look. "This thing is so stupid," I said to Anna May. "This is going to be in the background for the festival next week."

"Oh, would you stop worrying about it?" She dug around in her purse. "When do you get your car back?"

We stepped outside and were blasted with a strong, bitter wind. Nothing like a Cleveland January to give you that second wind. Literally.

"I don't know," I said, shuffling to her car. "Hopefully tomorrow. I haven't heard back from the mechanic yet today."

We drove to my place hardly speaking to each other. I was too busy obsessing over the thoughts from earlier, and Anna May . . . well, I don't know what she was thinking about. Probably law things.

She dropped me off, and I hurried inside, fighting against the wind. Kikko was going to love this.

As I suspected, not one for having her ears flap outside of a car ride, Kikko kept our walk short and tugged me back home where we were both relieved to be out of the cold.

Megan had brought home some chili from the bar, and I stuck it in the microwave. When it was ready, I joined her on the couch as she carefully added stitches to her blanket. Kikko watched silently from the end of the couch, her focus on my chili bowl.

"You know, I can't stop thinking about what Ryan told me . . ."

"Man, I wish I could have been there," Megan said, shaking her head.

I blew on my spoonful of chili, wishing it would cool down faster. "Yeah, maybe you would have thought of something to ask that I didn't."

"Do you think they were telling the truth?"

"It's hard to say. They were really anxious to get rid of me."

"What if they were just feeding you lines?" she asked. "You know, trying to steer you away from them."

"Completely possible. They did get kind of weird when I mentioned Marcia."

Megan's hands froze, mid-stitch. "See? It's just like I said before. What if everyone was in on this?"

"You really think this whole crew of people is out to get Brandon?"

"Yeah, they're all working together to eliminate their threat . . . and they all have different reasons for wanting to get rid of them, but they work together anyway . . . common goal and all."

"I think we've watched too many conspiracy movies."

"Yeah, but it sounded good, right?"

Megan and I wasted the night talking about the different possibilities that could have played out the evening of the murder. If there was anything we agreed on, it was that the casino and one of the ex-wives absolutely had to be involved. We also agreed on the fact that Carmen and Ryan were lying about something . . . we just didn't know what.

I woke up the next day feeling groggy and a little hoarse. The stress of work and solving the murder was starting to take its toll on me. As I inspected the dark circles that had formed under my eyes, I knew one thing I definitely needed. A vacation.

CHAPTER

28

Peter picked me up at the same time as he had for the past two days. We drove together with nothing but the radio on low. The one thing I have always appreciated about him is his ability to let people be themselves. He never forces conversations or situations, he is always respectful of people's space, and he will never ask too many questions.

I hugged my coffee cup, wondering what the day might bring.

An hour after my shift began, I got a call from the auto repair shop. They promised that my car would be ready by the end of the day. And as promised, they were able to get me a deal on the tires. It was minor, but at this point, I'd take anything.

Then around ten a.m., I got a text message from Carmen, who said that she'd found out the name of the guy who had been giving Brandon a hard time. She added she knew that he'd be at the casino that night and agreed to point him out if I could make it there during her shift.

She refused to tell me his name via text and I found that to be a little suspicious, but I wasn't in a position to argue.

I guess I knew what my plans were going to be that evening.

I replied and told her to meet me by the food court at our usual spot. I didn't have a plan for what I would say when I approached this man, but I had all day to think about it. Maybe something would come to me.

This would be my final trip to the casino. Once I learned the identity of the older man from the blackjack table, I would come clean with Adam, telling him everything I'd found out thus far.

However, I didn't get much time to think about the case, what might happen next, or anything else for that matter. Asia Village was filled with activity and the day flew by just as the others had. People were in last-minute prep mode, and it showed as the crowd flowed in and out of stores, bags in tow. Their empty stomachs brought them to the restaurant, and we had another packed house by lunch. A small crowd formed in the lobby as people waited for tables to be cleared.

Nancy and Anna May joined me shortly before noon, and I was thankful for the help. Right after they'd arrived, a group of twelve came in and requested the banquet area.

We kept the dining room fed and moving, hardly taking time to feed ourselves. I think the whole day I had a bite of dumpling and half a spring roll.

The auto repair shop called again around four o'clock and told me that I could pick up my car anytime before six.

Neither Anna May or Nancy could get away to take

me, so I poked my head into China Cinema and asked Kimmy. "I would, but my parents just left to get something to eat before I head home for the day. They should be back by five thirty if you want to wait around for them."

"That's okay," I said. "It's not that far to the auto shop, but knowing my luck we won't make it before they close, and I really need my car tonight."

How the heck was I going to get my car?

I stepped back out into the plaza and watched the mass of people crisscross among one another going from one store to the next. I scanned all the stores and the people I considered friends. Everyone was busy.

My eyes landed on the management office. Ian.

I hated the thought of asking him for another favor. Especially since the last one I'd asked for hadn't produced any results that would make him happy. But if I wanted to get to the casino, I needed my car, and that meant I would have to suck it up and ask.

He was sitting at his desk when I walked in.

"Hey, Ian." I stood in the doorway trying not to act uncomfortable.

He looked up from his paperwork. "Lana . . . what brings you by?"

I glanced down at my shoes. "I was wondering if you could do me another favor?"

"Depends on if you have any information for me," he said with a crooked smile.

I sighed. "On Constance, no. But, I might have something else after tonight." I still wasn't ready to tell him anything about what I'd learned. I didn't know if it would go anywhere and didn't want to get his hopes up. I was still lacking the hard evidence that I needed.

"Does the something later tonight have anything to do with our good friend Constance?"

"I'm not entirely sure."

"I see," Ian said with remorse. "Oh well, the meeting with Donna is all set for Thursday and it doesn't seem like there's anything else I can do about it. Looks like you'll be getting a new neighbor. And I'll be getting a new . . ." He stopped, searching for the right word. "Well, in the presence of a lady, I'll keep that comment to myself. What was the favor you needed?"

"Oh." I shook my head, bringing myself back around to the original reason I'd come by. "I was wondering if you could take me up to an auto shop to pick up my car. They said I could pick it up before six, but there isn't anybody to take me."

"What about your boyfriend?" Ian asked. He tried to keep his voice level, but I definitely noticed a hint of jealousy. "He's not available?"

"I didn't ask him," I said, lifting my chin. "It's okay; I can come up with something else. Thanks anyway."

He stood up. "No, no, I don't mind taking you; I just didn't want to step on any toes." He came around from behind his desk. "Give me a minute to lock up and we can be on our way."

I said a final round of goodbyes to everyone at Ho-Lee Noodle House, letting them know where I'd be if they needed anything. Let's hope no one needed anything. I had other plans.

Ian drove a brand-new Jaguar and I tried to remember a time I'd been in a car this luxurious. When I got into the passenger's seat, I felt like I melted right into the leather. It was cold through my clothes, but the material was so soft, it didn't matter.

"The seats are heated, just give them a minute," he said, adjusting some knobs on the center console.

"This is way nicer than my junky car," I said, running my hand along the dashboard in front of me.

He glanced over at me. "If you put your mind to it, you can have anything you want."

The potential of that sentence having a double meaning was too likely, so I just let it hang there. I kept my gaze fixed outside the window and avoided any awkward conversations that might take place.

We drove to soft jazz music and I enjoyed the smooth ride from the plaza to the auto shop.

When we got there he offered to stay and wait to make sure that everything was okay. But I insisted that he go on ahead.

At the counter, I paid for my new tires, cringing as I signed the receipt. I'd be putting in extra time once my parents got back from vacation to cover this cost.

I sank into my own seat, glad to have my car back, but wishing that it would magically heat like the one in Ian's car.

While I daydreamed about that distant moment when I'd have the money to enjoy the finer things in life, I made my way home for a quick change of clothes before heading to the casino.

CHAPTER

29

I found Carmen in the food court at our designated meeting spot, as promised. She paced back and forth in front of the burger place. I rushed over.

"What took you so long?" she asked, clearly agitated. "I have to get back to the bar before they wonder where I've been."

"Sorry," I said, trying to catch my breath. "Getting in was a nightmare. The woman in front of me couldn't find her ID and held up the line."

"Whatever." She turned away from me. "Let's go already."

We started to leave the food court, but just as we reached the escalators, a tall man with a distinct haircut caught my attention. There on his way down was my mysterious Captain Kirk! I squealed and Carmen gawked at me in disgust. "What is your problem?"

"That guy," I said, pointing at the man descending the escalator. "I've been looking for him!"

Carmen squinted her eyes in the direction I pointed. "Oh . . . well, great." She shrugged and continued on. "Come on, we have to go."

"Wait." I grabbed her arm. "You don't understand, that's the guy I was telling you about. The one who was with Brandon that night."

She jerked her arm away from me. "Yeah . . . so?" Her eyes darted in the direction she wanted us to go. "We have to hurry."

"But I saw them leave the plaza together. He could know something."

"I don't have time to waste while you go chase this guy down," Carmen said. "So what if he was with Brandon that night? They're probably gambling buddies or something. We need to go. Plus, I already told you, that guy disappeared long before I lost track of Brandon."

"You told me you thought you might know who he was . . . do you?" I asked.

"He looks familiar. That's all," she huffed. "Quit stalling . . . we have to meet Ryan at the blackjack table before it's too late."

Something bothered me about her insistence. It left me with a bad feeling I didn't care for. "Either way, I can't miss my chance. I have to get ahold of him. Who knows if I'll find him again?"

She groaned. "You know what, if you want to chase him down, go ahead. Just come find me when you're done."

We split up at the top of the escalator and I headed back down, keeping an eye on my mystery man. By this time, Captain Kirk was already back on the first floor.

I watched him take a left and head toward the craps tables.

There was hardly anyone going down when I got on, so I took two steps at a time, trying to speed up the process. An elderly man with a cane stopped me from totally jumping off the moving stairs. I waited with all the patience I could muster for him to get off so I could go around him.

Captain Kirk was well over six feet tall, so I was able to spot him easily once I made it off the escalator. I just had to catch up with him.

And I did. He was slowed down by a cluster of people standing in the narrow aisleway between the tables and the wall. I tugged on the back of his sleeve.

He turned around and looked down at me. "Hey," he said with such a casual tone, I almost felt like he'd been expecting me.

"Um, hi," I said. It hadn't dawned on me until this moment, but I had no idea what I was going to say to him. This wasn't part of the plan. With everyone else, I'd had a chance to craft some type of story or be somewhat prepared. I had no idea what to do with myself.

"You look familiar." He cocked his head. "Do I know you from somewhere?"

"I'm friends with Brandon . . . was . . ."

He stiffened. "That's right. You work at that Chinese plaza with him or something, right?"

"Yeah, that's me." I moved closer to the wall, letting a couple pass.

"Oh, okay. See ya," he said and then turned around to walk away.

"Hey," I yelled, tugging on his arm again. "Wait, I want to talk to you."

"I suppose you want to borrow some money, too," he said, folding his arms over his chest. "Well, I'm sorry, sweetheart, but I'm going to have to pass this time. That last broad was enough to make me rethink my line of employment."

"Huh? Borrow money?"

He looked around us, and then grabbed my arm, pulling me off to the side, out of the way of people walking by.

"Hey!" I yelled. "What do you think you're doing?"

He backed me against the wall and threw an arm out, shielding me from the crowd. He pressed his hand firmly against the wall next to my head. "Who sent you?"

My eyes widened. "Sent me? No one. I swear. I just wanted to ask you about Brandon."

His eyes traveled the length of my body. From afar, I'm sure it seemed like we were about to be inappropriate in public. "So you're not here to take out a loan?"

My brow crinkled. "A loan? No . . . I have no idea what you're talking about."

His body relaxed and he removed his hand. "Wait a minute . . . are you Katherine?"

I let out a nervous laugh. Ah-ha! So *this* was Bobby. My mystery men were the same man! "Nope, my name is Lana."

He shook his head. "Sorry, I got a weird call the other night and I thought you might be the same woman."

While we stood together in an awkward silence, I started to put all the pieces together. The times Brandon had been seen with this man, the trips they made to the casino together . . . the money that came out of nowhere . . . his unwillingness to introduce him to anybody. "You're a loan shark!"

He threw a hand over my mouth. "Shhhh . . ."

A few people turned our way, but they were too absorbed in their potential future winnings to pay us much attention so the glances were short.

"No one says that." He removed his hand from my mouth and straightened, rolling his shoulders. "I prefer the term *opportunity investor.*"

I pushed away from the wall, trying to straighten myself. "So Brandon wasn't actually your friend?"

"Nah." He shook his head. "A client. I liked the guy well enough, but it's best not to get emotionally attached to anyone that borrows money from you. That leads to a lot of messy outcomes."

"I see," I said. "Well, I hate to break it to you if you don't already know, but he died recently."

He nodded, scrubbing his chin with the back of his hand. "Yeah, I saw the whole thing on the news. Such a shame. The guy was young . . . and his wife was a knockout. I don't know why a guy like that would want to go and mess all that up."

"So I guess you're out some money then," I said, coming up with a new angle to this mystery. He might not have been a hit man like I'd originally considered, but maybe he'd had a hand in this whole thing after all. "How much did he owe you?"

"He didn't owe me anything. His debt was paid."

"He paid you off?" Well, there went that theory. But was this what had happened to the missing money? Had Brandon used his winnings that night to pay off Bobby?

"No, that crazy Chinese broad did." He looked away. "No offense or anything."

"None taken . . ." I said, unsure if he was sorry for calling her crazy or a broad. But I figured it wasn't the best time to have him elaborate.

"Who was this woman? Did you happen to get her name? Did she wear a black fur coat?"

"No, no fur coat," he said. He studied the ceiling, shaking his head back and forth. "Oh man, what was her name? Something like . . . Mary . . . or maybe Marie . . . yeah, Marie." He shook his head again. "Nah, that ain't right . . . wait . . . yeah . . . Mary. It was definitely Mary."

"Marcia, you mean?" I suggested.

"Yeah, that's it! Marcia!" He snapped his fingers, relief washing over his face. "That was going to bug me forever."

"When did she pay you?"

"The same night I saw Brandon for the last time."

"Wait . . . she was with the two of you that night?"

He nodded. "She met us here and she was out of her mind when she found out how much he owed me, which was a few tens of thousands, if you're wondering. She chewed into him for a hot minute and then cut me a check. Normally, I only accept cash. But for this amount, I was willing to make an exception. I left right away and went straight to the bank just in case she tried any funny business. It wouldn't be the first time."

That's all it took. This was the information I needed to know that she'd been lying for sure. I had an actual witness—someone placing her in the city the night that Brandon and Isabelle were murdered. Out of reflex, I reached out and hugged him. "You have no idea how much you've just helped me."

He stood there, still as stone. "Uh, yeah. You're welcome."

"Just one question," I said, letting go of him.

"What?"

"What's your name?" I asked, pretending not to know. He looked at me skeptically. "Bobby."

"Huh. I wouldn't have pegged you for a Bobby."

"What do I look like to you?" he asked, appearing genuinely curious.

"A James."

I didn't bother to find Carmen on my way out. I had everything I needed and I didn't think it was necessary to see the man she thought might be involved. Megan was probably right—it was probably something to throw me off the right trail. Now that I knew Marcia had been in town that night, I could almost be certain that there was some type of affiliation among her, Carmen, and Ryan. Especially since they'd gotten so weird when I'd mentioned her name.

I hightailed it to the parking garage and locked myself in the car. Something had been weighing on me since the murders: the break-in. Nothing had ever come of it because at the time, Carmen and her boyfriend had been the only likely suspects. At least in my book. But now, knowing that Marcia had lied about quite a bit, I wondered if she'd lied about going back to New York, too. With things in the state they were in, it was hard to believe that she'd run back before things got resolved. She probably had been here in the city this entire time.

I had to tell Adam right away. Once he knew that she'd been lying for sure about when she'd arrived in Cleveland, he could bring her in for questioning again. It might even speed up the process of him getting his hands on the tollbooth photos.

Things were starting to look up.

CHAPTER
30

On the way home from the casino, I tried calling Adam's cell phone, but he didn't answer. I left a cryptic message telling him that I had important information and that he needed to call me back. I knew I would have a lot of explaining to do and I didn't want to say too much without actually talking to him.

I'd have to implicate Bobby, and he probably would not be too happy about that, but he was the only one who could verify seeing Marcia. Aside from Bobby's wrath, I also worried about Adam's reaction, but that was something I would just have to deal with when the time came. This information was too important not to hand over. I still didn't have solid proof that she'd been at the actual crime scene, but hopefully the Bobby angle would be enough.

I pulled into the parking lot of my apartment complex and thought about calling Adam again. But it had only been a few minutes. I needed to calm down. I would walk Kikko and then give him another try.

After I parked the car, I sent Megan a text letting her know I had exciting news about the case. She was never going to believe it.

I got out of the car and practically ran with nervous excitement to my apartment. Kikko came waddling to the door, squiggly tail wagging. I gave her a quick pat on the head and searched for her leash, anxious to walk her so I could get back and call Adam. I decided to check my phone one last time before we headed out.

Damn . . . my phone was missing!

I rifled through my purse and my coat pocket, but it was nowhere to be found. I must have dropped it or left it in the car. Leaving Kikko behind, I trekked back to my spot, searching the ground on my way.

As I made it to the front of my vehicle, a car raced into the parking lot with its high beams on, blinding me with their light.

"Geez, jerk," I said, shielding my eyes with my hand. "Do you really need those bright lights? We're not in the freakin' country."

The car pulled up behind mine, hitting the brake abruptly, almost grazing my car in the process.

"Hey!" I yelled. "Watch my car!"

The lights flicked off and a shadowy figure got out of the car.

My stomach dropped when the person came into view.

Marcia.

"Hi, Lana," she said. Her voice a little higher than usual, and the peppiness in her tone sounded fake and sarcastic. "I hope I'm not catching you at a bad time. I was wondering if we could talk for a quick minute. It's about the store. You don't mind, right?"

"Oh, uh . . . can this wait?" I started to back away from my car. "I have a headache. It's been a long day and I was planning on heading straight to bed. Maybe we can talk about whatever it is tomorrow? Stop by the restaurant . . . I'll even give you lunch on the house."

She laughed. "No, I think we'll talk about this now." She maneuvered around the car, hopping onto the sidewalk. "Aren't you going to invite me in? It's cold out here, and we wouldn't want to catch cold."

I continued to back away from her as she closed the gap between us. "You know, my place is a mess and it's kind of embarrassing. I'd hate for you to see what a wreck it is."

She smirked. "I don't mind."

I heard the click of the gun before I saw it.

I froze as the realization of what was happening fully registered. A brief flashback from the night Charles An held me at gunpoint flittered through my mind. I slowly raised my hands in surrender.

"Move, Lana," she said through clenched teeth. "Besides the fact that it's freezing and you seem to have lost your manners, we don't want other people to hear our conversation, do we?"

"Fine," I said, trying to keep my voice steady. "Just don't shoot me, okay? We can work this out. I'll do whatever you want."

"We'll see how I'm feeling once we get out of the cold." She nudged me forward with a wave of the gun.

I shimmied to the door, keeping an eye on Marcia and her trigger finger. My hands shook as I unlocked the door. Once I stepped a foot over the threshold, Kikko came rushing to me, no doubt impatient to go on her walk. She took one look at Marcia and immediately set off in a bout of irritated yips.

Marcia's gun flicked to the ground where Kikko stood, barking at her. "Shut that thing up, or I'll shut it up."

"No!" I yelled, stepping in front of my dog. "Please, leave her alone. She doesn't know any better. You're a stranger. She always barks at strangers."

She pointed the gun upward, back at me. "Okay, shut her up then."

I picked up Kikko and cradled her in my arms. "Let me put her in my room." I kissed the dog's forehead and she returned the favor with a slurp to my cheek. I hurried to my room, setting her on the floor and shutting the door behind me.

Muffled barks came through the door. She scratched at the wood in protest.

When I turned around, Marcia was standing right behind me. Her eyes were wild and she appeared completely untethered. Nothing like the woman I had met on prior occasions. The gun was inches away from my chest. I could hardly breathe. If I passed out, I didn't know what would happen. I tried to inhale a slow breath, telling myself I would make it out alive. I had to. I wasn't going to go out like this. Not shot to death by a madwoman who was nicknamed "Manic Marcia."

When it was clear she had my attention, Marcia waved the gun at the living room. "Go, sit down. Make yourself comfortable."

I did as she said, moving in slow, measured steps.

"I have to figure out what I'm going to do with you."

She scratched the side of her head with the barrel of her gun. "You've put me in an odd position."

"I didn't do anything to you," I whispered.

"Oh, stop," Marcia spat. "I know exactly what you've been up to. I told you I have eyes around here. Do you think Carmen was so helpful out of the kindness of her heart?"

My mouth dropped. "Carmen?" They were involved with each other after all!

She laughed at the expression on my face. "I know quite a few people at the casino. This isn't my first rodeo, sweetie."

Carmen's willingness to help, and her attempt—with Ryan—to steer me toward Constance really had been part of the master plan. As I'd suspected, there probably wasn't even a disgruntled blackjack player. The whole thing was most likely made up to lure me to the casino so Marcia could confront me. If I'd gone along with Carmen, who knew if I would have made it home? Although that wasn't exactly making much difference at the moment. Marcia had still gotten to me before I could tell anyone the full story.

"So Carmen and Ryan helped you this whole time?" I asked. "Why? What did they get out of it?"

"Why, money, of course. I needed to be sure that any evidence of mine and Brandon's dealings was completely removed from that apartment. We couldn't have Constance finding anything to implicate me in his current life, could we? I didn't know if he was stupid enough to keep anything there. I approached Carmen and Ryan, who were both more than happy to do the job . . . for a price."

"So, the three of you killed Brandon and Isabelle. Then you lied about going back to New York . . . so you could move around without anyone knowing that you were here."

She laughed again. "Okay, you're smarter than I took you for. This whole time I was hoping that I'd had you in my pocket." She gave me the same innocent smile that she'd given me and Peter the first time we'd met her. "But I have to take points off for the whole Carmen-and-Ryan-helping-me-with-any-of-the-truly-dirty-work angle. They're just a couple of dumb kids who fit into my plans."

"But I don't understand why you did it. You loved Brandon."

"Ha! I loved him all right. A lot of good it did me." She began to pace the length of the living room, her agitation increasing with every step. "That man has ruined my life. Everything became about winning him back.

"He wanted to move to Cleveland . . . I paid for him to move to Cleveland. He wanted to open a stupid souvenir store. I paid for him to open the store. He *needed* a loft apartment." She turned to look at me. "Guess who paid for that?"

"You did," I said quietly.

"You got that right." She continued to pace and shook her head. "I did everything for that man. Everything!" she yelled. "And do you know what I got in return?"

"What?"

"Nothing. That's what," she said with a sneer. "Not a damn thing. Meanwhile, he's giving all of his affection to this little twerpy girl. You know what he told me? He told me he was going to stop gambling for her. He was going to settle down like he promised. Clear all his debts with this one big win. For her. *Isabelle*." She snorted. "She wouldn't even fight for him. That's how this whole mess happened. It's all her fault.

"If she'd had the guts to show me she loved him as much as I did, I might have respected her. I might not have had to provoke her. All I did was push her. I didn't know what would happen."

A light flicked in the window and I jumped.

Marcia stopped pacing and whirled around to face me. "Oh, don't you judge me."

I held up my hands in defense. "I wasn't."

She continued to pace and my eyes shifted back to the window, where I saw a motion of metallic blue flash past the window. Another small beam of light flicked on and off. It was code.

Marcia prattled on, oblivious to the light show outside. She was too busy justifying her actions. "Do you even know what it's like to love someone and see them with someone else . . . someone less deserving? Do you have any idea what that's like?"

"Actually, I do," I said, with renewed composure. My hands were still shaking, but there was hope I would make it out of this, and that was enough to keep me going. "It hurts. He took advantage of you on top of it. That's a terrible feeling. I wouldn't wish it on my worst enemy."

She whipped around to face me and tilted her head in surprise. "So you get it then? You see why I had to do it?"

"Oh, totally," I said, standing up.

She backed away, pointing the gun at me again. "What do you think you're doing?"

I held up my hands and stopped moving. "You don't have to point that at me. It's going to be okay now." My voice dropped to a whisper. "I understand everything you've been going through. Just between us girls, I would have done it, too," I said, trying to sound as sincere as possible. I needed her to believe me.

"All I did was push her, you know?" she said, her voice catching. "She wasn't supposed to hit her head that way. All those damn boxes were in the way. At first, I thought she was faking it, but then she stopped breathing . . . and I . . ."

"I know." I nodded to appease her. "Isabelle was a klutz that way." I inched a step closer.

She took a step back, tears welling up in her eyes. "I wasn't going to take the blame . . . not after everything else. But then he looked at me . . . oh God . . . I couldn't stand the way he *looked* at me . . ." A tear rolled down her cheek. The gun shook in her hand.

I took a deep breath, mustering up every ounce of courage and strength that my body possessed. This was not the time to fall apart. Not now. Letting my emotions get in the way would cloud my thinking. "I know . . . it must have been awful."

"All he had to do was love me. That's not so much to ask, right? I did everything for him. *Everything!*" Full waterworks poured from her eyes, and the gun faltered in her hand. It pointed at the floor—she'd removed her finger from the trigger.

"*Now!*" I yelled from the top of my lungs.

Kikko howled from the bedroom.

Marcia gawked at me in shock, mascara-stained tears streaking down her cheeks.

In a matter of seconds, the door flung open in a whirl of neon blue and ashen blond. "Take that, you psycho!" Megan yelled, swinging her new Maglite at Marcia's head.

Marcia hit the floor with a thud. The gun she'd been holding slid across the floor.

Megan let out a deep breath. "Are you okay? I could hear everything from outside the apartment! This chick is nuts!"

I held my chest, instructing myself to breathe like a normal person. "What are you doing here? I thought you were at work!"

"After I got your text, I responded and asked you to call me," Megan explained. "But then you never answered. So I called you, and you didn't answer then, either. I got worried and decided to come home. Thank God I did!"

I looked down at Marcia, who was out cold. "You have impeccable timing."

Megan followed my line of sight to the ground where Marcia was sprawled out. "Oh my God, I killed her!" she yelled, covering her mouth.

I knelt down to the floor and checked Marcia for a pulse. I let out a ragged sigh of relief. "Don't worry, she's still alive. Call the police. I'm going to get a sheet and tie her up."

"Yeah, 'cause when she wakes up, she's gonna be super pissed."

A few hours later, Megan, Adam, Kikko, and I sat in the living room with a box of pizza on the coffee table.

None of us had bothered to open it; we just stared at the floor, trying to process everything that had happened in the past few hours.

Megan was the first to speak. "I can't eat anything. I think I'm gonna go to bed. You guys save me some in case I wake up in the middle of the night with trauma munchies." She got up and zombie-walked to her bedroom.

I jumped up after her. "Megan . . . wait."

She stood in the doorway to her room and turned. She was visibly exhausted, and the dark circles under her eyes were proof of it.

"Thank you . . ." I said, looking down at my toes. "You saved my life tonight."

She laughed. "It was no sweat. I'd swing a flashlight for you any day."

Tears welled up in my eyes. I nodded and started to go back in the living room. "I'll let you go to sleep now. I just wanted to say that. Good night."

"Oh my God, give me a hug, you weirdo." She grabbed me and embraced me in a bear hug. "I love you, Lana Lee. Don't you ever forget that."

I held back my tears as best I could. We had gone through enough emotions tonight. "Love you, too, buddy."

She shut her door and I went back into the living room where Adam sat relaxing with Kikko. He scratched her head as he stared into space. There was no telling what he was thinking.

"So you're mad at me, I presume," I said, standing over him. "I was just about to tell you—"

He held up a hand and gestured for me to sit next to him.

I sat on the edge of the couch and he put an arm around me, pulling me close to him.

I tried to smile, but I could feel the tears forming in my eyes again. "I tried to stay out of trouble this time, I promise."

He laughed. "No, you didn't."

"Okay, well, I *thought* about it." I said, wiping away a stray tear.

"And for you, I'm guessing that's a big step in itself?"

"It is."

He sat up and turned to me, looking me straight in the eye. "I know there are some things that I need to work on as far as getting close to someone. But I hope you know that I care about you a great deal, Lana."

I felt myself getting lost in the intensity of his stare. I tried to look away, but he grabbed my chin, holding my face in place. "I'm not going anywhere. And I don't want you to go anywhere, either."

"Okay, I won't," I said.

"So, my answer is . . . I want to be mad at you, yes. Because I almost lost you . . . again."

"I know . . ."

"But . . . I'm just happy that I didn't."

We sat there for a minute gazing at each other like two smitten teenagers on their first date. I leaned in and kissed him softly, trying to savor the moment. This feeling: This is what life is about. The good things. The things that make you smile and the things that touch your heart.

When we parted, he smiled at me, and his eyes gave off that mischievous twinkle that I had come to adore. "Besides, I can always be mad at you tomorrow."

EPILOGUE

A week later, it was New Year's Eve, the Chinese edition, and I put on the red dress I had picked especially for the occasion. The plaza's party was starting in a few hours, and Adam was my date for the evening. He'd never celebrated Chinese New Year before, and I was excited to show him this part of my culture.

Things were still a bit on the shaky side with us, but they'd gotten better since the case had been resolved. Megan was adamant about finding out what exactly was keeping Adam from closing the relationship gap. But for the time being, I found myself happy with the progress we'd made.

In the short time since Marcia had been arrested and officially charged with the murders of both Isabelle and Brandon, some semblance of normalcy had returned to the plaza. Well, as normal as things could be these days.

Of course, that's not to say that the Mahjong Matrons didn't do their part in spreading the details of the gruesome ordeal, including me being held at gunpoint, around the entire plaza. The whole story made it into the *Plain Dealer*, and I was even mentioned in the article. A reporter had asked to do a separate piece on my firsthand account, but I gracefully declined. The New Year was a time for fresh beginnings and everyone was eager to put events behind them, including me.

Carmen and Ryan both got what was coming to them and from what I understood, they would be in prison for quite some time. It also turned out they had the missing money all along. After Marcia murdered Brandon and Isabelle, she'd taken the cash that Brandon had on hand and given it to the crooked couple. She'd instructed them to go on about their lives as normal until attention around the case had dissipated. No one had expected yours truly to stir the pot.

The situation with Constance Yeoh and her planned takeover of the souvenir shop ended up correcting itself. After she'd read the story in the newspaper, it was decided that Asia Village was a little too crazy for her tastes. She felt it was in her best interest to return to New York and start her designer purse shop there.

And as far as surprises go, she sure gave us one before she left. She ended up handing the property and all rights over to Rina. I hadn't thought Rina would accept, but apparently she had shown some interest in being her own businesswoman. I guess a slight respect had formed between the two women while they dealt with the deceased couple's apartment. Who would have thought?

Rina accepted under the condition that she could liquidate the store and turn it into a cosmetics shop. The memory of her sister was too strong in the store the way it was. Ian and the rest of the board happily approved and Ian did a silent dance of joy at the news of Constance leaving his life for good. Rina was scheduled to take over the store after the New Year festivities had ended and the paperwork was finalized. She planned to move to Cleveland in the next several weeks and even asked me to help her look for an apartment.

My parents had heard what happened from Esther before I even had the chance to update them. Now without anything to worry about, my parents had chosen to extend their stay in Taiwan for a little bit longer. My mother was so pleased with the way I had run things in her absence—considering the circumstances—that she told me she was thinking about retiring for real and making me the new restaurant manager indefinitely. After we'd both had a good laugh, she assured me that she wasn't kidding.

At the end of our conversation, she shocked me with the news that my grandmother would be coming back with them to the United States. She didn't clarify if it was a permanent stay or temporary, but I figured I would find out soon enough.

My phone chimed, bringing me back to the present. It was a message from Adam letting me know that he was on his way. I dabbed my lipstick and touched up my mascara before I slipped into my heels. I stuffed some backup shoes in my purse, just in case.

I sat at my dining room table and flipped open my laptop. Since I had a little time to kill, I signed onto Facebook. My brain had been dancing around with this idea since after Marcia's arrest. I finally felt ready.

With some apprehension, I typed in Isabelle's name and her profile popped up. I smiled back at her picture as her profile loaded. Her page had continued to fill with people leaving fond memories, and I imagined it would for a long time. Isabelle had been such a great girl.

I must have lost track of time because my phone chimed again. Adam had arrived and was waiting out in the car.

With a deep breath, I put the cursor in the comment box of Isabelle's page and typed the following message I'd been carrying with me for the past week. It read: *Justice has been served, my friend. May you forever rest in peace. Xoxo, Lana Lee.*

Read on for an exclusive excerpt of the next
Number One Noodle Shop Mystery

Murder
Lo
Mein

Available in April 2019
from St. Martin's Paperbacks!

CHAPTER
1

There I was, staring at my doom . . . surely, this was a fate worse than death. "I am in so much trouble. This is a complete and total nightmare!"

Kimmy Tran, childhood friend and fellow Asia Village employee, gawked at me as we stood side-by-side inside the enclosed plaza, staring at the cause of my nervous breakdown. The sloppy bun on her head wobbled as she lectured me. "Lana Lee, calm down. It's not that serious. You're a grown woman, for Pete sakes."

"There couldn't be a more horrible circumstance. Why is this happening to me?" I tugged on the locks of black and magenta-streaked hair that framed my face. "What did I do to deserve this?"

She puffed out her already chubby cheeks. "This is ridiculous, you need to relax."

Peter Huang, the head chef at my family's restaurant, walked up behind us. "What's up, ladies? What are we lookin' at?"

"This . . . this monstrosity," I said with a shiver. "This horrible, horrible monstrosity."

Peter adjusted his black ball cap, and tilted his head. With a chuckle, he asked, "What? The doughnut shop?"

As he said the word *doughnut*, I heard my stomach rumble. Standing before us was the newest tenant of Asia Village, Shanghai Donuts. They were due to open in the next few days, and sadly I knew that I would be their very first customer.

On top of my addiction to noodles and book buying, I had a weakness for doughnuts. For the most part, I was able to refrain from indulging on the delicious, round pastries of doughy goodness, but with the new shop opening up right next door, I had to wonder about the current status of my willpower.

At the age of twenty-seven—on the brink of twenty-eight—many warned me that my metabolism was on its way off the fast track. Those 'many' included members of my family who seemed to be tracking my eating habits.

I squeezed the side of my waist and felt the pounds I had put on since I'd started working at the restaurant. My pants were starting to feel tight. With my credit cards dancing on the edge of being maxed out, I found my two favorite food groups to be excellent stress relievers.

Peter laughed, giving my shoulder a nudge. "Don't worry, Lana, I'm sure you'll get sick of them after a while. You can't eat doughnuts every day."

"Says you," I grumbled.

He grabbed my arm and pulled me in the direction of my family's noodle house and also my current place of employment. "Come on, man, let's get to work, we have to prep for the noodle contest."

Kimmy looked between the two of us. "I can't believe it's tomorrow already. Are you guys prepared?"

They were referring to the Cleveland's Best Noodles contest that was set to be held at Asia Village. Peter had been prepping and perfecting recipes for weeks in anticipation of winning the competition.

"Super stoked," Peter replied. "This year we're taking first place. No more of this third place stuff. No, it says right there on the sign." He pointed above his head to the restaurant's gold-lettered sign.

It read: Ho-Lee Noodle House, #1 Noodle Shop. We served all sorts of Taiwanese and Chinese cuisine, but our specialty, of course, was noodles. And, Peter's noodles were the best in the whole city. I might be a little biased, but if you've tasted his cooking, I think you'd agree.

Kimmy gave Peter a flirtatious grin. "If there's anybody that will beat out the Shen family, it'll be you."

He blushed. "Um, thanks."

Peter and Kimmy were in the midst of a budding new romance. They weren't the likeliest of couples out there, but so far it seemed to be working for them.

Kimmy was a touch on the outspoken side and didn't mind being the center of attention—and that was putting it lightly. In recent history, to help her parents with some money problems they were having, she had taken a secret job at a strip club as a cocktail waitress. Needless to say, there were plenty of eyes on her there.

Meanwhile, Peter was a touch on the introverted side, keeping to himself and partaking in his solitary hobbies which involved video games of some type or something artistic, like painting or drawing.

We said our good-byes to Kimmy, who shuffled over two storefronts to her own place of business, China Cinema and Song, which she helped run for her parents.

I unlocked the door to the restaurant, and we stepped into the darkened dining room, making our way to the back with little effort. A few weeks ago, I had officially become the permanent restaurant manager, now taking care of the main responsibilities while my mother tended to my grandmother. A native to Taiwan, this was my grandmother's first trip to the United States, and her English was less than stellar. And that's me being nice about it.

The restaurant life wasn't what I had been searching for, but it was turning out better than I'd thought. My older sister, Anna May, wasn't thrilled with me taking over the family business, but with her well on the path to becoming a high-powered attorney, she didn't have much say in the matter. There might be a small part of me that takes pleasure in that fact.

Outside of the kitchen, I flipped on the lights, and the black and red dining area sprang to life. The touches of gold accent sparkled under the soft yellow lighting and bounced off the black-lacquered tabletops.

We passed through the kitchen and made our way to the back room, which had been turned into an employee lounge. A beat-up couch and small TV from my childhood still occupied the room, and I wondered if my parents would ever replace them.

"So," Peter said as he grabbed his apron from the hook, "I'm ready for the contest, but I want to test out my recipes one more time before tomorrow. Are you cool with taste-testing them for me?"

"Twist my arm," I joked. "Of course, I'll taste them. We can't let the House of Shen win . . . or Ray."

Ray Jin, last year's Cleveland's Best Noodles contest winner, beat out both us and our rivals, the House of Shen, at winning the coveted award.

The grand prize winner's restaurant would be featured in *Cleveland* magazine with a special profile on the chef and their award-winning recipes. Not only that, but the winning restaurant also won free advertising in the magazine for a year, a cash prize of five thousand dollars and an engraved plaque to hang in their restaurant.

In the five years that the contest had been in existence, we had always placed in the top five, but never made first. This had to be our year. I could feel it.

Peter shook his head. "No, didn't you hear? They asked Ray to be one of the judges this year."

"You're kidding!"

"I swear on my own life, dude."

"But what about all the rumors that spread around last year after the contest was over? So many people thought he cheated."

"Yeah, but no one could actually prove it. Especially when the whole scenario came from Joel Liu . . . totally made him look even more crazy than he already did. Losing that contest really put him over the edge."

"True, I just assumed they would want to avoid the controversy."

"They always make the first place winner a judge so they can't compete again, anyway. I guess he's no exception."

I contemplated that while we headed back into the kitchen and got into our morning zones. Peter revved up the appliances while I prepped the dining room before our first customers of the day arrived.

After all that had happened at Asia Village in the past handful of months, we needed something good to happen at the plaza. And winning this contest was it.

CHAPTER
2

Asia Village was my home away from home, and not just because the restaurant was conveniently tucked inside. No, these days, I spent a lot of time in the enclosed shopping center taking advantage of everything it had to offer. When I wasn't browsing the shelves of my favorite bookstore, The Modern Scroll, I was getting drinks with my newest friend, Rina Su, at the karaoke bar, The Bamboo Lounge. And you can't forget the salon, Asian Accents, where I always went to get my hair cut and dyed by Jasmine Ming, stylist extraordinaire. Aside from that, we had an Asian grocery, an herbal shop, a gift shop and just about anything else you could think of. It was your one-stop Asian shopping experience.

It was lunchtime at the plaza and my mother and grandmother had stopped through for some noodles before heading off to do whatever it was they did during the day. We were huddled in a circle in Esther's store, Chin's Gifts. Esther is my mother's best friend and my aunt of sorts. She does things like lecture me on my behavior and comments on my posture.

"If the Shen family wins this year, Ho-Lee Noodle House will lose face again," my mother told the group. "We must beat them."

"We will, Mom," I replied. "Don't worry about it so much. Peter and I have everything under control."

My grandmother, who was standing next to me, barely came up to my shoulders. I am not by any means a tall person—I come in at a solid five foot four. She observed my mother and me, watching our lips move, and tried to follow along. She blurted something rapidly in Hokkien and stared expectantly at my mother.

My mother replied, and they both nodded.

"What did she say?" I asked. My knowledge of the language was slipping and continued to dissolve as I got older from lack of use. I caught the word "eat" and that was it.

"She said that she would like to have lunch now. She is bored because she does not understand us."

I turned to my grandmother who met my glance with a smile. Her two front teeth were silver and they glistened in her mouth. She grabbed my hand. "A-ma . . . hungry."

"Okay, A-ma . . ." I pointed to the door with my free hand. "Let's go."

"Go!" She tugged on my hand to follow her.

We said good-bye to Esther, and headed out into the plaza. Construction for the noodle contest was under way, and a team of workers hustled to construct a temporary stage over the koi pond.

Ian Sung, our property manager, had insisted that the contest be held indoors in case of unexpected weather. A Cleveland spring could be extra rainy and he didn't want to take the chance.

"Hey guys!" Rina Su waved at us from the threshold of her new cosmetics shop. The Ivory Doll specialized in Asian makeup and skincare brands like Shisiedo, Wei East, and Amorepacific, but also carried more familiar brands like L'Oreal and Revlon. Since she'd moved in, my cosmetics collection had . . . gotten healthy.

Rina was the sister of a friend I'd made not long ago who'd been the victim of a senseless murder. Isabelle Yeoh, and her husband, Brandon, had opened a souvenir shop next to Ho-Lee Noodle House and it seemed like just yesterday that they had opened the doors to their first business.

After Isabelle and Brandon had been murdered, I'd met Rina at the memorial services, and we had bonded over the loss of her sister. An unexpected turn of events had led to Rina taking over the property that her sister and brother-in-law had previously owned.

However, with the nature of things as they were, Rina had convinced Ian to let her move the property over to a different empty space in the plaza. Now she resided in the spot which had formerly been owned by a man named Charles An. In case you were wondering what happened to him, well, he turned out to be a very bad man, and he's now sitting in a state correctional facility for first degree murder, and attempted murder. The attempted murder was on yours truly. The nightmares from that ordeal were still waking me up from time to time, but I tried my best to brush it under the proverbial rug.

That is also how I got stuck with Shanghai Donuts

right next to the noodle shop. My mom and sixty percent of the Village believed that the space was cursed. For once in my life, I wished that were true.

My mother grabbed my grandmother's arm. "We will meet you at the restaurant. Go talk to your friend."

I separated from my family, and walked over to greet my friend. "Hey Rina, whatcha up to?"

She pushed off the wall she'd been leaning against and gave me a hug. "Watching these handsome guys work their magic."

I laughed and followed her line of sight to the group of men working, completely oblivious to the two of us staring at them. "I see. Anyone in particular that you've got your eye on?"

"Not really, they're all pretty cute. That one there is the new community director, Frederick Yuan." She pointed to a slightly muscular Asian man in a white t-shirt and jeans. "He doesn't start until Monday, but he offered to help with the contest. Isn't that sweet?"

"I didn't know that Ian had picked someone for the job already."

"He made the decision yesterday. I guess he and Frederick go way back or something. I think he said they went to school together."

I watched him as he worked. He talked and laughed with the others as he helped lift one end of the stage. His biceps stretched the material of his shirt, and a sliver of tattoo was exposed.

"How's Adam?" Rina asked, breaking my stare.

"Huh, what?"

She laughed. "I asked, how's Adam?"

"Oh, right. Adam." I straightened and turned my back to the crew. "He's okay, I guess."

"I haven't seen him around lately. Is everything all right with you guys?"

Adam, also known as Detective Trudeau, was my sort of boyfriend guy. I say "sort of" because we had yet to seal the deal on the whole relationship bit. At present moment, we were dating and not seeing other people— at least, I wasn't. But lately, we had been seeing less and less of each other. "He's been busy with a case so he hasn't had much time to stop by and visit."

"Hopefully things lighten up for him soon. Starting new relationships can be hard if you don't put in the time."

"Yeah, you're telling me." I turned back around to the workers who were now taking a break. They had covered the koi pond with their makeshift stage and lounged on benches nearby. "Well, I better get to the restaurant, my mom and grandma are waiting on me."

"I'll talk to you at the contest tomorrow! I have my fingers crossed that you guys win!"

As I walked to the restaurant, I kept my eyes on the cobblestone pathway that trails through the plaza. I could feel four sets of eyes fixed on me as I walked by. Just as I was about to reach for the door handle of the noodle shop, someone yelled, "Hey!" and the natural reflex to turn and look kicked in.

Frederick Yuan was jogging up to me, a dimpled smile on his full lips. "Hey, hi, I'm Rick," he said as he halted inches away from me. He extended a hand. "You're familiar . . . why is that?"

I took his hand and he gave me a first shake. "I'm Lana . . . Lana Lee. I work here . . ."

"Great! I'm the new community director. I'm starting next week." His chocolate brown eyes focused intently on mine, and I could feel the heat rising up my neck into my cheeks. "It's nice to meet a friendly face . . . I look forward to seeing you around."

"Yeah . . . me too." I realized he was still holding onto my hand which was beginning to sweat. I jerked it away and hid it behind my back. "I'm sorry, I have to go. My family is waiting on me."

"Oh, don't let me hold you up. Just wanted to introduce myself." He jerked a thumb at the stage behind him. "Are you going to be at the contest tomorrow? Your restaurant is in the competition, right?"

I nodded.

"Cool, I'll see you then." He gave me a quick wink before jogging back to the other guys.

I turned on my heel and pulled on the door handle. Come Monday, Shanghai Donuts wasn't going to be my only problem.

I pulled into the parking lot of my apartment complex a little after six o'clock. Making my way to the apartment I shared with my best friend, Megan Riley, I noticed that her car was still there, which was unusual for a Friday night considering she worked at a bar.

When I opened the door, my black pug, Kikkoman, who normally greeted me upon arrival, was nowhere to be found. "Hello?" I scanned the room. "Where is everybody?"

"In here!" A muffled voice yelled back.

I locked the door and headed down the short hallway where I noticed the bathroom door was closed. The water was running and I could hear splashing. "What are you doing? Where's Kikko?"

"Open the door. You'll see."

I twisted the door handle and poked my head inside. Immediately I burst into laughter.

Megan twisted around from her kneeling position over the tub. "Today, this little girl decided to roll around in some other dog's poop."

I continued to laugh. On my dog's head was a mini-shower cap stretched over her floppy ears. She looked up at me and her mouth dropped open. "Kikko, is this true?"

Her little pink tongue flopped out and she panted in reply.

"I hope you're not missing work because of this." I leaned against the bathroom wall, watching Kikko squirm in the tub.

"Nope, I took off tonight so I could get up and go with you to the noodle contest in the morning."

"Aw, you did? That's so nice!"

"I know how much this means to you. With everything that's been happening, Asia Village needs a win."

"Exactly what I said earlier today. Business is still doing pretty good despite everything, but having an award-winning restaurant at the plaza would definitely help."

"Is Adam going to be there tomorrow?" she asked, glancing up at me. "You haven't mentioned him in a couple of days."

"That's because there's nothing to tell. And no, I don't think he'll be there tomorrow."

Megan pulled Kikko from the tub, carefully covering her in a towel. "He's still busy with that case?"

I nodded. "He sent me a few text messages, but nothing exciting."

"I'm sure once things are wrapped up, he'll be around again."

"Right now, my main concern is this noodle contest. We have got to beat the Shen family, no matter what."

She released Kikko from the towel and the little pug shook the remaining water from her body before zipping out of the bathroom. "Peter is the best cook in town, I'm sure there won't be any problems."

"There better not be. Or I won't hear the end of it from my mother."